MORE PRAISE FOR *FAR-SEER*

"Robert J. Sawyer's *Far-Seer* makes a lot of promises—and keeps them. A fascinating world, remarkable characters, and a problem of world-shattering proportions. What more can you ask for?"

—ROGER MACBRIDE ALLEN, author of *Ring of Charon*

"A landmark in hard science fiction. Succeeds on many levels: as a fascinating piece of world-building; as an action-packed adventure; as a coming-of-age novel; but perhaps most of all, as a book about the scientific method and the scientific mind."

—ANDREW WEINER, author of *Station Gehenna*

"Robert J. Sawyer's recipe for *Far-Seer:*
one enormous sense of wonder
one boatload of convincing and charming aliens
one planetful of accurate and fascinating science
one truly breathtaking premise
Mix well and stir.
Sawyer's a hell of a chef."

—JOHN E. STITH, author of *Redshift Rendezvous*

"A brilliant parable of the nature of scientific investigation, and its relation to art and faith."

—S.M. STIRLING, coauthor of *Man-Kzin Wars*

ROBERT J. SAWYER

ACE BOOKS, NEW YORK

This book is an Ace original edition,
and has never been previously published.

FAR-SEER

An Ace Book / published by arrangement with
the author

PRINTING HISTORY
Ace edition / June 1992

ISBN: 0-441-22551-9

Ace Books are published by The Berkley Publishing Group,
200 Madison Avenue, New York, New York 10016.
The name "ACE" and the "A" logo
are trademarks belonging to Charter Communications, Inc.

PRINTED IN THE UNITED STATES OF AMERICA

10 9 8 7 6 5 4 3 2 1

For Carolyn Clink
My Wife,
My Lover,
My Best Friend

ACKNOWLEDGMENTS

This manuscript went through many phases. Those who made sure the best side ended up being illuminated include Ted Bleaney, Carolyn Clink, Richard Curtis, Richard Gotlib, Terence M. Green, Peter Heck, Laurie Lupton, Alan B. Sawyer, and Andrew Weiner. I bow concession to them all.

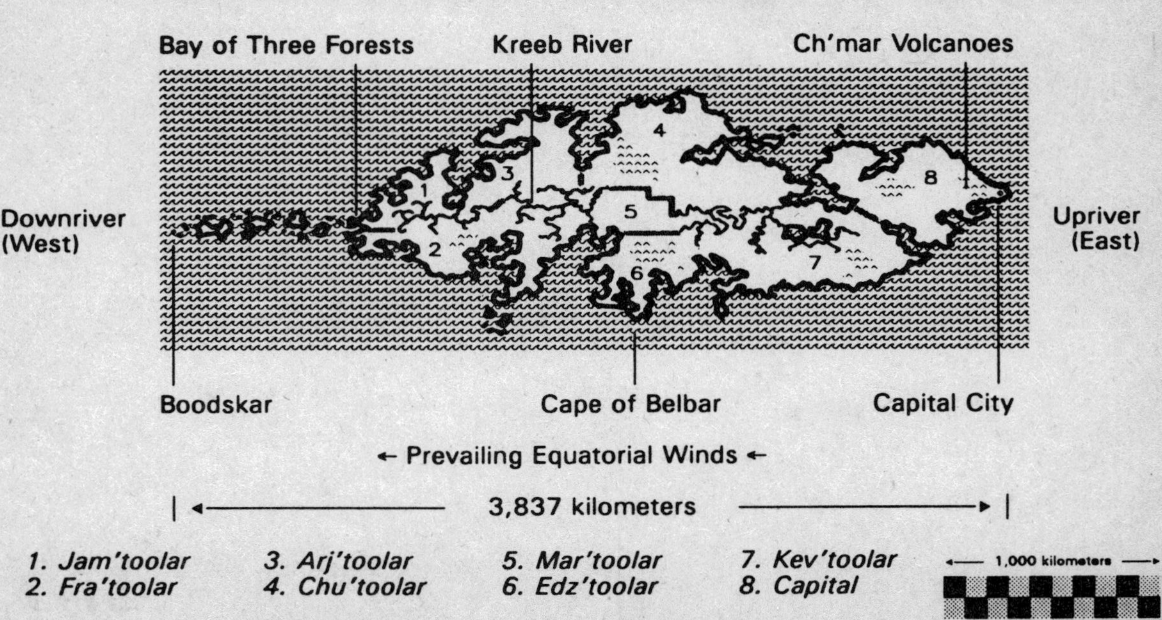
The Single Continent of the Quintaglio Home World
Bay of Three Forests
Kreeb River
Ch'mar Volcanoes
Downriver (West)
Upriver (East)
1
2
3
4
5
6
7
8
Boodskar
Cape of Belbar
Capital City
← Prevailing Equatorial Winds ←
3,837 kilometers
1. Jam'toolar
2. Fra'toolar
3. Arj'toolar
4. Chu'toolar
5. Mar'toolar
6. Edz'toolar
7. Kev'toolar
8. Capital
1,000 kilometers

Dramatis Personae

Capital City

Afsan	apprentice astrologer
Dar-Mondark	doctor
Dy-Dybo	prince
Det-Yenalb	chief priest
Gerth-Palsab	citizen
Irb-Falpom	land surveyor
Jal-Tetex	hunt leader
Len-Lends	Empress
Pal-Cadool	butcher
Tak-Saleed	master astrologer

The Crew of the *Dasheter*

Bog-Tardlo	sailor
Dath-Katood	sailor
Det-Bleen	priest
Irb-Hadzig	sailor

Mar-Biltog	sailor
Nor-Gampar	sailor
Paldook	sailor
Var-Keenir	captain

Pack Gelbo

Lub-Kaden	leader of a hunting pack
Val-Toron	rider
Wab-Novato	maker of far-seers

Pack Carno

Cat-Julor	creche mother
Det-Zamar	senior priest
Pahs-Drawo	likely Afsan's father
Pal-Donat	bloodpriest
Tar-Dordool	leader

Chapter 1

Afsan often escaped to this place. He remembered the first time he had run up this hillside, half a kiloday ago, after his original encounter with the formidable Tak-Saleed.

Formidable? Afsan clicked his teeth in humor, figuring that the choice of adjective was a sign that he must be getting accustomed to all this. Back then, after his introduction to the master astrologer, the word he'd used was "monstrous."

That first time he'd run up here his only thought had been to get out of the city, get back to his distant home Pack of Carno, back to the simple life of a country boy. He was sure he'd never get used to this dizzying, terrifying world of apprenticeship, of scowling imperial guards, of hundreds of people—ten or more gathered together in the same place at once! Afsan hadn't experienced crowds like that before, never felt such a wash of pheromones over him. He couldn't stand the tension, the constant fear that he was encroaching on another's territory or otherwise breaching protocol. He had found himself tipping from the waist so often it made his head spin.

But on that day, as on this, Afsan had been calmed by the magnificent view from here, tension slipping from his body, claws retracting so far that Afsan thought he'd never see them again, tail swishing back and forth in leisurely, contented movements.

The sun had set a short time ago. It had swollen to a bloated egg, changing from its normal white to a deep violet, before dropping behind the ragged cones of the Ch'mar volcanoes to the west of the city. A beautiful sunset, Afsan had thought, the wispy clouds a veil across the dimming disk, tinged with purple, with red, with deepest blue. But then Afsan found all sunsets beautiful, and not just because of the play of color across the clouds, although this evening that was indeed spectacular. No, Afsan welcomed sunsets because he preferred the night, craved the stars.

This will be a grand night for observing, he thought. The only clouds were around the volcanoes, and those rarely lifted. Overhead, the vast dome of the sky was immaculate.

Tonight was odd-night. Most adults slept on odd-nights. For that very reason, Afsan did not. He preferred the peace and tranquillity of the hillsides on those nights when—the thought came unbidden—it was as if they were his own territory.

Of course, Afsan owned nothing of value, and, having entered a life of quiet study, his chances of acquiring land were—how did the old joke go?—about as likely as one of the Empress's eggs being used as a game ball.

But even if he couldn't own land, he would always have the stars. The sky was darkening quickly, as it always did, and there would only be a short time of real night before even-day broke.

Afsan inhaled deeply. The air was as clear as the waters of spring-fed Lake Doognar back home, the smells of—he flexed his nostrils, wrinkled his muzzle—of wildflowers; the scent of a large animal, perhaps an armorback (although how one of those would get this high up a mountain he didn't know); urine on those rocks, likely from a much smaller critter; and, underneath it all, faint, but more prominent than when he'd first arrived in Capital City, the sulfurous tinge of volcanic gases.

He had been straddling a boulder, his tail hanging over it, to watch the sun go down. Now it was time to climb higher up the hillside. He did so, the three broad toes on each foot giving him excellent traction. Upon reaching the crest, he clicked his teeth in satisfaction, then continued partway down the other side, placing the bulk of the hill between himself and the torch-lit glow of Capital City. Afsan lowered himself to the ground, and lay on his side to look up at the panorama of the night sky.

As usual, Afsan found it uncomfortable with all his weight on his right shoulder and hip, but what alternative was there? Once he had tried lying on his belly in the sleeping position and had craned his neck to look up instead of forward, but that had given him a stinging crick.

Dekadays ago, he'd asked Tak-Saleed why there was no easy posture for Quintaglios to look at the stars, why their muscular tails made it impossible to lie on their backs. Saleed had stared down at young Afsan and declared that God had wished it that way, that She had made the stars for Her face alone to gaze upon, not for the pinched muzzles of overly curious apprentices.

Afsan slapped his tail sideways against the soil, irritated by the memory. He drew his nictitating membranes over his eyes. The purple glow of the twilight still filtered through, but that was all. Afsan cleared his mind of all thoughts of old Saleed, opened the membranes, and drank in the beauty he had come here to enjoy.

The stars scurried from upriver to downriver as the brief night raced by. Two of the moons were prominent at the start of the evening: Slowpoke and the Big One. The Big One was showing only a crescent sliver of illumination, although the rest of its disk could be seen as a round blackness, obscuring the stars. Afsan held his arm out and found that if he unsheathed his thumbclaw, its sickle silhouette appeared about the same height and shape as the Big One. The Big One's orange face was always intriguing—there were markings on it, details just a little too small, just a little too dim, to be clearly made out. What it was, Afsan couldn't say. It seemed *rocky,* but how could a rock fly through the sky?

He turned his attention to Slowpoke. It had been in one of its recalcitrant moods again these past few nights, fighting its way upriver instead of sailing downriver. Oh, the other moons would do that occasionally, too, but never with the determination of tiny Slowpoke. Slowpoke was Afsan's favorite.

Someday he would make a study of the moons. He'd read much of what had been written about them, including Saleed's three-volume *Dancing the Night Away*. Such a whimsical title! How unlike the Saleed he knew, the Saleed he feared.

Some of the moons moved quickly across the sky, others took several tens of nights to cross from horizon to horizon. All went through phases, waxing and waning between the extremes of showing a fully lit circular shape and appearing as simply a black circle covering the stars. What did it all mean? Afsan exhaled noisily.

He scanned the sky along the ecliptic, that path along which the sun traveled each day. Two planets were visible, bright Kevpel and ruddy Davpel. Planets were similar to the moons, in that they moved against the background stars, but they appeared as tiny pinpoints, revealing no face or details, and their progress against the firmament had to be measured over days or dekadays. A few of the six known planets also showed the strange retrograde motions that some of the moons exhibited, although it took kilodays for them to complete these maneuvers.

Near the zenith now was the constellation of the Prophet. Afsan had seen old hand-copied books that called this constellation the Hunter, after Lubal, largest of the Five Original Hunters, but as worship of them was now all but banned, the official name had been changed to honor Larsk, the first to gaze upon the Face of God.

Lubal or Larsk, the picture was the same: points of light marked the shoulders, hips, elbows, knees, and the tip of the long tail. Two bright stars represented the eyes. It was like a reverse image, Afsan thought—the kind one gets after staring at an object, then looking at a white surface—since the prophet's eyes and Lubal's, too, like those of all Quintaglios, must have been obsidian black.

Above the Prophet, glowing faintly across the length of the sky, ran the powdery reflection of the great River that Land sailed on in its never-ending journey toward the Face of God. At least, that was what old Saleed said the dusty pathway of light crossing the night was, but he'd never been able to explain to Afsan's satisfaction why it was only during certain times that the great River cast a reflection on the sky.

Saleed! Abominable Saleed! It had taken Afsan fifty-five days riding atop a domesticated hornface in one of the merchant caravans to get from Pack Carno, part of the province of Arj'toolar, deep within Land's interior, to Capital City on the upriver shore of Land.

The children were the children of the Pack, of course—only the creche operators knew who Afsan's actual parents might have been—and the whole Pack was proud that one of their own had been selected to apprentice to the court astrologer. The choice, presumably, had been made based on Afsan's showing in the most recent battery of vocational exams. He had felt honored as he packed his sashes and boots, his books and astrolabe, and set out for his selected future. But he had been here for almost five hundred days now. True, that was something of a record. As he had discovered after arriving here, Saleed had had six other apprentices in the last four kilodays, all of whom had been dismissed. But, even though he seemed to have greater endurance than the previous try-outs, Afsan's dream of contributing to the advancement of astrological research had been smashed by his master.

Afsan had idolized Saleed, devouring his books on portents and omens, his treatise on the reflected River in the sky, his articles on the significance of each constellation. How he had looked forward to meeting the great one! How disappointed he had been when that day finally came. Soon, though, Afsan would be leaving on his pilgrimage. He thanked God for that, for he'd be away from his master for a great many days—able to study in private, free from Saleed's critical scowl.

Afsan shook his head slightly, again clearing his thoughts. He'd come here to bask in the beauty of the night, not to wallow in his own misfortune. One day the stars would yield their secrets to him.

Time slipped by unnoticed as Afsan drank in the glory overhead. Moons careened across the sky, waxing and waning as they went. The stars rose and fell, constellations hustling across the firmament. Meteors flashed through the night, tiny streaks of gold against the black. Nothing gave Afsan more pleasure than to behold this spectacle, always familiar, always different.

At last, Afsan heard the *pip-pip* call of a wingfinger, one of the hairy flyers that heralded the dawn. He stood, brushed dirt and dead grass from his side, turned, and looked. A cool steady breeze played along his face. He knew, naturally, that the air was still—for what could move the air?—and, rather, that Land, the ground beneath his feet, was sailing ever so smoothly down the mighty River, the River that ran from horizon to horizon. At least that was what he'd been taught, and he had learned painfully that one does not question the teachings. And perhaps, he reflected, it *was* true that Land floated on the River, for if you dug deep enough, did you not often come upon water beneath the ground?

Afsan knew little of boats—although his pilgrimage would involve a long water journey—but he did understand that the bigger the boat, the less it rocked. Land was roughly oval in shape. According to explorers who had traveled its length and breadth, it was some 3 *million* paces from the harbor of Capital City to the westernmost tip of Fra'toolar province and about 1.2 million paces from the northernmost point of Chu'toolar province to the southern tip of the Cape of Belbar in Edz'toolar. Such a great rocky raft might indeed float reasonably smoothly down the River. And, after all, the journey was not always a steady one, for the ground shook, sometimes severely, several times each kiloday.

Still, the floating was the part he always had a little mental trouble with. But he himself had seen how the porous black basalts that covered so much of Land's surface could indeed be made to bob in a chalice of water. Besides, if there was a better explanation for the way the world really was, he couldn't think of it—at least not yet.

His stomach growled, and, opening his wide mouth, Afsan growled back at it. He understood that a ritual hunting party was going out today, and that meant he might get to eat something other than the usual fare from the imperial stockyards. He wondered what they would bring down. Thunderbeast, he hoped, for it was his favorite, though he knew that even the largest hunting packs had trouble felling those great animals, with their massive pillar-like legs, their endless necks, their lengthy tails. Probably something less ambitious, he thought. Perhaps a shovelmouth or two. Stringy meat, but an easy kill, or so he'd heard, even if they did almost deafen you with the great bellowing calls they produced through the crests of bone on their heads.

He ambled back up to the top of the hill. From there he could look in all directions. Below him lay sleepy Capital City. Beyond, the wide expanse of beach—sometimes completely submerged, but now uncovered almost to its maximum extent. Beyond that, the River, its waves lapping against the black sands.

The River was, Afsan reflected for the thousandth time, like no river he had ever seen inland, nothing like the Kreeb, upon whose north side his Pack of Carno roamed. The Kreeb, which formed part of the border between the provinces of Arj'toolar and Fra'toolar, was a meandering channel of water. But this river—*the* River—spread from horizon to horizon. That made sense: it had to be immense for Land to float upon it.

Those who had traveled all around Land claimed that from no point were the River's banks visible. But it must be a river—it *must* be. For that is what the teachings said. And, indeed, hadn't one of the great explorers—Vek-Inlee, was it? Or long-clawed Gar-Dabo? One of them, anyway, had discovered what she claimed was one bank of the mighty River, all ice and snow, just like on the tallest mountaintops of Land, after sailing far, far to the north. And another explorer—and that person's name completely escaped Afsan at the moment—had eventually confirmed that the northern ice was one of River's banks by sailing an almost equal distance to the south and bringing back accounts of a similar icy shore there. But those stories were often discredited, since they were accompanied by claims that if you sailed far enough north or south, the River flowed backwards, and that was clearly ridiculous.

Afsan stared out at the deep waters of the River. Soon, he thought, soon I shall sail you.

Far out to the east, where the sky and the River met, a purple glow was growing brighter. As Afsan watched, the tiny and brilliant bluish-white sun slowly rose, banishing the stars and planets and reducing the dancing moons to pale ghosts.

Chapter 2

The workplace of Tak-Saleed, senior court astrologer in the service of Her Luminance Empress Len-Lends, was located deep in the labyrinthine basement of the palace office building. Afsan descended the tightly wound spiral marble ramp, the polished banister smooth and cool beneath his palm. Because of landquakes, stone buildings usually didn't last long, but this one had managed to remain more or less intact since it was built, here on the site of the prophet's triumphant return from first gazing on the Face of God. That had been 150 kilodays ago, and the building showed it. Deep scratches were worn into the ramp by the toeclaws of countless Quintaglios. The ramp should have been replaced, but the royal marble quarry near the Nunard rift had been closed after the most recent series of landquakes, and a suitable alternative source of pristine white stone had yet to be found.

As he continued down the curving ramp, Afsan thought again how wrong it was for the chief astrologer not to be quartered on the topmost floor, as close to the heavens as possible. On the first day they had met, he'd asked Tak-Saleed why he worked out of sight of the sky. Saleed's reply still burned in Afsan's mind. "I have the charts drawn up by my exalted predecessors, eggling. I need not see the stars to know that they are moving in their prescribed courses."

Afsan rounded out onto the basement level and hurried

down the wide corridor, its length illuminated by ornate lamps burning thunderbeast oil. His claws clacked against the stone floor.

Along the walls, behind protective sheets of thin glass, were the famed Tapestries of the Prophet, telling the story of Larsk's voyage upriver to see the Face of God. Around the periphery of the tapestries were horrid renditions of Quintaglios bent in aggressive postures, tails balancing heads. These were the nay-sayers, the evil ones, the *aug-ta-rot* beings, the demons who *knew* that Larsk had told the truth but lied about it in the light of day. Afsan looked at their twisted faces and outstretched arms. Each demon had his left hand held strangely, with the thumb over the palm, the claws extended on the second and third fingers, and the fourth and fifth fingers splayed.

The images were flat, with all the characters depicted in plain profile, and no perspective to the form of Larsk's sailing ship. Many illustrations were still done this way, but Afsan had begun to see an increasing number that used the three-dimensional drawing techniques recently developed by the religious painters of Edz'toolar province. Still, despite their flatness, the tapestries were captivating. Ever since he had begun working here, Afsan had meant to arrive early one morning and spend some time examining the finely painted leather sheets with their colorful images of a time 150 kilodays past.

But today was not the day. As usual, Afsan was late. He bounded down the corridor, his tail slapping up and down. Saleed had finally given up berating Afsan for the noise he made running down the halls.

Afsan came to the great *keetaja*-wood door to Saleed's office, the astrologer's cartouche with its pattern of stars and planets and moons carved into the golden grain. Suddenly there were voices coming from within, loud and harsh, as if engaged in an argument.

Afsan paused, his hand on the fluted brass rod that worked the locking mechanism. Privacy was deeply valued. The territorial instinct could never be completely overcome, and when one was alone behind a closed door it was presumably by choice. But, Afsan decided, since Saleed obviously was *not* alone, no harm would be done by assessing the situation before stepping into it. He placed his other hand to his right earhole, forming a cup to funnel the sounds.

"I have no use for your toys." That was Saleed's voice, deep, sharp, like a hunter's polished claws.

"Toys?" A gravelly voice, pitched even lower than Saleed's. The Quintaglio word was *ca-tart,* with the final consonant accompanied by a clicking of teeth. Whoever had spoken it was clearly angry: the terminal click was loud enough to be heard through the thick wood, like rocks clacking together. "Toys!" shouted the voice again. "Saleed, the shell of your egg must have been too thick. Your brain is damaged."

Afsan's nictitating membranes fluttered over his eyes in amazement. Who could possibly speak to the court astrologer thus?

"I am an obedient servant of my God," replied Saleed, and Afsan could picture the old astrologer raising his wrinkled muzzle haughtily. "I don't need the help of the likes of you to accomplish my work."

"You prefer to go on spouting the dogma of ages past, rather than really learning something about the heavens?" The voice carried a strong note of disgust, and Afsan expected to hear the sound of a tail slapping against the marble floor. "You are an embarrassment to the Empress."

Whoever this stranger was, Afsan liked him. He pressed his ear harder to the door, eager to catch every word. The dry wood creaked. Shocked, Afsan's claws jumped to attention. There was nothing to do but walk right in as though he had just arrived.

There was Saleed, standing behind his worktable, leaning on his withered arms, green skin spotted yellow and black with age.

Opposite him was the stranger, barrel-chested, wearing a red leather cap over the dome of his head. The stranger had a ragged yellow scar running from the tip of his muzzle to his left earhole. He wore a gray sash over his torso. The sash was perhaps a handspan wide at the shoulder, but narrowed to half that at his hip. Capital City was a port town, and Afsan recognized the sash as the mark of a master mariner.

Quintaglios continue to increase in body size until death, although the rate did slow as time went on. The stranger was about the same size as Saleed—double Afsan's mass—so

Afsan judged him to be approximately the same age as the old astrologer. His green hide, though, showed none of the age mottling Saleed's did.

"Ah, Afsan," said Saleed. He glanced at the newfangled timepiece on the wall, its pendulum swinging back and forth like the codger's dewlap. "Late again, I see."

"I'm sorry, master," said Afsan quietly.

Saleed hissed, then swished his tail in Afsan's direction. "Keenir, this is my latest apprentice, Afsan—proudest son of far Carno." The last five words were ladled with sarcasm. "Afsan, pay honor to Captain Var-Keenir."

Var-Keenir! Here? If even half the stories he had heard were true— Afsan tipped from the waist in respect, lifting his tail from the ground. "I cast a shadow in your presence," he said, and for the first time Afsan felt the tired old greeting might actually carry some truth.

Keenir turned his head to look at Afsan. Since Quintaglio eyes are solid black, one can't tell where another is looking unless the other also turns his head. Afsan always turned his head to look at adults, but few adults repaid the courtesy to those adolescents who did not sport the tattoos of the hunt or the pilgrimage (and those adults who lacked the hunter's tattoo were accorded no respect by anyone). That Keenir had turned to look at him made Afsan like him even more.

"If you can keep your claws sheathed while working with Saleed, then it's I who should pay honor to you," said Keenir, the voice so deep it reminded Afsan of the call of a shovelmouth. The mariner stepped forward, leaning heavily on an ornate carved stick to support himself. It was then that Afsan noticed that most of Keenir's tail was missing. There was only a handspan's worth of yellow new growth on the green stub. He could look freely at the injury, for there was no way for Keenir to tell where Afsan had focused his eyes, but he took care to show no other expression on his face or with the movement of his own tail. Afsan judged that Keenir's tail must have been chopped off only a hundred days ago or so, perhaps in whatever accident had scarred the sailor's face. "So you would be an astrologer, eh, boy?" said Keenir.

"That is the profession selected for me," said Afsan, and again he bowed in respect. "I would be honored to succeed at it."

"I wish you luck," said Keenir pointedly, and turned for the door. "Saleed," he said over his broad shoulder, "the *Dasheter* sails in a dekaday. Until then, I'm staying at The Orange Wingfinger. If you change your mind about this new tool, send word."

Afsan clicked his teeth quietly. He had never known Saleed to change his mind.

"Young Afsan," Keenir said, "a pleasure to have met you. Your light will glow brightly as time goes by, of that I'm sure." There's no way Keenir could have bowed—without a tail to balance the weight of his head, he would have fallen over—but something in his warm manner gave the impression that he had done so nonetheless.

Afsan beamed. "Thank you, sir."

The sailor hobbled out the door. The ticking sound of his walking stick on the marble floor faded into the distance.

Afsan didn't like asking his master questions, but he had to know what brought the great Keenir to the palace.

"He is a dreamer," replied Saleed, who—much to Afsan's surprise—failed to reprimand him for impertinence. "He has a device he claims lets him see detail on distant objects, a metal tube with lenses at either end. Apparently a glassworker on the opposite shore of Land built it for him. Keenir calls it a 'far-seer.' " Saleed spat the compound word. His hatred for neologisms was well-known.

"And?"

"And the fool thought it might have application in my work. He suggested I turn it on the moons—"

"Yes!" crowed Afsan, and then shrank, expecting a rebuke for interrupting his master. When the sharp words did not come, he continued meekly. "I mean, it would be wonderful to find out what they are."

"You know what they are," said Saleed, slapping his tail against the floor. "They are the messengers of God."

"Perhaps Keenir would let me borrow his far-seer for my pilgrimage," said Afsan. "Then I could use it to examine the Face of God." The words came tumbling out, and Afsan began to shrink the moment they were free in the air.

"Examine?" Saleed roared, his voice erupting from his giant, ancient chest, shaking the wooden furniture in the room. "Examine! An eggling does not 'examine' the Face of

God. You will bow down and worship before It. You will pray to It. You will sing to It. You will not dare to question It!" He pointed his scrawny freckled arm at the doorway. "Go now to the Hall of Worship and pray for forgiveness."

"But, master, I meant only to better see my creator—"

"Go!"

Afsan's heart felt heavy. "Yes, master." Dragging his tail behind him, he left the dimly lit room.

Chapter 3

Afsan hated the Hall of Worship. Not all such halls, mind you: he did have fond memories of the small, cheerful one his Pack had built on the shore of Lake Doognar. But this one in particular was loathsome.

The Hall of Worship at the imperial palace! He'd expected it to be holier than any room he'd ever been in, for here the very Empress balanced in prayer, the regal tail held firm and rigid parallel to the ground. Here, the Master of the Faith, Det-Yenalb, spoke directly to God.

There was no real difference between this hall and the one he'd attended as a child. Both had the same circular layout, although this one was five times the diameter of Carno's. Both had the same wooden floor, although poor Carno's was deeply scratched with claw marks, whereas this one constantly received fresh planks, stained a pale green, from the nearby *madaja* grove maintained solely for that purpose. And both halls were divided in half by a channel of water, representing the mighty River on which Land floated. In the hall of his youth, the channel had been just wide enough to accommodate supplicants in single file. But here Afsan had often seen processions of Quintaglios wearing broad leather sashes marching six, seven, and even eight abreast.

But now the huge hall was empty. Major services were held every fifth even-day and whenever a boatload of pilgrims returned from gazing directly at the Face of God. Afsan's footfalls echoed in the chamber as he entered from the sinner's doorway, set at right angles to the channel of water. This was significant, he knew: those who came through this entrance, passed beneath this arch of blackest basalt, had turned as far from the natural flow of life as was possible.

He walked to the mock river and tested the ankle-deep water with his toes. As usual, it was uncomfortably cold, although he had heard tell that when the Empress was to walk here it was heated. Afsan stepped into the channel of water and leaned forward, his torso parallel to the floor, his tail swinging up to balance his weight. He'd never been good at this, and he had to splay his legs slightly to make it work, but it was considered disrespectful to drag one's tail in the holy water.

The last thing he wanted to do was appear disrespectful, for he knew that High Priest Det-Yenalb might be watching even now from his secret place, high above. Afsan kept his muzzle pointed ahead, as the posture of respect demanded, but he rolled his black eyes upward. Painted on the bowl-shaped ceiling was an image of the Face of God, swirling and colorful. But one of the black circular God's eyes was really a window through which Yenalb sometimes watched, or so Afsan had heard from a court page. Afsan would make sure that Saleed would get a good report of his penance.

Afsan had started in the middle of the river channel, as sinners must, and was now working toward the west end. The symbolism had been explained to him kilodays ago at Carno's Hall of Worship, the first time he'd had to undergo this humiliation. He'd bitten off a playmate's finger during a game. The other boy—what had ever become of Namron, anyway?—had regenerated the digit in a few dekadays, but he'd also tattled to the creche master about Afsan. Anyway, walking to the west end meant walking into the fading light of dusk, reminding one of the darkness that awaited sinners. Even then, Afsan had enjoyed the night, but he had been restrained enough not to point that out to the creche master.

At the end of the channel, balancing all the while, he bobbed his whole body three times. It was an emulation of the instinctive gesture of territoriality, and, in this context, meant, as the sacred scrolls said, *here I draw the line, I will allow darkness to come no farther*. After the ritualized bobbing, he turned tail and began the slow march the other way, splashing down the river toward the east, toward dawn, toward light, toward knowledge.

Knowledge! Afsan clicked his teeth in rueful humor. How little knowledge we have. What do we really know of the planets? Of the moons? How can Saleed turn down an opportunity to study them in detail, to learn their secrets?

"*Boy! Your tail!*"

Afsan's heart jumped, and his fingerclaws unsheathed in surprise. Having lost himself in thought, he'd let his tail dip into the water. He quickly pulled it up and then swung his head around to find the source of the voice, echoing in the domed chamber.

It was the wrong thing to do. With legs splayed, tail swung way up, and head turned around, he lost his balance. He came flopping down belly-first into the river, splashing holy water everywhere. The impact hurt—he could feel the free-floating riblets across the front of his belly pressing in on his organs. He quickly got to his feet, and, fear on his face, hurried onto the *madaja*-wood flooring, the sound of drips hitting the planks echoing much too loudly in the Hall.

He scanned around for the source of the voice again. There, at the head of the mock river, standing where the sun would rise, was Det-Yenalb, a mid-sized male with an exceptionally long muzzle and earholes that seemed a bit too high on the side of his head. Yenalb wore the swirling, banded, colorful sash of his office.

"Your Holiness," Afsan stammered. "I'm sorry, I didn't mean—"

"You didn't mean to make a mess." Yenalb didn't seem to be angry. "I know."

"I'll clean it up right away."

"Yes, I'm sure you will." The temple master looked at Afsan. "You're the young one from Arj'toolar province, aren't you?"

"That's right, sir. Afsan is my name; my home Pack is called Carno."

"Afsan. That's all? A boy your size should have a praenomen syllable by now."

Afsan cast his head down. "I have not earned my name

prefix yet, although I have chosen the one I hope to merit: Lar."

"Lar," repeated Yenalb. It was derived from Larsk, the name of the prophet. "A high standard to aspire to. And, yet, of course, you would not be here at the palace if you were not already exceptional. You're Tak-Saleed's latest, aren't you?"

"It is my honor to be his apprentice."

"I'm sure it is," said Yenalb. "Afsan, you must take care. God talks to Her children in many ways. To priests, such as myself, She talks directly, in words spoken so only we can hear. To astrologers, such as your master, Saleed, She talks in the complex motions of the stars, the planets, and the moons. To others, She talks in subtler, less direct ways. Has God spoken to you?"

Afsan's tail swished in sadness. "She has not."

"I see you bear no tattoo. When is your pilgrimage?"

"I am to take it in the near future, although I have not yet scheduled a voyage."

"You are of the age, though, are you not? You look the right size."

"Yes, it has been ten kilodays since my hatching."

"Then you must go soon."

"I've been waiting for the right moment to discuss this with my master."

"If memory serves, I've seen you in Saleed's company before. Somehow, I doubt a moment when you feel comfortable with him will come." Yenalb clicked his teeth together a few times to show the remark was meant as a jest. Afsan tipped his head in concession. "Well, the *Dasheter* sails soon. Would you care to travel with Var-Keenir, boy?"

"Would I! That would be terrific—!"

Yenalb clicked his teeth again. "I have some influence with Saleed. I'll speak to him."

"Thank you."

"Not at all. You obviously need some enlightenment, or you wouldn't have been marching the sinner's march. And nothing is more enlightening than gazing directly upon the Face of God."

"So I hear."

"Good. Now, do the march again, properly this time, then get a mop and clean up the water." Yenalb turned to go, but then spoke once more. "Oh, and Afsan, you should try to do your hunt before your pilgrimage."

"Why?"

"Well, the pilgrimage is dangerous."

"So is the hunt, I'm told." Again, Afsan regretted speaking so plainly to an elder, but Yenalb dipped his head politely.

"The hunt is less dangerous," the priest said, "as long as you don't join one of those crazy parties that still adhere to the teachings of Lubal. Go after something that eats plants and you'll be fine. No, we lose more people on the pilgrimage than we do on the ritual hunt. Riverquakes mean there are times when boats don't return at all. If anything were to happen to you during your long voyage, and you hadn't participated in a hunt yet, your soul would arrive in heaven without having completed either rite of passage. That's bad."

"How bad?"

"Well, we all look forward to the afterlife, to a place where we will shed the instincts that keep us from working well together the way a snake sheds its skin. In heaven, at God's side, with infinite territory, we will constantly enjoy that special camaraderie and those heightened senses that one normally only experiences during a pack-hunt. But you must be primed for that, must have experienced the cooperative spirit of the hunt in this life in order to be able to adopt it as your native mode in the next. And, as for the pilgrimage, well, you must in fact see God in this mortal existence if you are to recognize Her in heaven. She does not—She does not look like one of us."

"I'm looking forward to gazing upon Her face," said Afsan.

"Then I shall go arrange it." And with that, Yenalb turned tail. Afsan watched the old priest's back as he disappeared down a corridor.

Det-Yenalb made his way out into the blue-white light of day. He paused on the ramp leading down from the Hall of Worship, reflexively sniffing the air. The palace grounds were huge. They had to be.

The veneer of civilization, thought the priest. He snorted. *God had told us to live and work together, but even to this day, it's hard for us to do so.*

The territorial instinct was strong, and although the creche masters worked to break it in the egglings, no one ever lost it completely. Yenalb could sense the others around him, smell their skin, hear the clicks of their claws on the paving stones. There, across the courtyard, young Henress, smaller even than this Afsan, the problem child from Carno. And, there, flopped on her belly under a flowering tree, old Bal-Hapurd, torpid after a meal. Normally Yenalb would take the shortest path to Saleed's office, since all but the Empress would move out of his way, conceding territory to the priest. But dealing with Saleed required planning. Yenalb took a circuitous route, avoiding everyone. He could not afford to have his concentration disturbed by his own reflex responses to others in his path.

At last he entered the palace offices, went down the spiral marble staircase, passed the Tapestries of the Prophet—pausing to bow territorial concession to the likeness of Larsk and to shield his eyes from the lying demons that formed a ring around the tapestry—and finally stopped at the golden *keetaja*-wood door to Saleed's office. Yenalb took a moment to admire the astrologer's cartouche. The symbols were much the same as in Yenalb's own. That was proper, for was not the study of the stars, planets, and moons akin to the study of God? But there was something about the layout of Saleed's that Yenalb found appealing.

Yenalb's claws drummed against the small strip of metal at the edge of the door. The clicking they made against the copper was quiet enough not to be threatening, but distinctive enough that anyone on the other side would realize that someone wanted to come in. Saleed made a questioning bark, Yenalb identified himself, and permission to enter was granted. The priest pressed on the fluted brass bar that opened the door.

Saleed, taller by a handspan than Yenalb—the result of the twenty kilodays difference in their ages—was lying on his dayslab, his belly pressed against the wooden boards. The slab was at an angle halfway between horizontal and vertical, taking Saleed's weight off his legs and tail. Supported by a stone pedestal, the slab came up to Saleed's shoulders, letting his head look comfortably down onto his desk, and his spotted arms dangle down onto the desktop, angled to be parallel to the dayslab.

Saleed had twin pots built into his desk, one for ink, the other for solvent. He was finishing a glyph at the end of one line on a sheet of writing leather, the ink-dipped claw of his longest left finger steady and firm as it delineated the intricacies of a scientific symbol Yenalb did not recognize. Yenalb bowed territorial concession to the astrologer; Saleed replied by lifting his hands to show that, except for the one he was using for writing, his claws were sheathed.

"I cast a shadow in your presence, honorable astrologer," said Yenalb.

"And I in yours," replied Saleed without warmth.

There was silence between them for a moment. At last, impatience honing his words, Saleed spoke again. "And what business do you have with me?"

"Your latest young apprentice—Afsan, is it? He came by the temple this morning."

Saleed let out his breath noisily. "I sent him there. He had blasphemed."

"Well, he can't be that bad," said Yenalb lightly. "You're not tossing him out on his tail like your last five."

"My last six," said Saleed.

"In any event, Afsan marched the River. He is cleansed."

Saleed nodded and turned his head to look at Yenalb. "Good."

"But he has not yet taken the pilgrimage."

"That's right."

"He's nearly up to my shoulder. A boy that size is old enough for the journey."

"There is more to maturity than height, Yenalb. You know that."

"Granted. But what better way for him to mature than to take the voyage? Your old creche-mate Var-Keenir is in town, did you know that?"

"Yes. Keenir and I spoke this morning."

"The *Dasheter* sails in a dekaday on a pilgrimage tour."

"I see." Saleed pushed up into a standing posture, letting his weight fall onto his tail. The wood of his dayslab creaked in relief. "And you, Yenalb, who have seen the boy occasionally at service, have spoken to him once or twice, you feel you know what's good for him better than I, who has been his master for half a kiloday now. Is that it?"

"Well . . . "

"And now you have the fangs to come in here and set me straight?"

"Saleed, I have only the boy's welfare at heart."

"And I do not? That's your contention, isn't it?"

"Well, you're not known for being the gentlest soul—"

Saleed slapped his tail against the floor. "I am training the boy's mind. I am teaching him to think."

"Of course, of course. I meant no slight."

Saleed lifted his tail from the floor and bobbed his torso once, a slow, deliberate gesture, a clear signal that he felt Yenalb had crossed into territory Saleed considered his own.

Yenalb backed away. "My apologies, astrologer. I meant only to suggest that you might perhaps see fit to let Afsan voyage with Keenir."

Saleed was not mollified. "Yenalb, perhaps you should place a little more faith in me. *Ask Keenir.*" He drummed his now unsheathed claws against his thigh. "He will tell you that I have already arranged for young Afsan's passage aboard the *Dasheter.*"

Yenalb's nictitating membranes fluttered over his eyes. "You have?"

"I have."

"Saleed, I—I'm sorry. I didn't know."

"Your business here is concluded?"

"Yes, but—"

"Then perhaps you will do me the honor of withdrawing from my area."

Swishing his tail in wonderment, Yenalb did just that.

Chapter 4

The hunt! Afsan excitedly slapped his tail against the floor of the Hall of Worship. All young Quintaglios looked forward to joining in a pack, setting out in the ritual quest for food.

And yet, there was trepidation, too, for the hunt was difficult and dangerous. But if Afsan were to take his pilgrimage soon, then he must make arrangements to join a pack right away.

Most of the apprentices at the palace were older than Afsan—he was, after all, a relatively new arrival in Capital City—and all but a few bore the tattoo of their successful first kill. Afsan's hand went to the left side of his head, above the earhole, the spot where the tattoo would go. Who else did he know who did not have the tattoo?

Dybo.

Of course. Dybo, shorter by three finger-widths than Afsan himself. Dybo, who had such a flair for music and poetry, but who had often enlisted Afsan's aid in his studies of mathematics and science. Dybo, whose penchant for mischief had gotten Afsan in trouble on many occasions, although, of course, Dybo himself always emerged unscathed.

Dybo, the crown prince.

Surely Dybo could be talked into going on a hunt. His blood-red sash of royalty, after all, was a hollow honor in the view of some people, for it had not been earned, but the tattoo of a hunter carried weight everywhere and with everyone. Yes, a prince could get away with not having it, but some would always compare him to the others who never acquired it, the beggars who had to fight with the wingfingers for whatever meat remained on discarded carcasses.

Most people enjoyed killing their own food now and then, Afsan knew, finding it invigorating and cathartic. Some made careers of hunting—Afsan had heard it said that those who might otherwise be too violent for living peacefully with others were often assigned that vocation. But to forgo the Ritual Hunt, one of the prime rites of passage, was to never know the camaraderie of the pack, and, therefore, to never really be considered a part of society.

Yes, Dybo would be the answer. His rank could get them both bumped to the top of the waiting list to join a pack. But where to find him? Afsan looked up at the bright white sun, so small as to be not much more than a searing point of light. It moved quickly across the sky—not quite fast enough for its progress to be perceived at a glance, but with enough rapidity that a few tens of heartbeats later the change would be noticeable. Noon would be here shortly.

Dybo, like most people, slept odd-nights, meaning that tonight he would be up. Usually one wouldn't eat until just before going to sleep, since torpidity settled in after a large meal. But Dybo wasn't like everyone else. His appetite was well-known, and he might very well be off devouring food.

Afsan headed down the ramp that led out of the Hall of Worship into the courtyard. A reflex sniff of the air, a quick scan of the grounds to ascertain who was where, then he hurried off to the dining hall.

As he entered the vestibule, he checked the container into which shed teeth were discarded. Only ten or so bright white Quintaglio fangs were at the bottom, their curved, serrated shapes ranging from the length of Afsan's thumb to longer than his longest finger. So few discards meant that most of the palace residents had not yet eaten today. Afsan paused for a moment to admire the container, a flowing shape of intricately painted porcelain. He clicked his teeth together. At the palace, even a garbage pail was a work of art.

He headed into the first dining room. There were cracks in the stone ceiling from the big landquake of a few kilodays ago.

The dining tables, with their central ruts to drain blood, were worn, the wooden tops pitted with claw marks. Four people were eating there, three females and a male, each separated as widely as possible from the others, each noisily working over meat-laden bones.

Afsan bowed concession to the one he had to pass most closely and entered the inner dining room. There, as he had hoped, was Dybo.

The crown prince didn't look particularly regal just now. His muzzle was caked with drying blood as he worked over a joint of hornface meat. His chest was covered with animal grease, blood splatters, and not an inconsiderable amount of the prince's own drool. That the prince was a lusty eater was well-known. And why shouldn't he be? Stockyards of plant-eaters were kept adjacent to the meal hall, and the Empress's child got nothing but the finest cuts. Indeed, Afsan felt envy at the sight of the hip joint, mostly cleaned of flesh now by a combination of Dybo's teeth and claws. Apprentice astrologers got such fare only on holidays.

"I cast a shadow in your presence, Dybo," said Afsan. The greeting was usually reserved for one's elders. But honor must be paid to any member of *The Family,* that special group that knew who its blood relatives were, that tiny elite who were direct descendants of the Prophet Larsk.

Dybo, his chest supported by a dayslab angled over the table, looked up. "Afsan!" He scooped an ornate bowl of water from the table and drained it in a massive gulp. "Afsan, you shed skin of a snake!" Dybo smiled in delight. "You gizzard stone from a spikefrill! You shell of your former self! By the Face of God, it's good to see you!"

Afsan clicked his teeth lightly. Dybo's exuberance was both amusing and embarrassing. "I'm always glad when my studies permit me time to see you, too, Dybo."

"Have you eaten? You're looking as scrawny as a wingfinger." Afsan was thin for a Quintaglio, but it was only in comparison to Dybo that he might be thought of as scrawny. The prince's appetite came at a price.

"No," said Afsan, "although I will eat soon. I like to sleep even-nights."

"Right, right. At some unspecified time in the future, you

must tell me what it is you do while the rest of us are sleeping. Great mischief, no doubt!"

Afsan clicked his teeth in jest. "No doubt."

"Well, then, you must eat, my friend, eat so that you will sleep soundly. You see, while you are the only one sleeping, the rest of us are out doing things we won't tell you about." Dybo's teeth clattered in heavy laughter at his own joke. "Eh, Afsan! Someday you'll wake up and find your tail tied in a knot!"

"If I do," said Afsan, "I'll simply cut it off and make the most likely suspect swallow it whole."

"Yuck. Not while I'm eating."

It was Afsan's turn to laugh. "What other time is there?"

Dybo nodded slight concession. "When indeed, my friend?" He pointed to the hip joint. "This one is pretty well finished. I'll have it put out for the wingfingers to pick over. But I could use a little more, and I'm sure you'd enjoy a fine piece of meat."

"That I would."

"It is done, then!" Dybo slapped his palm against the side of the dayslab. "Butcher!" he called. "Butcher, I say!"

A Quintaglio clad in a red smock appeared in a doorway. He was long-of-limb, almost insectile, and his muzzle had a drawn-out, melancholy look.

"Bring another hip joint," commanded Dybo. "A nice, bloody one, not yet drained. And water."

With a loping stride, the butcher went off to do as the prince had asked.

"There, Afsan. We'll get some flesh on you yet. Now, what brings you here? Not to sing again, I hope! I do like you, you malfunctioning bowel, but, by the moons themselves, if I have to listen to you sing again, I'll stick pebbles in my earholes to drown out the noise."

Dybo's musical ability was almost as enormous as his appetite, but even Afsan conceded that his own was virtually nonexistent. Still, the young astrologer loved the sound of music, admiring the mathematical precision of it.

"Well," said Afsan, "in a way, I do want to talk to you about my singing."

Mock horror ran across the prince's face. "No! By the eggshell of God, no!"

"And about God, too. You see, I wish to take my pilgrimage."

Dybo slapped his palm against the dayslab again. "Excellent! About time, you puffed dewlap! You may be a skinny thing, but your height betrays your age. It's time we shipped you off on a boat."

"Indeed so. But—"

At that moment, the butcher reappeared. With his long arms, he managed to place the hip joint on the table without stooping, positioning it over the drainage trough. This joint was even bigger than the one Dybo had been gnawing on before. Steam rose from the flesh; the animal had been killed moments ago. Afsan looked up at the butcher. His long snout was bloodied. He had slain the beast himself.

"Thank you, butcher," said Dybo, who had never been good at names. Even Afsan, who had been here less than five hundred days, knew this lanky fellow was Pal-Cadool.

"Yes," said Afsan. "Thank you, honorable Cadool."

The butcher bowed, and with that insect-like walk of his, strode off to get the bowls of water.

"Well, don't just stand there, you crusty growth," Dybo said to Afsan. "Lie down. Eat."

Afsan lowered himself, push-up style, onto the angled surface of another dayslab, letting the wood take his weight. "Dybo, I want you to go on the pilgrimage with me."

Dybo's face was already buried in the carcass, ripping hot flesh from bone. He came up, gulped down what he'd taken, and then stared at Afsan.

"Me?"

"Yes, you. You do have to go sometime, don't you?"

"Well, yes. Of course. I haven't given it much thought yet, though. But my mother would never let me sail on some scow—"

"I'm going on the *Dasheter*. With Captain Var-Keenir."

"Are you, now?"

"Yenalb has lifted some dragging tails for me."

"The *Dasheter,* you say. By the prophet's claws, that's a fine ship! We could have a grand time aboard her, that we could! Think of the fun we'd have!"

"I have. Will you come?"

"My mother will have to say yes. The Family belongs to the people, after all."

"The people might find they got a lot more to eat if you weren't around for three hundred days or so."

Dybo released gas from his belly. "That's probably true," he said, then clicked his teeth in laughter. "Very well! Let's assume we'll do it."

"Excellent. The *Dasheter* sails in a dekaday."

"That soon?" Dybo used his claws to worry a gob of flesh from between his teeth. He examined the errant meat, skewered on the polished curve of his middle-finger talon, then nibbled it off. "Well, why not?"

"There's one more thing, Dybo."

"You've got my food. You've got my company. What more could you possibly want?"

"Yenalb says one should take the hunt before going on the pilgrimage."

"Does he, now? Well, I suppose that makes sense. But the hunt—" Dybo looked away.

"You're afraid?"

"Afraid?" Dybo's voice sounded hollow. "You are addressing the son of the Empress, you would-be astrologer."

"That I am. Well, if you are not afraid, then why not join me in the hunt?"

"It's just that—"

Pal-Cadool had returned bearing a platter holding bowls of water. Dybo fell silent.

"How is the meat?" asked Cadool, his words, like his frame, elongated.

"Excellent," said Dybo, still slightly tremulous.

"Young Dybo," said Cadool, each word a ponderous, lengthy sound, "it's not my place to comment, but I overheard a bit of what you two are talking about, and, with your permission, I have something to say."

Dybo looked up, surprised. It was as though he was seeing Cadool as an individual for the first time. "Speak, butcher."

Cadool dipped his muzzle, now wiped clean, to show that he was looking at the hip joint on the table. "Nothing, young prince, tastes better than meat you have killed yourself."

Dybo looked up at Cadool. The butcher's muzzle retained its normal green color, so the prince knew that he was telling the truth. Dybo looked back down at the meat, flared his nostrils, enjoyed its smell. "Well, in that case, I must try it. Afsan, a-hunting we will go!"

"You're not afraid?" said Afsan.

Dybo dug into the meat in front of him. "I've endured your singing, excrement from a shovelmouth. What could be more frightening than that?"

Chapter 5

Well, thought Afsan, *among other things, meeting the Empress herself could be more frightening than my singing.*

Afsan had seen Empress Len-Lends many times, but always from a distance. Her stern visage oversaw most official events and she often greeted returning packs. But now Afsan was to have an audience with her. He would never forget the expression on Saleed's face when he had arrived at the astrologer's office that morning.

"Young Afsan," Saleed had said, a tremulous note in his voice, "the Empress commands your presence at her ruling room right away."

Afsan's nictitating membranes danced across his eyes. "The Empress wishes to see me?"

"That's right," Saleed said with a nod. "You've either done something incredibly bad or incredibly good. I don't know which it is."

Afsan headed up the wide spiral ramp into the light of day, then crossed the courtyard to the ornate building that housed the room from which the Empress ruled. Guards flanked the entrance ramp, but they were there only to fend off wild beasts that might wander into the city. They wouldn't think of challenging another Quintaglio, even one as young as Afsan, for to challenge one's territory was to force a fight, and civilized beings did not fight.

Instead, Afsan merely was expected to nod concession to the guards, and he did just that, hurrying up the ramp and through the vast archway that marked the entrance to the main palace building.

There was no sign of decay here. Yes, the landquakes hit this building as hard as any of the others, but it, at least, was repaired quickly after each tremor. Afsan made his way down the Hall of Stone Eggs. Its walls were lined with thousands of rock spheres that had been cut in half and polished to a lustrous sheen. The inside of each hemisphere was lined with beautiful crystals. Most of the crystals seemed to be clear or purple, but some were the same bright bluish-white as the sun itself and others were the green of Quintaglio hide.

Afsan had heard of this great hall. Its beauty was legendary; even the priests of Carno spoke of it. But Afsan had no time to pause and enjoy its wonders—it would not do to keep the Empress waiting. He hurried past the hemispheres of sliced stone, wondering how something as plain as an uncut egg could contain such beauty within.

The Hall led into a vast circular chamber, its round floor banded with polished rocks of different colors. There were four doors leading from the chamber, each with the cartouche of the occupant carved intricately into the rich red *telaja*-wood from which they were made. The Empress's cartouche was used on every official proclamation—including even the notice Afsan had received summoning him to Capital City—so he had no trouble recognizing which door he wanted. But before knocking, he paused to admire this particular rendition of the cartouche. Five handspans high, it was carved in exquisite detail. The symbols of the Empress were rendered in bas-relief and the background, carved out to take advantage of the rich grain of the wood, represented the swirling, mesmerizing Face of God.

At the top of the cartouche's oval boundary there was the egg, said to be that of the Prophet Larsk himself. Its shell was marked by a thin reticulum of cracks, showing that it had at one time been open, but now was resealed, signifying that the prophet might indeed one day be born again, might return to the people to make known more new and wondrous truths.

Below the egg was the serrated sickle of a hunter's tooth, and, to its right, the tighter curve of a hunter's claw—a reminder that whenever a Quintaglio hunted, the Empress went with him or her in spirit, for it was through her strength that even the most ferocious of beasts would end up as food.

Beneath these was a field of wavy lines, representing the great River upon which Land floated, and an oval shape in the center, representing Land itself.

And at the bottom were two profile views of Quintaglio heads facing away from each other, bowed in territorial concession, indicating that no matter which side one moved to, all territories found there were the Empress's. Usually the heads were rendered in silhouette, and Afsan had always taken them to be generic faces, but here they were brought out in striking individual detail. Afsan's heart jumped when he realized that the face on the left, wrinkled and mottled with age, was none other than Tak-Saleed, court astrologer, and that the one on the right, with its long muzzle and high earholes, was Det-Yenalb, the chief priest of the temple. What Afsan had interpreted before as saying *all people will concede to the Empress* was much, much more: *even the stars and the church must bow concession to me*. Afsan swallowed hard and drummed his claws against the metal plate in the doorjamb, the *tinking* sound made louder by a hidden hollow behind the copper sheet.

Afsan waited nervously. At last, a reply came: "*Hahat dan,*" a short form of the words meaning "Permission to enter my territory is granted."

Afsan worked the lever that opened the door and stepped into the ruling room. It wasn't what he'd expected. Yes, there was a throne, an ornate dayslab angled perhaps a tad closer to vertical than normal, mounted high on a polished basalt pedestal. But in front of it was a plain, unadorned worktable, covered with papers and writing leather. The figure lying on the throne slab had her head tipped down, drawing glyphs. Afsan did not want to interrupt, so he stood quietly just inside the doorway.

There was no doubt that this was the Empress: the great dome of her head was richly tattooed. Afsan noticed that the worktable was mounted on little metal wheels. It could apparently be easily removed when official functions were being performed here.

At last the Empress looked up. Her face, although youthful,

was weary. A ragged band of brown skin ran across the top of her head and down over one eye—an unusual pattern, clearly visible beneath the tattoos. She squinted at Afsan. "Who are you?" she said at last, her voice thick and cold.

Afsan's heart skipped a beat. Had this all been some terrible mistake? Was he not expected here? "Afsan," he said in a soft voice. "Apprentice to the court astrologer, Tak-Saleed."

The Empress tilted her head in acknowledgment. "Ah, yes. Afsan. Saleed must like you. You've been here, what, four hundred days?"

"Four hundred and ninety-two, Your Luminance."

"A record, I should think." There was no humor in her tone. "And in that time you have become a friend of my son, Dybo?"

"It is my honor to be so, yes."

"Dybo tells me you wish him to undertake the pilgrimage and the hunt with you."

Afsan's tail swished nervously. Had he overstepped propriety in asking this of Dybo? What punishment would befall his impertinence? "Yes, Empress, I have."

"Dybo is a member of The Family and prince of this court. But, of course, he does, at some point, have to go through the rites of passage."

Afsan didn't know what to say, so he merely bowed concession to the Empress.

"Come closer," she said.

Should he run to her, his tail lifting from the ground? Or walk more slowly, thus letting his tail drag? He opted for the latter, hoping it was the right choice. Normally one could approach to within the body-length of the larger of the two individuals in question without prompting a reflex reaction. Afsan felt that coming that close to the Empress, though, would be wrong. He stopped a good ten paces shy of her.

Lends nodded, as if this was as it should be. Then she held up her left hand, the three metal bracelets of her office clinking together as she did so. "I will allow him to go with you, but," she unsheathed her first claw, "you will," and then her second, "be," the third, "responsible," the fourth, "for his," the fifth, "safe return."

She let the light in the room glint off her polished claws for several heartbeats as she flexed her fingers. "Do I make myself clear?" she said at last.

Afsan bowed his agreement, then left the Empress's ruling room as fast as he could.

Chapter 6

Spitting dust, Afsan forced himself to climb higher. He had wanted Dybo to come with him. But Pal-Cadool, the butcher who for three days now had been telling the boys stories about the hunt, had been shocked at that suggestion. "One must go alone to join a pack," he'd said in that drawn-out way of his. Dybo had gone earlier today. Afsan had had to wait until his duties to Saleed were discharged. He had not seen Dybo since the young prince had departed, nor, from what he could gather, had anyone else.

It was late afternoon, the sun already bloated, purple, and low. When he'd started the climb, Afsan had been conscious of the background noises: the mating cries of shovelmouths pumped through their intricate crests; wingfingers shrieking as they scooped up lizards; ship's bells and drums far off in the harbor. But the climb was arduous, and soon all other sounds were drowned out by the thudding of his heart.

The Hunter's Shrine was atop a giant rock pile, fully as high as any of the Ch'mar volcanoes. But this cairn hadn't been formed naturally. Legend had it that each of the Five Original Hunters—Lubal, Katoon, Hoog, Belbar, and Mekt—had brought one stone here for every successful kill throughout their lives. The priests of their sect had continued the practice thereafter. Of course, worship of the Five had all but vanished ever since the Prophet Larsk first gazed upon the Face of God, now some twelve generations ago, and so the pile did not continue to grow.

Which was fine by Afsan. It was far too high already. He clattered over slabs of stone. Some were ragged; others, smoothed by rain, by tilting and chafing together, or by the scouring of Quintaglio claws. His hands scrabbled for purchase, his feet dug in where possible. He moved quickly over precarious parts, the slabs shifting beneath his weight. Afsan hadn't labored this hard in kilodays. That he wore a backpack didn't help. The straps of shovelmouth hide cut into his shoulders.

Afsan wondered how many turned back before reaching the summit, still a dizzying height above him. And what of poor Dybo, chubby Dybo? Had he failed in the climb? Was he hiding somewhere, ashamed?

Afsan was above the low coastal hills that shielded Capital City from the continual east-to-west wind. Here, up high, the evidence for Land's breakneck journey down the River was plain: the air bit into Afsan's hide like needles of ice. He had hoped the breeze would cool him, for he was close to overheating, but instead it just made him more miserable.

Far above, canted at an angle, he could see the summit and, at its crest, the Hunter's Shrine.

The Shrine, appearing small from this distance, was a stark frame, like a wooden building abandoned before completion. Afsan's knuckles, shredded on the rocks, continued to find rough handholds to hoist himself higher still. For a long time the building seemed to grow no closer, but at last he was near enough to hear the wind shrieking through its gray members. With a final effort, Afsan scrabbled to the top of the rocky cairn.

In front of him the stones were scarred by a gridwork of shadows as the sun, swollen and dim, dipped behind the Shrine. The strange twisted girders were stained a deep purple in the waning light. Rising to a standing posture, Afsan shifted the weight of his pack and forced himself over the remaining distance to the Shrine.

He was exhausted, his breathing deep and ragged. To steady himself, he grabbed one of the beams that made up the Shrine, a short cylinder knobbed at each end. His nostrils were full of grit; his knuckles were bleeding; his knees were scraped, his tail likewise; chips had been knocked out of the chitinous sheaths that covered his clawbones.

The beam was hard and cool. It glinted in the fading light, apparently coated with resin. Afsan stood back a few paces to get a good look at the Shrine. It was by no means huge: twenty paces in length, half that in breadth, and perhaps twice his own height. The design was an eerie lattice, a twisted skeletal structure.

Skeletal. By the prophet's claws, the thing was made of bone! Afsan staggered back, seeing the nightmare edifice with new eyes. Gnarled columns of a hundred vertebrae rose over his head. Femurs joined to form archways; ribs and assorted smaller bones traced out geometric shapes. Through the wide gaps between the bones, Afsan saw a large sphere of Quintaglio skulls at the center of the Shrine, empty eye sockets facing out in all directions.

His tail was swishing back and forth uncontrollably. Every instinct told him to run, to get away from this evil place, to scramble back down the tilting, clacking rocks to safety.

No.

No, he could not.

It was a test. It must be. The whole thing: the impossible climb, the terrifying building. A test, to eliminate those not fit for the rigors of the hunt, those too squeamish to face death.

And yet. And yet. And yet.

Afsan hadn't been able to find anyone who had seen Dybo since he had headed out. Much of the ritual of the hunt was still based on the old worship of the Five Original Hunters, and priests of Lubal had been known for many a perversion, not the least among them cannibalism.

But no. He would not give in to his fear. Afsan stepped to the Shrine's opening, a door frame of shoulder blades. The chill wind whistled through the structure, an eerie, plaintive call, like the dying breaths of all those whose bones now surrounded him. He peered into corners in the purple twilight. Afsan's backpack carried a gift—an astrolabe he had brought from Carno—but he didn't know where to leave it.

"Hers is the white skull, at the front of the sphere."

Afsan jumped, twisting at the apex of his leap. He hit the ground, claws extended, facing the intruder. A figure stepped from the shadow: bulky, with an ebony leather hunting tunic whipping against her body.

Afsan's voice sounded hollow, even to himself. "Are you Dem-Pironto?"

The large dark figure silhouetted against the swiftly growing night did not reply.

"I'm looking for Dem-Pironto," Afsan said again. His nostrils caught the intruder's odor and he realized that this was a female. Her pheromones were different from any he'd ever detected. There was something about them—something that caused him to feel an edginess, a wariness. Afsan felt energized, even after the exhausting climb. He took off his backpack, grateful to be free of its weight. "I've brought a gift for Pironto," he said, pulling at the gut ties. "No one would give me guidance as to what would be appropriate, but this object has much meaning to me, and to my intended profession." Her eyes were on him, unblinking. Afsan wished she would speak, knew he was babbling. "It's a device for measuring celestial angles," he said, pulling an ornate object into view, a trio of freely spinning concentric brass rings. He held it out so she could see the polished metal, the fine care lavished on its manufacture.

"A hunter knows his or her course without mechanical aids." The words were talon-sharp.

Afsan spluttered. "I—I'm sorry." He tried to fathom her expression. "I meant no disrespect." There was silence between them, silence except for the screaming wind. At last, Afsan said again, "Are you Dem-Pironto?"

The dark figure stepped sideways, blocking the exit arch. "Dem-Pironto is dead," she said at last. "She died yestereven-day. She died so others could eat."

Dem-Pironto, leader of the imperial hunt, dead? "How?" asked Afsan, curiosity getting the better of prudence.

"Gored, she was, by a triple hornface. An honorable passing for a hunter."

"My gift—?"

"—is of little use to her now."

Afsan sighed. He set the astrolabe on the rocky ground.

"Not there, eggling." The female pointed, claw unsheathed, to the sphere of skulls. "Place it near her skull. Pironto's is the white one, there, facing out from the middle."

Afsan's heart skipped a beat. The monstrous collection was wider than he was tall: two hundred skulls arranged in concentric spheres. Each skull was twice as long as it was high, with large eyeholes, gaping pre-orbital fenestrae halfway down the snout, and elliptical nares. The lower jaws consisted of separate left and right bones, able to split wide when swallowing. The muzzles were packed with serrated daggers.

Afsan always found skulls frightening: eyeless receptacles, the discarded canister of the mind. These skulls seemed to float a distance above the ground, each somehow not touching the ones near it. A support, then, he told himself, perhaps thin glass or crystal, invisible in this waning light. He reached a hand forward to feel the space between skulls, but jerked it back, deciding he'd rather not know if he was wrong.

"I've never seen such a place as this," Afsan said aloud, his back to the stranger. He was grateful even for the sound of his own voice, something warm and alive interrupting the shrieking winds. "A structure made of bones."

Skulls in the inner concentric spheres had darkened over great time to a deep brown, but the skull of the late Pironto was easy to spot: it was whiter than all the others.

Afsan stooped and placed the astrolabe on the ground beneath the overhanging bulge of the sphere of skulls, directly below Pironto's snout. It disconcerted him as he rose to catch a glimpse of the brass rings of the astrolabe, an object he had cherished since childhood, through the gaping holes in her skull and the skulls beneath.

The stranger was silent for several heartbeats. "They are the bones of hunt leaders from the past," she said at last. "Here rests the hunting spirit of each."

He turned to face her. "Hunting spirits? I thought that was a myth."

"You are so blind." The stranger spread her arms wide. "I hear them." She closed her eyes. "Irb-Stark and Tol-Tipna. Sar-Klimsan the Scaly and Hoad-Malat. The smooth-skinned Klimsan and Tol-Catekt. And my predecessor, Dem-Pironto."

Afsan swished his tail in comprehension. "You are the new hunt leader."

"I am." Her voice was pure glass. "Jal-Tetex is my name."

"I cast a shadow in your presence."

In the gathering darkness, that was far from literally true. Jal-Tetex's black eyes did not betray where they were looking, but nonetheless Afsan had the uncomfortable feeling that he was being assessed from head to toeclaw, from the front of his muzzle to the tip of his tail. At last Jal-Tetex spoke again. "No doubt you do. What do you know of the hunt?"

Afsan couldn't remember the exact words to the Scroll of the Hunt, but he came up with what he thought was a good paraphrase. "It is the ritual through which we purge emotions of hate and violence. It is the endeavor through which we gain self-sufficiency. It is the activity that brings us together in camaraderie and cooperation."

"And who is the greatest hunter of all time?"

Afsan's tail twitched. A trick question? There were *five* original hunters. To pick one as better than the others might be considered blasphemous. Even though the religion of the hunt was all but extinct, there was deep respect for all five. Lubal was the one whose cult still had the most adherents, and those who didn't understand fine distinctions often referred to the Worship of the Five and the Lubalite Cult as one and the same. Still, to name only one— And then it hit Afsan: "Why, you, Jal-Tetex, as imperial hunt leader. You are the greatest hunter."

Afsan saw Tetex's jaw work, but he couldn't tell over the howling wind whether she was clicking her teeth in amusement. "You'll go far at the palace," she said at last. "But you're wrong. The greatest hunter of all is The One yet to come, the one foretold by Lubal: 'A hunter will come greater than myself, and this hunter will be a male—yes, a male—and he shall lead you on the greatest hunt of all.' "

Afsan had heard the story before, and mentally whipped himself with his tail for not remembering it in time. "Of course," he said. "The One."

Tetex seemed satisfied. She nodded slightly at Afsan. "And you are?"

"Afsan, from Carno Pack, part of Arj'toolar province. I am a student astrologer, apprenticed to Tak-Saleed."

"Why do you climb the rocks of the Five? Why do you come here?"

"I wish to join the next hunting pack."

"Afsan, did you say?" Her face was impassive. "You're a friend of Prince Dybo, aren't you?"

"That's right."

"Dybo climbed the rocks earlier today. He brought a gift of precious stones."

Afsan was delighted that his friend had made it. "Dybo has access to great wealth."

"Not to mention influence," said Tetex. "You used that influence to get bumped to the front of the queue."

"Well—"

The wind whipped, but it was her voice that stung. "Egg-ling, do you seriously believe that princely influence will save you should something go wrong on the hunt?" Afsan said nothing. "Look there!" She pointed at the floating skulls. "Those were all great hunters, with kilodays of experience. Every one of them killed on the hunt. There are others who were swallowed whole, for whom we don't even have a skull by which to remember them."

Afsan stood tall. "I am not afraid."

"Fear is important, young one. Fear is the counselor. Those who don't know when to fear wind up dead."

Afsan was confused. "I am not afraid," he said again.

"You lie!" Tetex's voice cut across the shrieking wind. It was now dark enough that the color of Afsan's muzzle would not have betrayed him if he were telling a falsehood.

"I am not afraid of the hunt," said Afsan quietly, his tail twitching uncomfortably among the ragged gray rocks.

"Are you afraid of me?" Tetex demanded.

Afsan was defiant. "No."

Suddenly Tetex was moving, a black blur against the gath-ering night. Afsan's claws sprang from their sheaths: she was charging at *him,* attacking another Quintaglio. He didn't know what to do; one does not attack one's own kind. But instinct, mighty instinct, took command in his hesitation. He dived to the left, avoiding the impact of her body, twice his own bulk. But Tetex pivoted, her tail slicing the air as she wheeled around. She caught Afsan's arm and flipped him, sending him sailing. He crashed into the gridwork of bones that made up the nearest wall and tasted salt blood in his mouth. Penned, no way to resolve the territorial ambiguity, he leapt forward, arms up, claws out, jaws agape. Tetex ran directly into his leap, muscular legs propelling her. They smashed together. Afsan landed on his back, an agonizing position, his tail bent aside. Tetex's triple-clawed foot slammed into his chest above his heart, pinning him. She flexed her toes, the claws sending sharp pains into his chest.

The tableau held for a semi-ten of heartbeats, wind whipping around them. Finally Tetex spoke again. "Do you fear me now, astrologer?"

Afsan's eyes narrowed in shame. He spoke in a whisper barely audible above the wind. "Yes."

Tetex pulled her foot from his chest, and then, to Afsan's amazement, stooped to offer him a hand in getting back on his feet. "Good," she said. "Learn to listen to your fear. Perhaps then you will survive." Tetex nodded concession to Afsan, and he felt the instinctive reflexes drain from within him. She looked up at the stars, at the rising constellation of the Prophet/Hunter. "We leave at first light tomorrow."

Chapter 7

Up ahead, Jal-Tetex had stopped moving. The grass came to the middle of her chest. Afsan, ten paces behind, immediately stopped as well. Dybo, just behind Afsan, continued ahead for a step or so before he realized what was going on, then he, too, came to a halt.

Tetex held up her right arm, the five fingers splayed, the claws sheathed. A symbol in the hunter's sign language: she had again detected the trail of their quarry.

What, wondered Afsan, had given away the beast they were tracking? A footprint? Trampled vegetation? The animal's pungent wind? Whatever it was, the discovery made his heart pound.

There were six others in the hunting party besides Afsan, Dybo, and Tetex. Three were veterans, each half again as big as Afsan. The other three were also on the hunt for the first time. Afsan had not discussed with Dybo his meeting with Tetex at the Shrine, but his respect for the rotund prince had increased, knowing that he had endured the cruel climb and the sight of the bones of dead hunters.

Tetex clenched her middle digits, leaving only her first and fifth fingers exposed, and these she extended as far as she could. The sign meant *thunderbeast*.

Thunderbeast! There was no tastier prey. Next, Tetex rotated her hand at the wrist, then turned it back. Once.

Twice. Three times. Each twist signified a gradation in size: small, medium, large. The animal that Tetex had detected would be food enough for the entire palace to have a feast. Afsan could hear Dybo clicking his teeth in delight.

Tetex turned to the right and began moving through the high grass. The three other experienced hunters moved as one to keep pace with her. Afsan, Dybo, and the trio of tyros were momentarily confused, then, one by one, they followed the rest in stalking the great beast.

The terrain here, like most places on Land save the Mar'-toolar plains, was mountainous. Banded patterns of buckled rock were exposed everywhere. The pack was heading uphill, and soon Afsan himself could see some of the signs that Tetex was following. The long grasses were not just compressed; in many places they were pulverized. Smashed groundfruits could be seen here and there.

Excitement mounted within them. Afsan realized that the same pheromone he had detected yesterday radiating from Tetex was the cause. Those rare females who were in perpetual heat made the ideal hunt leaders, their scent arousing normally dormant instincts within the pack. It affected males and females the same way, sharpening their senses, readying them for battle.

The sun, tiny and brilliantly white, beat down upon them. The experienced hunters moved with great stealth, making no more sound in the grass than did the rustling of the constant east-to-west wind. Afsan and the other young ones made more noise, but their kilodays of training playing the stalking game were paying off. The sound still wasn't enough to herald their arrival.

Afsan could feel the sack of his dewlap waggling in the breeze, dissipating heat. He held his tail slightly aloft, exposing its entire surface to the air. Onward, onward, up one side of a hill and down the other, again and again, following the signs of the thunderbeast's passage.

Throughout it all, Tetex kept the lead. At last, she held up her hand again. This time, claws were unsheathed. Afsan searched his memories for the significance of that signal, but, glancing down, he saw that his own claws had slipped out into the light of day, as well. The excitement of the hunt, he thought. Instinct at work.

Tetex waited several heartbeats, perhaps to be sure she had everyone's attention. She then touched her middle finger to her thumb, creating a circle. *I see it.*

Afsan heard Dybo behind him surge forward a step, and then immediately come to a halt. He'd wanted to rush up and view their intended prey, but, thankfully, his training came into play before his action could have alerted it.

Tetex now held up both arms, showing both hands. Each member of the hunting pack was represented by a finger on those hands: the experienced hunters by those on the left hand, the neophytes by those on the right. By extending the appropriate finger, Tetex was able to indicate a specific hunter. She held up the first finger on her left hand, then pointed to a spot perhaps thirty paces from where she was now standing. The largest of the experienced hunters moved to that position. Using similar signals, she deployed her other two practiced killers.

She then held up the first finger on her right hand, indicating Dybo, and pointed to a position far to the east. Dybo bobbed concession and moved off in that direction. Next, she positioned two more of the first-timers, both females, at points midway along the crest of the hill. Then came Afsan's turn. He was delighted that Tetex motioned for him to stand near her.

Afsan moved through the tall grass to his assigned position. At last he could see into the valley, see what they had come to kill.

Thunderbeast: a four-footed mountain of flesh; brown, with blue mottling on the massive back; an enormously long neck; ridiculously small head; pillar-like legs; a great whip of a tail.

And this one was a giant! To the thing's shoulder, it was eight times Afsan's height; to the top of its neck, now extended to browse leaves from the *hamadaja* trees around it, the beast stood fully twenty times as tall as Afsan. To walk the length of its tail would take forty paces.

The thunderbeast had not yet seen them. The neck was poking into the topmost part of one tree, defoliating it rapidly. These beasts spent most of their waking time eating, moving huge quantities of vegetation past their peg-like teeth, through their narrow throats, down those long, long necks, and into their rumbling guts.

The prey was ideally situated for the attack. About fifty paces away, it had walked partway into a loose stand of trees. *Hamadajas* had unbranching bone-white trunks that exploded into leaves only at their tops. The trees were evenly spaced, forming a natural pen for the creature. Only the tapering tail stuck out, free of obstructions.

Tetex looked left and right, sizing up her team. At last, she held up her arm and gave the rapid hand chops that signaled the attack.

Stealth was no longer required. The only easy way out of the valley was back up the hillside, and that was the direction from which the nine Quintaglios were coming. Tetex let out a roar, the massive sound erupting from her chest. She charged, back parallel to the ground, tail flying out behind.

Afsan followed. He was surprised to find himself roaring in excitement, too. The ground shook as the seven others charged, as well.

The thunderbeast's head was buried in the leaves. That would muffle its hearing, buying them a little time before the giant creature would respond.

Suddenly the end of the neck swung around, the tiny head and the dull brain within reacting slowly to the nine puny creatures barreling toward it. Afsan could see the black eyes—obsidian black, the most intelligent-looking thing about the animal—go wide in astonishment. The beast began to back away from the trees, each footfall sending a tremor through the ground. Afsan looked over his shoulder. Chubby Dybo, his gut in the running posture barely clearing the soil, was bringing up the rear.

Tetex was first to reach the thunderbeast. She leapt onto the animal's right flank just ahead of the rear leg. Her claws dug like pitons into the mountain of its abdomen. Rivulets of blood ran down the thing's sandy hide. One of the other experienced hunters arrived next, his greater stride letting him outrun Afsan. He, too, leapt onto the beast, his jaws digging into its flank. Afsan watched in amazement—

—which was a stupid thing to be doing. Suddenly, out of his peripheral vision, he became aware of a beige wall barreling along, slicing the air with a massive *whoosh*. The tail—no thin line from this close, but rather half the height of Afsan himself—came toward him. He turned and ran, trying to get out of its way, but it struck him from the rear, knocking the wind from his lungs.

His vision exploded into patterns of light. He felt himself being lifted up, knocked flying by the impact, and, heartbeats later, saw the ground far below. Afsan brought his arms up to cover his face. The hard ground rushed toward him—

God protect me!

—and all was blackness for an instant.

His whole body ached. He had landed in shrubbery, the thorns scratching his hide. His right leg hurt as he put his weight on it.

He was now thirty paces from the thunderbeast. The monster was slapping its side with its tail, attempting to dislodge the tiny Tetex. Several other members of the pack had secured themselves to the beast's side and were ripping chunks of flesh from it. Even round Dybo was gnawing at the thing's right rear ankle.

By the prophet, this was a monster! Afsan had never heard of a thunderbeast so big. Perhaps they had bitten off more than they could swallow whole.

No, thought Afsan. He would not fail at his first hunt. *He would not.* He tipped forward into the running posture and rushed toward the beast.

The ground was slick with blood. The creature, still very much alive and fighting, had many small rips in its belly, although, as yet, the internals seemed intact.

The thunderbeast's tail flicked again, and Afsan saw one of the other youngsters—Punood, was it?—go flying the same way he had. But Punood had received a more vicious blow. Even over the pounding of his own footfalls, Afsan had heard the cracking of Punood's bones as the tail impacted, killing him instantly, and, moments later, the splat as his corpse slammed against distant rocks.

I won't be distracted. Afsan clenched his teeth, feeling the uneven interlock of their serrated tips. *I won't look back.*

The beast lifted its right forefoot. One of the older hunters had been maneuvering to get at the soft flesh beneath the shoulders, but now the round footpad with its five stubby claws was coming down upon her, the circular form casting a shadow on the hapless Quintaglio. In a few moments, she'd be crushed to death. The hunter began to run, but the leg, like a giant hammer, pounded down. It missed her body, but pinned her tail. Even at this distance, Afsan heard the snap of vertebrae. The Quintaglio's legs went out from under her, and she slammed chest-first into the ground. The thunderbeast realized it had done only half a job, and lifted its left forefoot as a prelude to bringing it down to stamp the life out of the prone hunter.

Chubby Dybo, tendons from the thunderbeast's rear ankle hanging like reeds from his mouth, rushed into the scene. He spat the tendons aside and with one massive chomp sheared through the downed hunter's tail just below where it joined her torso.

The thunderbeast's foot smashed down, kicking up a cloud of dust. When the view cleared, Afsan could see that the formerly pinned hunter had made it to safety several tens of paces away, the stub of her tail bright red with her own blood. Dybo, too, had managed to avoid the crushing foot.

The thunderbeast was confused about what had happened. Afsan was close now, very close.

When you charge, think of what angers you, Tetex had said before the hunt.

Saleed. Afsan inhaled deeply. *Abominable Tak-Saleed.*

He folded his legs beneath his torso and pushed up with all his might, divots flying from the ground as he leapt into the air.

Afsan tasted his own blood as he slammed into the beast's right front leg just above the knee. He scrambled, digging in claws for traction, pulling himself higher and higher up the massive thigh. The hide was tough, and he had to kick to get his claws to pierce it, but he was making progress.

The beast apparently sensed something in this new attacker. It bent from the hips, rising up on its hind legs. Afsan had heard that thunderbeasts could do this, especially when the forefeet were balanced against the side of a tree, to reach particularly lofty vegetation. But in a desperate effort to save its own life, the animal had found the strength to surge up without such support. Afsan felt wind flow over his body as the beast's torso rose into the air.

Afsan dug in, desperately holding on. Surely the creature could maintain this semi-erect posture, with its tail bent at almost a right angle, for only a few moments.

A few terrifying moments . . .

The animal's front crashed down, the forelegs pounding the dirt. Over his shoulder, Afsan saw that Tetex and two others had been knocked off the beast's side, and one of those two didn't look like she was going to get up again. Afsan turned his attention back to the beast. Its flesh spread out in front of him like a wall. He scrambled up onto the shoulders.

The neck curved up in front of him, dizzyingly, rising into the sky like a giant beige snake. It measured twelve times Afsan's own body length. He looked back. Hunt leader Tetex had leapt onto the creature's side again. She'd ripped a gaping hole through the pebbly skin and was at last getting at the entrails. The beast's tail swung wildly left and right, knocking hunters off as it went. Afsan could feel the mountain of flesh beneath him expanding and contracting with each breath.

Suddenly everything moved again, and Afsan feared he would become nauseous. The shoulders bounced, almost tossing him off. The creature was walking, desperately trying to find some way to escape.

The surrounding trees limited its mobility, but it had apparently spotted a path through the grove. Afsan felt muscles rippling beneath him as it marched forward. Once out of the stand of trees, it would be able to roll on its side, crushing Tetex and the others.

Once again, Afsan conjured a vision of his master, Saleed. Strength grew within him, power pumping through his blood vessels. He stretched his arms wide, digging claws into the massive base of the thunderbeast's neck. His arms encircled only a tiny portion of it. He pulled himself up, dug his toe-claws in, reached his arms farther up the neck, and pulled up again.

Off the shoulders now—

He dug in again; pushed farther up, feet ripping into the flesh for traction.

Again.

Again.

Afsan could feel the creature's pulse, a rapid beating beneath the thick hide. Again he reached up the neck, again he pulled himself up, shimmying his way.

The beast was making good progress toward the clearing. Small tree trunks snapped as it barreled ahead. Afsan pulled,

pulled, pulled, afraid to look down, afraid to see how high up he now was.

The neck was tapering slowly; Afsan's arms encircled it halfway now. But the tiny head was still dizzyingly high above him. He climbed harder.

Suddenly the thunderbeast's front end was free of the trees. The creature swung its neck in a wide arc. Afsan did look down now, and screamed. The ground swept by in a blur, air whipping over his body. He continued to climb, clawing. Blood from the wounds made by his hands flowed down the snaking tube, making it harder for him to get traction with his feet.

The neck swooped down. Afsan saw the ground swelling upward. Then the neck swung back up, and Afsan felt his ears pop. He clawed ahead.

Another swoop. Another painful popping. Diving down, swinging up, dizzying, dizzying . . .

Fingerclaws on his left hand clicked against those on his right. He could now encircle the entire neck.

The neck swung to the left, and Afsan saw the beast's brown and blue abdomen looming in. But before he could be squished against it, the neck reached the limit of its flexibility. It swung back to the right, curving outward, sweeping Afsan through the sky.

The head was only a small distance away now. The squared-off snout was visible as the creature's face swung from side to side, the giant black eyes, bigger than Afsan's fists, batting opened and closed. The thunderbeast let out a scream, in response no doubt to Tetex's handiwork far below. Afsan could feel the neck expand and contract as the low rumbling erupted from the animal's throat. He gave one massive pull and brought himself to the end of the neck. The head, ridiculously tiny on a beast of such bulk, was smaller than Afsan's own torso. It spread out before him, wrinkled. The beast's nostrils, high on a dome of bone between the eyes, flared uncontrollably. The creature's mouth, still open from the scream, showed pink innards and peg-shaped teeth.

Afsan loosened his grip so that he could slide around to the underside of the neck. There he opened his jaws wide, as wide as they could go, his left and right mandibles popping from their sockets, and with all the strength he could muster he chomped down on the soft flesh on the underside of the neck. The thunderbeast gasped. Afsan bit again and again, cutting through the neck at its thinnest spot. Blood geysered out of the widening cavity, liquid crimson fists beating against him. Another massive bite, and then another, and another. Afsan felt hot air rush out of the hole he had made, forced out by the bellows of the creature's lungs, far, far below.

Craning, Afsan could see that the beast's nostrils had stopped flaring, that its black eyes had closed for the final time. All at once, Afsan felt the rigidity go out of the neck, and, like a massive flexible tree trunk, it came hurtling toward the ground, air rushing about him as it did so. Just before the neck hit, Afsan leapt off, lest he be crushed beneath it. He kicked away with all the horizontal force he could muster. While still airborne, he heard and felt the thunderous slam of the great weight of flesh as it hit, and then everything went silent as Afsan himself smashed into the dirt.

Chapter 8

"How is the eggling?" Tak-Saleed's voice betrayed no special concern as he looked down at the unconscious Afsan, lying flat on his belly on a marble surgical table, the youngster's head stretched out so that the bottom of his jaw was against the cold stone.

Most denizens of Capital City had left to enjoy the spoils of the hunt—more thunderbeast meat than many of them had ever seen in one place. But Saleed, giant and ancient, was too old and too slow to go so far for a meal. One couldn't unequivocally interpret his having stayed behind as showing any particular worry about his fallen apprentice, and yet he had come here, come to the hospital, where those trained in medicine did what they could for the hunters who had been injured during the day's spectacular kill.

Unfortunately they couldn't do much. Oh, they cleansed wounds with water. Some lacerations were wrapped with leather. Broken bones were braced with splints. Mangled extremities were cut off with twist-saws so that they could be regenerated. The saws were different from the cleavers Pal-Cadool used; these wrenched and tore so that blood vessels would seal. With a simple severing, a Quintaglio would bleed to death.

But, excepting bruises and minor cuts, Afsan's limbs were intact. His injuries were internal, to the head and torso. It was known that the sap of certain plants could relieve infections, that holding a *makaloob* root in the mouth might reduce nausea, that the venom from some lizards if applied in moderation could deaden pain. But to rouse one knocked unconscious, one who'd had a ladle of blood spill from his right earhole, one who even now breathed shallowly—that was a matter beyond doctor or priest.

Saleed switched from looking down his wrinkled muzzle at Afsan to facing the doctor, Dar-Mondark. Mondark seemed deep in thought, working his lower jaw backwards and forwards, the clicking made by pointed teeth passing over each other an audible indication of his cogitation. At last he answered Saleed's question. "He has been unconscious since they brought him back from the site of the kill. His shoulder took the brunt of his fall—see the bruising there?—and we have shifted his shoulder blade back to where it should be. But the side of his head was also banged severely. We tried placing *halbataja* leaves on his brow. That helps about one time in twenty, but there was no response."

Mondark knew more about the inner workings of the Quintaglio body than anyone else. For kilodays, he had been dissecting cadavers, trying to understand what each organ was for and how it worked; why extremities could regenerate, but eyes, for instance, could not; what blood was for; and so on.

The hospital room was heated by a cast-iron stove burning coal. When the body was warm, internal processes occurred more quickly, so this would normally speed any healing that might occur naturally. The crackling of the flames was the only sound for several heartbeats. Finally, looking as if he had been wondering whether to say what he was about to, Mondark went on. He gestured with his head. "High Priest Yenalb is here. And Crown Prince Dybo came in with Afsan, and said he would return soon. Even that lanky palace butcher—Cadool, is it?—stopped by. And now our humble facilities are graced by he who reads the stars for the Empress. Why is this youngster so important?"

Yenalb was bent over Afsan. He had used a carefully honed and polished fingerclaw to pierce the skin above Afsan's left earhole, making a swirling pattern. Now he was smearing in purple-black pigment, filling in the hunter's tattoo. Normally the high priest would only personally tattoo members of The

Family, but Yenalb must have felt a degree of responsibility for Afsan's injuries. If Afsan did not survive, at least he would make it into heaven bearing the mark of one rite of passage.

Saleed wrinkled his muzzle as if he found such questions distasteful. "Afsan is my apprentice," he said at last. "He has—he has a remarkable mind; a genius one rarely sees."

"Judging by his heroics today," said Mondark, "it would appear that he has a great future as a hunter."

"No." Saleed let the syllable hang between them for a time. "No, this is his first and his last hunt. His mind is too keen, too valuable, to waste on such animal concerns."

"The people need to eat."

"The people are going to need much, much more than just fresh meat if we—" Saleed stopped short. Mondark opened his mouth slightly, a questioning gesture. Apparently Saleed felt he couldn't just end there. At last he said, "There are tough times ahead, Doctor. Tough times, indeed."

Mondark's tail swished back and forth. His claws unsheathed. *Fear.* "You have read a portent in the sky. The stars foretell our doom!"

Yenalb stopped working on Afsan's tattoo and looked up at the astrologer. For a moment, Saleed closed both his eyes. He apparently was uncomfortable, as though, perhaps, the medic had read him too plainly, had taken his meaning too clearly. Or perhaps not, for after a moment Saleed clicked his own teeth in gentle humor. "You may be taking me too literally," he said at last. "Just because I'm an astrologer doesn't mean I always speak of heavenly revelations. Perhaps I meant, in a general sense, that our progress as a people simply depends upon the sharp minds of our young."

Mondark seemed about to speak again when Afsan, prone before them, let out a small groan, a sound coming more from deep in his chest than from his throat. Yenalb quickly moved out of the way and the medic loomed in, bringing his earhole to Afsan's chest.

"Well?" snapped Saleed.

"His heart is beating more steadily." Mondark laid his palm across Afsan's forehead. "He's managed to raise his body temperature well above the ambient, meaning his metabolism has strengthened considerably." He shouted, "Paturn, bring bowls of blood!"

Mondark's team was well-trained. Within moments a young male appeared bearing a tray full of simple clay hemispheres filled with red liquid. Paturn was no older than Afsan himself, judging by his size. He set the tray on a counter and brought the first bowl to Afsan, forcing Afsan's jaws open and letting the blood trickle into his short muzzle and down his throat.

Mondark stepped back from the marble surgical table and motioned for Saleed and Yenalb to follow. Softly he said, "The animal blood will help rehydrate him, and its taste usually arouses the spirit. He's fighting for consciousness now."

Paturn drained three bowls down Afsan's throat, although much spilled out of his gaping muzzle and pooled on the tabletop. Suddenly Afsan spluttered. Paturn immediately ceased pouring blood into him and turned Afsan's head aside so that his throat would drain onto the tabletop.

"Is he coming around?" asked Yenalb.

Mondark bent over Afsan and firmly gripped the boy by the shoulders. Saleed's nictitating membranes blinked in surprise. "Such physical contact often forces a reaction," said Mondark, almost apologetically.

But Afsan's coughing stopped almost as quickly as it had begun. Mondark shook him gently, but to no avail.

The doctor swore quietly. "Roots."

"Have you lost him?" Saleed demanded.

Mondark straightened. "I don't know."

Suddenly there was another voice in the room. "You had better not lose him, Mondark."

Heads swiveled. "Prince Dybo—" Bows of concession all around.

"I said I would be back," said Dybo. He looked at Yenalb. "I am pleased you came," he said. And then he turned to Saleed. "It's good to see you here, as well, astrologer."

Saleed dipped his muzzle. He looked uncomfortable and moved quickly to the doorway. He nodded concession to Mondark. "You've looked after him well. My thanks." And then, off-handedly, he added, "Oh, and don't tell Afsan I was here, please." And with that, the old astrologer hurried down the corridor as fast as his age and bulk would allow.

"What have you done for him, Doctor?" asked Dybo.

"Everything possible," said Mondark.

Dybo then turned to Yenalb. "And you?"

"I have used every prayer I could think of," said the high priest.

The prince waddled over to the surgical table. "Then let me try."

Darkness . . .

And a sound.

Music?

Yes, music. A ballad: *The Voyage of Larsk.*

So beautiful. Compelling.

He sailed to the east,
River's waters tossing his boat,
A steady wind,
And, at last, rising from the waves . . .

Rise up to the music.

No. Sleep.

Yes! Awake!

But the darkness is so warm, so inviting . . .

Can't give in to it.

Wake up! Break out into the light.

So difficult, like cracking through an eggshell without a birthing horn.

Better to sleep, to relax, to rest.

So tired.

No . . .

No!

Force the outer eyelids open. Light filters through the inner membranes. An effort, such an effort: open those, too.

Such beautiful music.

"Dy-bo . . . "

The prince stopped singing and thumped his tail in joy. "Afsan, you plugged earhole! I knew you wouldn't leave us."

Afsan managed to click his teeth together weakly. "Finish the song."

Dybo leaned back on his tail. And sang some more.

Chapter 9

Afsan and Dybo walked down the cobblestone streets of Capital City.

"You were amazing!"

Afsan bowed slightly. "I did only what needed to be done."

"Nonsense! It's the talk of the city, and I hear the newsriders are having a great time with it. No one has ever seen such skill, such innovation, on a first hunt."

"You are too kind."

"And that lanky palace butcher—what's his name?"

"Pal-Cadool."

"Cadool, yes. Every time he brings me food, he asks about that hunt. It's funny listening to him. He's intimidated by my station, but he can't help but ask about your kill. He keeps saying he wishes he had been there to see it. I've told him three times now about you shimmying up that endless neck, ripping out the thunderbeast's throat. He loves the story!"

"And no doubt it gets better with each retelling," Afsan said lightly.

"No, this tale needs no embellishment. I thought we were doomed."

"Well," said Afsan, "Cadool probably misses the organized hunt. After all, most of his time is spent simply slaughtering animals in the stockyards. A true ritual hunt is a rare thing. I understand that most people only participate once a kiloday or so. And I wouldn't doubt that Cadool gets to do so even less often, given his palace responsibilities."

Dybo slapped his belly in good humor. "Well, that's true enough. Feeding me is a full-time job!"

Clicked teeth. "Exactly."

"Still, it's not just Cadool who's impressed. Even Tetex admits that she had overestimated her skill in taking on that monster. When I become Emperor, I should make you leader of the imperial hunt!"

Afsan stopped dead, his jaw hanging open. "What? Surely you wouldn't do that—I, I'm an astrologer, a scholar."

Dybo stopped too and spoke gently. "I'm teasing you, you gizzard stone of a plant-eater. I know the stars are your first love; I wouldn't take them away from you."

Afsan sighed with relief and began walking again. "Thank you."

"But it *was* a remarkable kill . . . "

"You forget that it almost killed *me,*" replied Afsan.

"Well, yes, you took a nasty fall. But you had so much brains to begin with, I knew that even getting half of them knocked out wouldn't be a problem."

Afsan dutifully clicked his teeth.

Soon, they were looking down upon the harbor, the steady wind ruffling their sashes. Along the shore were many *jerboksaja* trees, distinctive because their branches all grew in great trailing arrays off to the west, shaped that way by the constant unidirectional wind.

Twenty sailing ships were moored in the harbor, ranging from small pleasure vessels to big cargo carriers. The great River spread out to the horizon, its waters choppy close to Land but looking smooth farther out. Twisty wisps of cloud were visible, but otherwise the sky was its usual deep, clear mauve.

Several kinds of animals were on the beach. A caravan of hornfaces, not unlike the one Afsan had journeyed with from Carno, stood by one of the cargo ships, long horns projecting from above their eyes and the tips of their nose beaks, a great frill of bone rising from the back of each head to shield the neck. Nearby, a small thunderbeast was being used as a crane, a cradle hanging from its long neck lifting what looked like a blast furnace off the deck of a three-mast ship. Wingfingers swirled in the air above the beach, individuals occasionally swooping down to snatch something to eat.

Quintaglios were milling about, too. Merchants from Capital City, crowding closer than protocol would normally allow, were shouting offers at the captains of the cargo ships. They were trying to secure the best of the latest shipments of copper and brass tools from Fra'toolar, of gold bracelets and pendants bearing the marks of workers from the Cape of Belbar, and of that rarest of commodities, cloth, from the plantgrowers of the Mar'toolar plains.

The *Dasheter,* with its double-diamond hulls, was easy to spot among the other ships. Its four masts—two on the port side of the forehull, two on the starboard side of the afthull—stood higher than any of the others in the harbor.

Most of these ships moved cargo from coastal communities. They could be small since they put into port every few days, letting passengers and crew off to run and hunt. Afsan remembered the story of the *Galadoreter,* blown far out into the River by a storm, unable to land for dekadays. With no way to release the territorial instinct, the crew had fought until everyone aboard had died in a crazed territorial battle. The ship, its decks littered with rotting Quintaglio carcasses half eaten by wingfingers, had blown back to shore near the mining town of Parnood.

But the *Dasheter* was a long-voyage vessel. Even though meant to carry only thirty people, it was huge. Afsan looked down at its twin hulls: two vast diamonds joined by a short connecting piece. Everywhere, space was maximized. True, a Quintaglio would feel uncomfortable penned in any place that was not clearly his or her own territory, but the four decks of the *Dasheter* afforded as many square paces per person as possible. Intellectually one would always know that others were nearby but if tricked physiologically into feeling alone, instinct should be kept at bay.

The *Dasheter*'s vast red sails were angled parallel to the steady wind caused by Land's travel down the River, preventing them from moving the ship. In the center of each sail was an emblem of the Prophet Larsk, for it was his famous voyage that the *Dasheter* was going to retrace. The first sail had Larsk's cartouche; the second, his name in ancient stoneglyphs; the third, his head silhouetted against the swirling

Face of God, an image derived from the famed Tapestries of the Prophet that hung not far from Saleed's office; and the fourth, the crest of the Pilgrimage Guild, founded by Larsk himself, and to which Var-Keenir and all other mariners of note belonged.

"It's a beautiful ship," said Dybo.

Afsan nodded. "That it is."

Coming up from the harbor was the *Dasheter*'s identification call. Loud: five bells; two drums. Soft: five bells; two drums. Loud: five bells; two drums. Over and over again.

"The journey will take a long time," said Dybo.

"Anything worthwhile takes time," said Afsan.

Dybo looked at him. "My, aren't we profound today." He clicked his teeth in humor. "But, yes, I suppose you're right. Still, it's frustrating. Why does God look down upon the world from so far away?"

"She's protecting us, no? Looking out for obstacles upriver, making sure the way is safe."

"I suppose," said Dybo. "Still, why does She never come and look directly down on Land? There are dangers here, too."

"Well, perhaps She feels that the people here are well looked after by the Empress. It is, after all, through God's divine will that your mother rules."

Dybo looked out at the water. "Yes, indeed," he said at last.

"And one day, you will rule."

Again, Dybo stared out toward the horizon, the steady wind blowing in his face. He said a word, or at least Afsan thought he did, but the wind stole it away before it reached Afsan's earholes.

"Does it scare you, Dybo? The responsibility?"

Dybo's gaze came back to look at Afsan. The chubby prince was strangely subdued. "Wouldn't you be scared?"

Afsan realized that he was upsetting his friend, and that was the last thing he wanted to do. He bowed slightly in concession. "Sorry. But, anyway, your mother is only thirty kilodays old or so. I'm sure she'll rule for a long time yet to come."

Dybo was silent for a time. "I hope so," he said at last.

• • •

Dybo, as crown prince, was ushered aboard the *Dasheter* first, amid a clacking together of honor stones by the ship's crew. Afsan had to queue with the rest of the passengers, but it wasn't long before his turn to board came.

A wooden gangway led from the dock up to the foredeck of the *Dasheter*. Afsan, his sack of belongings slung over his shoulder, was about to step upon it when he heard his name called by a deep voice. He turned and, much to his surprise, saw Saleed shambling toward him.

"Master?" said Afsan, stepping away from the gangway.

Saleed got within two paces of Afsan, closer than one would normally approach another in a public place. He reached into a pouch at the hip of his blue and green sash and withdrew a small object wrapped in soft hide. "Afsan, I—" Saleed looked uncomfortable. Afsan had never seen the astrologer thus. Irritated, yes. Angry, often. But uncomfortable? Ill at ease? Never.

"Afsan," Saleed said again. "I have a, a present for you." He opened up the knot of hide. Within lay a six-sided crystal, deep red, about the length of Afsan's longest finger. It seemed to glow from within.

Afsan was so surprised, he did nothing at first. Then, finally, he reached out to take it. He held it in front of his face, and turned toward the sun. The crystal blazed.

"It's beautiful," Afsan said. "What is it?"

"It is a traveler's crystal, boy. It is said to bring luck. I—I took this one on my own first pilgrimage."

Afsan, tail swishing in wonderment, said, "Thank you."

"Be safe," said Saleed, and with that, the old astrologer turned tail and walked away.

Afsan watched his master's back awhile, then walked toward the wooden gangway. He stepped on it, feeling the planks moving slightly as the *Dasheter* rose and fell on the waves, and walked up onto the deck of the ship.

The *Dasheter*! Afsan exhaled noisily. A more famous ship one could not imagine. Keenir's exploits were the stuff of legend, and his ship was well-known even far inland.

Afsan leaned back on his tail for balance, unused to the slow heaving of the deck. A ship's mate, wearing a red leather cap, much like the one Keenir had been wearing that day in

Saleed's office, gestured to Afsan. "Come along, eggling. Can't stand there all day."

Afsan looked over his shoulder and realized that someone else was on the wooden gangway, standing patiently halfway across, not wanting to invade Afsan's personal space. Afsan nodded to the fellow behind him. "Sorry!" He quickly moved farther onto the deck.

The mate moved closer to Afsan. "Your name, young one?"

"Afsan, late of Pack Carno, now of Capital City."

"Ah, Saleed's apprentice. Your cabin is on the topmost of the aft decks on the port side. You can't miss it; it has a relief of the Five Hunters carved into its door."

Afsan bowed concession. "Thank you."

"Best stow your gear, boy. We sail soon. You'll find on the back of your door a list of ship's chores you are expected to perform. There's also a prayer schedule; services will get more frequent as we approach the Face of God, of course."

"Thank you," Afsan said again, and headed off to find the door carved with the Five Hunters.

Walking the deck was disquieting. Like all Quintaglios, Afsan had lived through several landquakes. Once, indeed, he had seen a large building topple only paces away from him. The undulating of the deck reminded him of the angry shifting of the land. He had to make a mental effort to tell himself *not* to seek open ground.

Afsan crossed the connecting piece between the fore and aft hulls of the boat, and found a ramp leading to the decks below. Down here, it was dark and musty. The walls, floors, and ceilings groaned constantly, almost as if alive. He had no trouble finding his cabin. The carving of the Five Hunters was exquisite. Afsan could picture the artisan laboring for days over the planks that made up the door, using fingerclaws as fine tools to chisel out chips of wood.

Each of the Five was rendered in distinctive detail: Lubal in the running posture, back horizontal, tail flying; Belbar in mid-leap, hand and foot claws extended; Hoog baring her fangs; Katoon tipped over so that her tail stood up like a tree trunk as she picked over a carcass; and Mekt, wearing a priestly robe, head held way back, throat expanding in a swallow, the last handspan or so of a tiny, thin tail still protruding from her mouth. Afsan was puzzled. It looked like an awfully small meal for such a great hunter.

And then there were the strange hand gestures, visible in the renditions of Lubal and Katoon: fingers two and three with claws extended, four and five spread out, the thumb placed against the palm.

Afsan had seen that odd configuration somewhere else, but where? *The Tapestries of the Prophet.* The *aug-ta-rot* beings. The demons.

Odd, thought Afsan, that a ship that often retraced the journey of the prophet would sport carvings from the cult of the hunters, a cult Larsk himself had diminished from being the major religion of the people to just a series of rites adhered to mostly by those, like Jal-Tetex, who hunted regularly. Still, the *Dasheter* was not exclusively a pilgrimage ship.

The cabin behind the carved door was small, with a workbench, a single lamp, a trough for storage, a bucket full of water, and a small window, currently covered by a leather curtain. There was plenty of room for sleeping on the floor.

Afsan unpacked his sack, filling the trough with most of its contents. On the desk, he placed his sky charts, his prayer books, and some other books he'd borrowed from Saleed for pleasure reading. In the center of it all, he placed Saleed's traveler's crystal.

On the back of the door was the promised schedule of chores. Nothing too complicated: galley duties, cleaning the decks, and so on. He walked across the cabin, pulled back the curtain over the porthole, and stared out at the busy docks.

Suddenly his door creaked open. Afsan felt a twitching at the tips of his fingers, but checked the reflex immediately. Only a member of The Family would enter a room without warning. Turning around, he said, "Ho, Dybo."

"Ho, yourself, you muddied tail of a shovelmouth." The prince placed his hands on his hips and surveyed the room. "Not bad."

"Yours is bigger, no doubt."

Dybo clicked his teeth. "No doubt."

"When do we sail?"

"Any moment," said Dybo. "That's why I came to get you. Come on, let's go up on deck." Without waiting for Afsan's reply, Dybo headed out the doorway. *Sometimes,* Afsan reflected, *he really does act like a prince.* Afsan followed. Although Dybo was rotund, he was still much less bulky than an old Quintaglio, so the timbers of the deck made no special groaning under his weight.

They went up the ramp and out onto the main deck. Crewmembers were hurrying about, making final preparations. Captain Var-Keenir was walking back and forth, his face still hideously scarred, his tail still shy of its proper length, his steps still aided by a cane. He shouted orders in that incredibly deep and gravelly voice of his. "Lock off that line!" "Stow that cable!" "Angle that sail!" It appeared to Afsan that the crew already had everything under control, that Keenir was really just working off his own impatience. Since he had no tail to lean back on, he couldn't do many of the jobs himself. But at last Keenir called out the order everyone was waiting for: "Hoist the anchor!"

Five mates worked the wheel that pulled the thick metal chain aboard. As soon as the anchor lifted free of the harbor's floor, Afsan felt the ship move. The mates continued hoisting until they'd brought the five-pointed holdfast onto the deck. A large puddle spread from it.

Quintaglios worked the rigging for the sails, and the great ship sped along, but, Afsan noticed, not to the east, but rather to the northeast. Of course: the ship would have to tack into the wind, zigzagging its way up the River, sailing alternately northeast then southeast, crisscrossing to the Face of God.

Soon, thought Afsan, looking far ahead, *soon I will know your secrets.*

Chapter 10

Afsan restrained himself for all of the first day of the voyage, although he saw Keenir several times, his cane ticking against the creaking timbers. Keenir would often go up to the pointed bow and use his cross staff to measure angles in the sky, making sure the *Dasheter* was on the right course. The captain had looked at Afsan once with an expression that might have been recognition. But the voyage would last many days—130 or so out to the Face of God, 10 beneath the Face, and perhaps 110 to return. Afsan knew his chances of success were better if he did not seem greedy.

He watched Land dwindle as the sailing ship moved farther upriver. The Ch'mar volcanoes made a jagged line like Quintaglio teeth.

It wasn't long before Land disappeared beneath the horizon. Gone was Capital City and every other place Afsan had ever been. All that was left was water, choppy and blue. The red sails whipped in the steady wind, a wind strong enough to make Afsan close his eyes when he faced into it.

That first night was even-night, when Afsan normally slept. In fact, half of those aboard were being told to sleep that night, in an effort to keep the confined population—eight crewmembers and twenty-two pilgrims—out of each other's way. But even with his porthole open, Afsan was unable to slip into unconsciousness. The sounds of the ship, the yawing back and forth—it was all too strange for a youngster from Carno. He lay on his belly on the floor, waiting for the night to end.

Every now and then Afsan would hear a tapping coming from above, growing fainter and fainter, then progressively louder, a wooden *tick-tick-tick* against the background sounds of the ship. Afsan eventually figured out what it was: the captain's walking stick striking the deck. He seemed to be pacing, endlessly pacing.

At last morning came, heralded, even here, far out in the River, by the calls of wingfingers. But these were louder calls than those Afsan was used to hearing back on Land—deeper calls, the calls of much larger flyers. Afsan stretched, growled to himself, and rose.

Water was plentiful aboard the *Dasheter*—bucketfuls could be hauled aboard easily. It was somewhat salty, but nothing that Afsan's salt glands, between his eyes and nostrils, couldn't handle. Excess salt would be eliminated from the small openings over his pre-orbital fenestrae, on either side of his muzzle. That gland was the only part of his body he really had to wash regularly, the only part that might give off an unpleasant odor. As for the rest of his thick, dry skin he simply rinsed off any visible dirt. Then he donned his sash, yellow and brown, colors worthy of an apprentice, and headed out of his quarters, up the groaning ramp, and onto the deck.

The sun was rising on the eastern horizon, up ahead, with almost visible speed. The *Dasheter*'s red sails snapped salutes at the dawn.

Some crewmembers were hauling food nets aboard. The morning's catch included fish; some small aquatic lizards, their shapes streamlined like those of the fish; and several coiled mollusks, clusters of tentacles sticking out from their ornate shells. Some of the mollusks, already dying, were squirting ink onto the *Dasheter*'s deck.

Afsan wasn't hungry, but others were. They grabbed things to eat, trying to get them still wiggling, with some fight left in them. First to go were the aquatic reptiles. The dorsal fin was the best part, since it was solid meat, completely free of bone. A mate named Nor-Gampar grabbed one with both hands, seizing its long, toothed snout in his left, and gripping it just above the tail with his right. In one shearing bite the delectable fin was gone. Afsan watched long enough to see if Gampar would then help himself to everybody's second favorite part—the upper portion of the tail fin. It, too, was solid meat, for the reptile's backbone bent downward and reinforced only the lower prong of the tail. Gampar did indeed bite that off next.

Afsan walked across the connecting piece that joined the *Dasheter*'s fore and aft diamond hulls. It rose up like a bridge spanning a creek, and as he got higher above the waterline the swaying of the ship seemed even more pronounced. Spray hit his face.

On the foredeck he found Keenir, standing hands on hips, near the point of the bow, looking out at the waters ahead.

Afsan approached as close as he dared—four paces away. The yellow scar on Keenir's face looked fierce in the sunlight. The captain turned to look at him, blinked once or twice, then nodded slightly. It wasn't a bow of concession, but it certainly wasn't a challenge, either.

Encouraged, Afsan spoke. "I hope the day brings you a successful hunt."

Keenir looked again at the boy. After a moment he clicked his teeth. " 'Successful hunt,' eh? Seems an odd thing to say aboard a sailing ship."

Afsan felt his dewlap tightening in embarrassment. The ritual greeting did seem incongruous in this setting. "I only meant to wish you a good day."

"Well, if we find something for me to hunt, it will be a good day, indeed, youngster. A grand day." He looked back out at the waters. "You're Afdool, aren't you?"

Afdool meant "meaty legbone." Afsan meant "meaty thighbone." It was a forgivable mistake, especially since Afsan was by far the less common name.

"Uh, it's Afsan, actually."

"Afsan. Of course. Saleed's apprentice. I hope you last longer than your predecessors."

"I already have." Afsan instantly regretted saying that; it sounded boastful. But Keenir did not seem to be offended. "Your master and I go back a long time, boy. We were creche-mates. But he was never as skinny as you are. What's a slip like you doing with a name like Afsan, anyway?"

"I did not choose the name."

"No, of course not. Anyway, I thank you for your good wishes. Successful hunting to you, too, young Afsan—whatever it is that you seek."

"Actually, sir, there is something I seek."

"Eh?"

"The far-seer, sir—"

"The far-seer?"

"Yes. You remember, you had it that day we met in Saleed's office."

"Indeed." Keenir's tail swished. "Saleed thought it had no applicability to his work. Would he approve of you using it?"

Afsan felt his posture drooping. "Um, no, sir, he wouldn't. I'm sorry I asked." He turned to go.

"Wait, good Thighbone, I'd be delighted to let you use the far-seer."

"You would? But why?"

"Why?" Keenir clicked his teeth in glee. "Simply *because* Saleed would disapprove. To my cabin, lad!"

Chapter 11

The far-seer was marvelous. Before dark, Afsan practiced with it, looking up at the *Dasheter*'s riggings, catching sight of old Dath-Katood snoozing in that little bucket atop the lead mast, the place from which he was supposed to be watching for—for Afsan knew not what, but Captain Keenir had insisted that there be someone in the lookout's perch day and night. Afsan had heard grumblings that Keenir was obsessed with having the waters watched, and that, in the view of at least some of the crew, it was a waste of time. Apparently Katood was one of those who felt that way, and so was taking advantage of the quiet and warm sun for a rest. Afsan wondered how Katood's stomach stood the swaying of the mast at that height.

Afsan also briefly turned the far-seer onto the sun itself. That had been a mistake. The sun was always glaringly bright and hot, but, except when seen at the horizons or when partially obscured by clouds, it was hard to tell that it was a disk rather than simply an incredibly bright point. But through the far-seer, the radiance was amazing, and Afsan's eye had stung with pain. For the rest of the day, he had dark afterimages floating in front of him.

There was little else to look at in the daytime. Waves through the far-seer looked much like waves close up. It was briefly amusing to examine things through the wrong end of the tube, and see them as though from very far away. Land was quite hilly, so this reverse view was an unusual perspective. Afsan had never seen another Quintaglio from such an apparent distance. Still, even looking at them this way, Afsan could tell some of his shipmates apart. Dybo's round shape was unmistakable and Captain Keenir's stubby tail betrayed him when seen in profile.

At one point, Afsan saw a giant wingfinger in the distance. Its wingspan was perhaps as great as the length of the *Dasheter*. The graceful tawny shape in the circle of light at the end of the far-seer never flapped its leathery wings. Rather, it seemed to glide forever, rising and falling on currents of air. Afsan wondered if the huge creature spent its whole life aloft, skimming the surface of the water to scoop up fish or baby serpents. The freedom of its flight captivated Afsan, and he watched for a good daytenth before losing sight of it.

Four moons were visible as faint ghosts in the purple sky. It was not unusual to see a few during the day. Afsan turned the far-seer on each of them, but the images were washed out by sunlight.

Patience, he told himself. *Night will be here soon.*

And, indeed, it did come quickly. The sun, purple with the age of the day, egg-shaped, veiled with wisps of cloud, slipped below the horizon. Darkness gathered rapidly, and a few pinpoints of light appeared. Afsan, of course, knew which were stars and which were planets. He chose a star, the bright one that represented the shoulder in the constellation of Matark, the hornface upon which the great hunter Lubal had led her disciples into battle. A few twists of the far-seer's tube, already cool in the night, brought the star into crystal focus. Afsan was disappointed that, although the image was perhaps sharper than what he was used to seeing, it revealed no detail: just a yellowish-white pinpoint of light.

Undeterred, he aimed the brass tube at Kevpel, one of the planets, a speck in the firmament that, to the unaided eye, appeared no different from a regular star.

Afsan staggered backwards, almost tripping over his own tail. He put down the far-seer, rubbed his eye, and tried again. The planet showed as a disk—a disk!—in the eyepiece. No doubt: it was a circular object, a *solid* object. He marveled at the sight for some time before he realized that there was more to the image than he'd at first realized. Off to the left of the disk, there were three tiny specks of light in a line, and on the right side there were another two specks, one of which was so faint, Afsan wasn't absolutely sure it was even there.

He swung his gaze closer to the horizon, not far from where the sun had gone down, and turned the far-seer on Davpel. Again, Afsan was shocked by what he saw. This planet showed a white crescent face! Did the planets go through phases the way the moons did? Incredible.

And what of Bripel, the only other planet visible tonight? Afsan trained the magnifying tube on it. The *Dasheter* chose that moment to roll violently under a wave, and Afsan heard the creaking of the hull, the snap of sails, the pounding of water. When the ship had calmed itself, he searched again for Bripel. What he saw he could not believe. There were *handles* on the sides of Bripel, hollow curves protruding to the left and right.

He lowered the eyepiece to contemplate. One planet apparently went through phases, just like the moons do. Another had an accompanying collection of lesser points of light. A third had handles, like a two-fisted drinking cup.

Afsan shook his head. It was all too much to absorb at once. But, already, one thought burned in his mind. He couldn't give up using far-seers upon return to Capital City, regardless of what Saleed demanded. There was more to the universe than Saleed knew, more than Afsan had ever imagined. He was determined to learn its secrets, no matter what.

Chapter 12

"Godglow!" shouted Dybo, pointing to the eastern horizon. At once, every head turned to look. Afsan couldn't see what his friend was referring to. The sun, purple and fat, had set on the opposite horizon less than a daytenth ago, its sinking below the waves accelerated by the *Dasheter*'s steady drive to the east. Afsan's eyes had already adjusted to the darkness of night, or so he'd thought, for he could see many stars, the sky reflection of the River, three crescent moons, and bright Kevpel, one of the enigmatic planets he had been examining on previous nights with the far-seer.

"Where?" came the skeptical cry from one of the other pilgrims.

Dybo was adamant. "There! See how it banishes the stars!"

"I don't see anything," said the skeptic.

"Douse the lamps, you hornface dropping! It's there!"

Afsan and some of the others hurried to the glowing oil lamps mounted high on the gunwales and quickly turned off their flames. Darkness enveloped everything, broken only by the twinkling stars and bright moons overhead. No, no, that wasn't quite right. Afsan stared intently at the distant horizon. There *was* a glow there, a faint, ethereal luminance, barely perceptible. Dybo must have had keen eyes indeed to have detected it while the lamps were still ablaze.

"I still don't see anything," said a voice from the darkness, the same gainsayer as before.

Afsan worked his muzzle to form the words "I do," but was so moved by the wondrous sight that no sound passed his throat. He tried again, overcompensating, speaking too loudly for such an awesome moment. "I do!"

Hushed whispers of "Me, too" filled the air, then everyone fell silent. They watched, intent, for most of the night before any real progress became visible. The glow spread left and right across the horizon line, illuminating the crests of distant waves. As it grew brighter it took on discernible color, a pale yellowish-orange. It was dimmer than the early morning glow that heralded the dawn, and completely the wrong hue, but still it gave Afsan the feeling that something huge and bright and powerful was lurking just below the horizon.

Near him, one of the other pilgrims began to rock backwards, balancing against her tail, a low thrumming sound coming from deep within her chest. Afsan glanced at the other's fingers. Her claws were still sheathed; this rocking was the beginnings of rapture, not a fight-or-flight instinct.

"God made us," said the pilgrim softly. A few others echoed the chant. "God gave us the Land." Several pilgrims were reciting the prayer in unison now. "God gave us the beasts upon the Land." Three or four others were rocking back on their tails. "God gave us the teeth of a hunter, the hand of an artist, the mind of a thinker." The glow was slightly brighter now, covering most of the horizon. "For these gifts," said the crowd, now only Afsan's voice missing from the chorus, "God asks but one thing." But by the next verse, Afsan found himself joining in the chant. "Our obedience. And that we give with joy."

They rocked together for the rest of the brief night. Even though it was even-night, when many of them should have been sleeping, they pressed on in their worship, the ship rolling back and forth along the waves, the sails snapping in the steady wind.

When dawn came, the sun rose in the east directly out of where the Godglow had been, its blue light replacing the yellow radiance. They took turns scanning the eastern horizon, the tiny, furiously bright sun tracking across the sky, but no more Godglow was to be seen. That night it returned, and ship's priest Det-Bleen led them through many prayers, but it wasn't until shortly before sunset the following day that Dybo's voice went up again. "There!" he cried, loud enough for all to hear above the sounds of the ship, the thunder of the waves. "There! The Face of God!"

All eyes turned to the eastern horizon. The assembled group cast long shadows in front of themselves on the deck as the sun lowered to touch the waters behind them.

At the very edge of the eastern horizon a tiny point of yellow appeared. A few individuals gasped. Afsan was content simply to stare in wonder. It took most of the night before there was more than just a point, before there was something that had a discernible shape. It soon became clear to Afsan that he was seeing the leading edge of a vast, circular object.

According to Captain Var-Keenir, they would have to travel four thousand kilopaces more before the Face would clear the horizon. Tacking alternately port and starboard, that would take thirty-two days, the Face rising by just three percent of its total height for each day of sailing.

Time passed. The *Dasheter* continued east. The Face crawled up the sky from the horizon, a vertically striped dome growing wider and wider. It swirled with colors, yellow and brown and red and mixes of those in every imaginable combination: oranges and beiges and rusts, pale shades like dead vegetation, deep shades like fresh blood, dark shades like the richest soil.

Every morning, the sun emerged from *behind* the Face, a tiny blue point rising up into the sky, the Face illuminated only along its upper edge as the sun rose from it, as if from behind a vast round hill on the horizon.

It was a glorious double dawn, the top of the Face lighting up as the sun rose over it. As the day progressed, illumination pulled downward over the Face like an iridescent eyelid sliding shut over a dark orb.

Each day, dawn came a little later, the sun having to climb higher to clear the spreading dome of the Face of God. Afsan took advantage of the prolonged nights to do more observing.

That the Face was not always fully lit fascinated Afsan. In the afternoon and at night, it was indeed a bright dome on the horizon, but every morning only its upper edge was illuminated, a thin line arching up from where the water met the sky, the part of the Face beneath the line dim and violet.

And sometimes none of the Face was lit at all.

It didn't take Afsan long to figure out what was happening, but the thought staggered him nonetheless.

The Face of God, the very countenance of his creator, went through phases, just as the moons did, and, as he had seen through the far-seer, just as some of the planets did.

Phases, waxing vertically from top to bottom. Part lit, part dark.

Phases.

The Face of God continued to rise, broadening each day, a vast dome lifting from the distant waves, until at long last, eighteen days after Dybo had first spotted the Godglow, the Face's widest part cleared the horizon. That event, too, was marked by a prayer ceremony. It was mid-afternoon and the Face's entire visible hemisphere was illuminated: a half circle, a vertically striped dome, standing where the River met the sky.

Afsan retained enough of his astrologer's senses to gauge the object's size: some fifty times the width of an outstretched thumb. He looked to the east and held both arms out horizontally so that his left hand touched the southernmost tip of the Face and his right hand touched the northernmost. Tipping his muzzle down, he saw that his arms were making an angle equal to an eighth of a circle.

Afsan had always admired sunset, had studied the wonders of the night sky, had recently seen more marvels than he'd ever imagined through the far-seer. But he was left dumb by this sight, the single most beautiful thing he had ever seen; indeed, he knew at once that this was the single most beautiful thing he would ever see.

As the *Dasheter* continued east, the Face appeared to rise slowly, the part intersecting the horizon growing narrower and narrower as the vast circular form lifted higher into the heavens. Gorgeous colors rolled up and down it in loose vertical stripes.

The top-to-bottom cycle of phases fascinated Afsan. When the entire dome was lit up, as it was each midnight, it seemed, paradoxically, like a false dawn. The sky should have been at its blackest. Instead, all but the brightest stars on the western horizon were drowned out by the eastern rising of the Face.

When the Face was a waxing crescent, the illuminated top part rose from the waves like an archway, beckoning the pilgrims to enter.

But when it was a waning crescent, only the lower part lit, the points of the crescent rose up from the horizon like the curving horns of some great beast lurking below the edge.

Mixed signals.

Inviting.

Threatening.

The *Dasheter* sailed toward the Face of God, Afsan wondering what they would find.

Afsan saw that the Face did have features, after a fashion. No nostrils, no earholes, no teeth. But there were the famed God eyes, black circles as dark and round as Quintaglio orbs, spaced randomly in a tight vertical band up the center of the rising sphere.

And perhaps there was a mouth, for a huge white oval, measuring a fifth of the Face's total height, crawled up the right side each day.

Finally, three dekadays after they had first seen the Face of God, its trailing tip broke free from the watery horizon. It was after dark, the Face half full, its bottom lit up. The glowing curved edge lifted from the waves. Afsan had stopped breathing, waiting for the moment of separation. When it happened, he gulped cool night air.

Lovely. Afsan had never had cause to use that word to describe anything in his life, but the sight of the Face of God was indeed lovely. He stared at it, its lower half aglow, its upper half a vast purple dome against the night, the whole circular object floating just above the edge of the water, its reflection on the waves a rippling yellow arm reaching out to the pilgrims.

No, thought Afsan, no, the Face was not quite circular. Even discounting the fact that it was only partially illuminated, it still wasn't perfectly round. It was narrower than it was tall, squished horizontally.

Egg-shaped.

Of course! What better form for the creator of all life?

Sunrise was breathtaking. The Face was a thin crescent on its bottom half as the searing point of the sun rose from the waves just below it, then the whole sky dimmed again for more than a daytenth as the sun was hidden behind the great dark bulk of the Face. Then a second dawn occurred as the brilliant blue-white light finally rose out of the top of the Face, its upper edge now a bright crescent.

Afsan was always circumspect when using the far-seer. He recalled the trouble he'd gotten into at the palace when he'd suggested to Saleed that he might use such a device to examine the Face of God. Whenever Det-Bleen was on deck, Afsan did no observing. He occasionally overheard other pilgrims and members of the crew making derisive remarks about his obsession with looking through the brass tube, but Afsan didn't care. The sights were glorious.

Through the far-seer, in close-up, there seemed almost infinite detail in the swirling bands of color that ran up the illuminated part of the Face of God. The bands weren't sharply defined. Instead, they faded away into little eddies and curlicues. The mysterious God eyes were just as round and black and featureless as they appeared without the far-seer. Under magnification, though, the great mouth, that swirling white oval sometimes visible moving up the Face, looked like a whirlpool.

It was wondrous. Each tiny circular segment of the Face was intricate, each band of color complex and fascinating.

Actually Afsan quickly became convinced that he wasn't seeing a solid surface. Not only did the Face go through phases, but its visible details shifted from day to day, the configurations flowing, structures drifting. No, Afsan suspected he was seeing either clouds of tinted gas or swirls of liquids—or something, anyway, other than a solid object.

Again he tried to reconcile this with his expectations. Earlier he'd thought of the Face as a great egg, but now it seemed immaterial, fluid. And yet was not the spirit a diaphanous thing? Was not the soul airy and insubstantial? Wouldn't God Herself simply be a great immaterial spirit?

Wouldn't She?

• • •

The *Dasheter* continued to sail east day after day, its identification call—a semi-ten of drums, a pair of bells, loud then soft, time and again—hailing the Face of God. As the ship moved on, the Face rose farther. At last, eighty days after it had first been sighted, the heart of the great circular form, cycling through its phases once each day, stood at the zenith. The Face, sprawling across a quarter of the sky, inspired awe in Afsan and the other pilgrims.

It was overpowering, compelling, hypnotic. Afsan could not help but stare at it, and, when so doing, he lost track of time. The colors swirling in broad bands were like nothing he had ever seen.

No, he reflected, no, that wasn't quite right. He had seen similar colors, similar vibrancy, once, kilodays ago. Lost in the deep woods of Arj'toolar province, upriver from where Pack Carno was roaming, he had eaten a strange fungus growing only on the north sides of trees. A Quintaglio does not eat plants, he had reminded himself at the time. But he had been unable to catch any small animal, and, lost for three even-days and two odd, his belly was rumbling and he could taste his own gastric acid at the back of his throat. He'd need something to take the pain off, something to sustain him, until he found his way back to Carno or until someone found him.

He'd seen small scaly creatures nibbling at the fungus, chewing it, rather than swallowing it whole. He'd tried to grab the little lizards but, to Afsan's humiliation, they scampered away every time he tried to sneak up on them. Even worse, they didn't scamper very far—just enough to be out of reach of a single lunge.

Children do silly things, and Afsan, like many others, had tried eating grass and flowers in his youth, only to become terribly sick, his stomach cramped for days.

But this fungus, this strange beige lump growing on the side of the trees: it wasn't a regular plant, it wasn't green. Perhaps it wouldn't pain him so to eat it. And, by the prophet, if he didn't eat something soon, he would die. The lizards seemed to manage it well enough.

Eventually hunger got the better of him. Afsan crouched down beside the tree and snapped off a piece of the fungus. It was cold and dry and had a crumbly texture along its broken edge. He brought it up to his muzzle. It smelled musty, but otherwise innocuous. Finally he placed it in his mouth. The taste was bitter, but not too unpleasant. Still, he was a hunter, not an armorback. He had no molars to grind the plant with, but he used his tongue to bounce it around in his mouth, perforating and tearing it with his pointed teeth. Perhaps working it thus would make it pass through his digestion better than the grasses he'd tried when he was even younger.

At first, everything seemed fine. The fungus did seem to take the edge off his hunger.

But then, suddenly, Afsan felt light-headed. He rose to his feet, but found he couldn't keep his balance. He staggered a few steps, then decided he'd be better off lying down. He let himself down to the ground, and lay on his side on the cool dirt, a blanket of dead leaves beneath him, discrete shafts of fierce white sunlight coming through the canopy of treetops above his head.

Soon, the sunlight began to dance, the beams sliding back and forth, intertwining, coalescing, fragmenting, changing colors, now blue, now green, now red, now fiery orange, shifting, undulating, rainbows incarnate, swinging back and forth. He felt as if he was floating, seeing colors as he'd never seen them before, brighter, cleaner, more powerful, impinging directly on his mind like thoughts crisp and clear, pure and lucid.

It was similar to the delirium that accompanies fever, but with no pain, no nausea, just a cool sense of tranquillity, of liquid peace.

He lost all track of time, of place. He forgot he was in a forest, forgot his hunger, forgot that night would soon be here. Or, if he knew any of that, it did not seem to matter. The colors, the lights, the patterns—they were all that mattered, all that had ever mattered.

At last, he did come out of it, late into the night. It was cold and dark, and Afsan was very, very afraid. He felt physically weak, mentally drained. The next morning, a hunting party from Carno came across him. They gave him a leather cloak, and individual hunters took turns carrying him back to the village on their shoulders. He never told anyone about the fungus he had eaten, about the strange hallucinations he had experienced. But that event, six kilodays in the past, was the only thing he could compare to the hypnotic effect of staring into the swirling, roiling Face of God.

Every day, ship's priest Det-Bleen led a service. As the sun rose higher, the Face grew darker and darker, until only a crescent sliver was illuminated on the side toward the rising sun. A little before noon, with the sun arcing high across the sky and the crescent of illumination all but gone, the pilgrims would begin to chant.

The sun, a tiny point compared to the great mauve circle of the unilluminated Face, came closer and closer and closer to the vast curving edge, and then, and then, and then . . .

The sun disappeared.

Gone.

Behind the Face of God.

God was dark and featureless.

The whole sky dimmed.

Moons, normally pale in the light of day, glowed with their nocturnal colors.

Bleen would lead the pilgrims in prayers and songs, urging the sun to return.

And it always did, about one and a quarter daytenths after it had vanished. The brilliant blue-white point emerged from the other side of the Face of God, lighting the sky again.

Afsan watched this spectacle every day. As the sun slid toward the horizon, toward dusk, the Face, rock-steady at the zenith, would grow more and more illuminated, waxing from the side nearest the sun in the bowl of the sky. By the time the sun touched the waves of the River, the Face of God was more than half lit again.

Afsan was always amazed by the beauty.

And puzzled.

But he knew he'd be able to figure it out.

He knew it.

Chapter 13

There has to be a way, Afsan said to himself, pacing the length of his tiny cabin. *There has to be a way to make sense of my observations.*

Stars, planets, moons, the sun, even the Face of God itself. How did they fit together? How did they interrelate?

Afsan tried grouping them into categories. The sun and the stars, for instance, were apparently self-illuminating. The planets, the moons, and, yes, the Face of God, seemed to shine by reflected light. No, no, it wasn't that easy. *Some* of the planets seemed not to be self-illuminated, judging by the fact that they went through phases. But others, notably those highest in the night sky, did not go through phases. Perhaps those planets were self-illuminated. But that didn't seem right. Two types of planets? Surely it was more likely that they were all the same.

And what about the moons, those fast-moving disks in the firmament? They all went through phases, and with the far-seer every one of them showed surface details, even tiny Slow-poke.

Afsan strained to think. In all his life, the only sources of light he'd ever observed were things aflame. Even the sun appeared to have the heat and brightness of a burning object. Candles, lamps, fires produced by campers for heat—on none of these had he ever observed surface details. No, the moons must be shining by reflected light. And what could the source of that light be? The sun seemed the only candidate.

The thirteen moons were spherical—of that much Afsan was sure. He could see surface features that rotated around. Indeed, even without the far-seer, such details were obvious. Saleed had a globe of the Big One in his office, after all, made by Haltang, one of Afsan's predecessors, from naked-eye observations.

And the planets? Although still indistinct in the far-seer, they seemed to be spherical, too.

Well, if the planets and moons were all ball-shaped, and all illuminated by the sun, then the phases must be simply the effect of seeing part of the lit and unlit sides simultaneously.

He clenched his hand into a fist and held it up to the cabin's flickering lamp. Moving it back and forth, left and right, he could indeed alter the amount of the visible portion that appeared to be illuminated, ranging from none, if he rose to his feet and placed the fist between his face and the lamp, to almost all, if he interposed the lamp between his eyes and hand.

Afsan let himself down onto the floor, laying his belly against the reassuring solidity of the wooden planks. Why, he asked himself again, do only some of the planets go through phases?

He stared at his cabin wall, the timbers creaking slightly, as they always did, under the tossing action of the waves. In one of the timbers was a knot, a darker swirling pattern of grain. Over time, it had dried and shrunk away from the surrounding wood so that it almost floated freely within the wall plank. Afsan had grown fond of this knot over the 130 nights he'd spent in this cabin. It wasn't exactly a piece of art, but it did have a random aesthetic quality to it, and the swirling grain reminded him of the patterns across the Face of God.

But, of course, unlike the Face of God, the knot was always completely visible. It didn't go through phases—

—because it was farther from the source of illumination than Afsan himself was!

Of course, of course, of course. Afsan felt his blood surging. He pushed himself up to his feet again. Some of the planets were nearer to the sun than he was and some were farther away. That made perfect sense.

Except.

Except, how could it be thus? The perspective was all wrong. Surely it must be, rather, that in order of increasing distance from the great mass of Land we had some planets, and then the sun, and then some more planets.

The paths they traveled in must be closed loops—probably circles—since astrological charts showed that the planets always came back to the same point in the sky, each in its own time. And those that underwent phases completed their circular paths more quickly than those that did not.

Further, those that underwent phases never varied from their circular paths, whereas those that didn't show phases would periodically go into a backwards motion. They would move in the opposite direction across the sky for a space of many days before returning to forward motion.

Afsan headed up on deck, the great circle of the Face of God almost fully illuminated overhead, even though it was the middle of the night. He'd wanted to get something from the galley to help him visualize all this, but the spectacle made him stop in his tracks, lean back on his thick tail, and stare at the zenith, at the banded sphere covering a quarter of the sky.

It was the middle of the night.

The *Dasheter* and the River were in darkness.

The sun was invisible, having set many daytenths ago, off to the west.

It was the middle of the night.

And the Face of God was fully illuminated.

Afsan stared and stared and stared, his brain churning like the waters around the boat.

The middle of the night.

The Face aglow.

God eyes moving up the widest part.

Like shadows . . .

He broke away from the mesmerizing sight, and, rubbing the base of his neck, headed off to the galley. All sorts of kitchen equipment were lying around: tools for scraping meat from bones—none could go to waste aboard a sailing vessel; metal basins for washing those tools; cutting boards and cleavers; salting trays; mallets with hundreds of metal teeth, used to tenderize the salted meats; racks of spices, important on long voyages to hide the taste of meat past its prime;

devices for scaling fish; and so on. No one was in the galley, though, so Afsan simply helped himself to what he needed. In a storage trough he found glass flasks holding hard-boiled wingfinger eggs in brine. He grabbed a couple of flasks and headed back to his chamber. As he crossed the deck, he again looked up at the enigmatic, swirling Face.

Once back in his cabin, he removed his lamp from the brass hook that normally held it in place. Gingerly, for Afsan knew how careful one must be with any source of flame on a wooden boat, he set the lamp on the creaking timbers in the center of the floor. He got pieces of decorative clothing out of his storage trough, including his prayer neckband, the multi-pouched waistband he used for carrying things, the red leather cap he'd received after his first day's chores, symbolizing his honorary membership in the *Dasheter*'s crew, and three of his apprenticeship sashes. The leather sashes showed signs of alterations by the palace tailor. Pog-Teevio, the previous apprentice astrologer, who had lasted all of thirty days before Saleed had sent him back to Chu'toolar, had been older and much stockier than Afsan.

Afsan set these pieces of material at various places on the floor. He then opened a flask and pulled out a wingfinger egg. He wiped off the brine and put the egg on one of the pieces of clothing he had placed on the floor, the folds of fabric preventing the egg from rolling despite the pitching of the ship. He continued until he had nine laid out. Some he put near the lamp, some far away, some toward the port side of the chamber, some along the starboard. Afsan then stood in the center of his collection of eggs, towering over the flickering lamp, and looked down.

By the prophet's claws, it made sense! He could see that no matter where it was in the tiny room, exactly half of each egg was illuminated, just as he suspected half of each planet was illuminated by the sun. Afsan then lay on the floor, the timbers cool beneath him. Although Afsan sanded the part of the floor he slept on from time to time, most of the rest was ticked and scarred by his footclaws and those of previous pilgrims.

He felt the ship swaying slowly back and forth beneath him, felt his stomach rise and fall on the crest and troughs of waves. Taking care not to get slivers from the boards, Afsan positioned himself next to one of the tiny eggs, his muzzle flat on the floor. From this point of view, those eggs between him and the lamp representing the sun were almost invisible—at most a narrow crescent was illuminated. That one over there, perpendicular to the lamp from him, was a gibbous shape, more than half lit up. And there, another egg gibbous in the opposite way. And that one, on the other side of the lamp, illuminated almost fully. And that one, all but lost in the glare of the flickering flame.

Could it be? Could it be? The sun at the center of the planets? But that made no sense. If the sun was at the center, then the planets would have to move in circular paths around it, not around Land. That was absurd.

Absurd.

The ship groaned beneath him.

Afsan then thought about the moons. This model would not work for them, could not explain their appearance. The moons had to be illuminated by the sun, too, just as the planets were. But they couldn't be moving in circular paths around the sun. They were so big, so much closer, apparently, to Land than the planets, and completed their phase cycles in a matter of days, not kilodays. But they must be traveling in circular paths, too, for did they not endlessly move across a narrow band of the sky? What could they be revolving around?

Afsan slapped his tail against the deck. The eggs jumped. What could it be?

He got up, moved to his workbench, pulled out a few of his precious writing leathers and his pots of ink and solvent, and began to scribble notes, sketch configurations, try various calculations. It was long, long after the sun had risen, its bluish-white rays jagged around the edges of the leather curtain over Afsan's porthole, that he finally rinsed off his middle fingerclaw, washing away the ink, and stared at what he'd drawn, at the only arrangement that seemed to work.

Sun at the center.

Planets moving around the sun.

Moons moving around one of the planets, casting small round shadows on it.

And Land itself on one of those moons!

It all fit.

He knew he was right, knew this must be the truth. He

clicked his teeth in satisfaction. But then the *Dasheter*'s bells-and-drums identification call split the air. Suddenly he realized what time it was and he ran off to perform his shipboard chores.

Chapter 14

The *Dasheter*'s four sails had been furled upon the ship's arrival here, directly beneath the Face of God. The great sheets, each with a symbol of the prophet, were now rolled into tight bundles tied against horizontal booms at the top of each mast. The brass pulleys and pivots of the rigging were lashed down so that they wouldn't endlessly clink together.

Webbings of rope ran up the side of each mast, the interweave loose enough to allow a hand or foot easy purchase. Standing on the ship's foredeck, wooden planks creaking beneath him, Afsan looked up at the lead mast. Although he knew it to be of constant thickness from top to bottom, the mast seemed to taper as it reached for the sky. The rope webbing hung loosely to one side, the breeze only occasionally strong enough to move the heavy cords. The mast swung dizzyingly from port to starboard and back again, the topmost part slicing through the sky like an inverted pendulum. At the pinnacle was the lookout's bucket, so tiny, so far way.

And behind it all, gloriously, the Face of God, now slightly less than half lit in the morning sun. Bands of orange and beige roiled across its oblate shape.

Now that they'd arrived at the halfway point of their voyage, new lists of chores had been distributed. For the duration of the trip, Afsan would be responsible for a shift in the lookout's bucket every ten days. Today was his first.

The climb up to the bucket looked arduous and frightening. Still, whoever was up there now—Afsan half closed his nictitating membrane to cut the glare from the Face high above—Mar-Biltog, it looked like—would already be mad that Afsan was late in relieving him. Given the tight confines of the ship, displeasing another was never prudent, and Biltog was particularly short-tempered. Afsan reached out to grab the web of ropes.

By hand and foot, he pulled himself up. His tail lifted from the deck, and he felt the weight of it dangling behind him. He tilted his head up to counterbalance it.

The climb was indeed difficult; Afsan was not used to such effort, and having been aboard the *Dasheter* for over 130 days now, with no room to run, he was perhaps a tad out of shape. The sun, bright over his shoulder, felt good on his back as he continued up. But with each successive body-length of height, the mast swayed through wider and wider arcs. It was uncomfortably like scaling the neck of that giant thunderbeast. Afsan briefly closed his inner and outer eyelids, trying to fight vertigo. He'd resisted motion sickness throughout the voyage so far; he'd be strung up by his tail sooner than give in to it now—especially since, with the swaying of the mast, he'd probably leave a wide swath of vomit on the deck below.

Higher and higher still. The mast, brown and old, still showed the chopping marks of the blades that had hewn it. Afsan decided it was better to focus on those marks rather than on the sight of the bucket swinging wildly back and forth between the lit and unlit hemispheres of the Face of God. Unlike the thunderbeast's weaving neck, the rocking back and forth of the *Dasheter* was fairly regular. With an effort of will, Afsan found that he could anticipate it, and that helped quell his stomach.

His hands were getting tired and sore from the climb. His feet were too callused to be hurt by the ropes, but Afsan had forgotten just how heavy his own tail was. Still, he pressed on and at last made it to the top of the mast.

The webbing came right up to the lip of the bucket. The bucket itself was made of vertical planks arranged in a circle. Biltog, standing within, did not look happy.

"You're late," he said.

Afsan couldn't execute a proper bow while still holding on

to the climbing web, but he dipped his head as much as he could. "My apologies. I simply lost track of time."

Biltog snorted. "If there's one skill I'd expect an astrologer to have, it would be precise timekeeping."

Afsan dipped his head again. "I'm sorry."

Biltog nodded curtly and hauled himself out of the bucket, grabbing onto the web of ropes next to Afsan. For his part, Afsan swung first one leg and then the other into the bucket. It was good to be able to lean back, putting all his weight on his tail.

His job up here was simple: scan the horizon for anything out of the ordinary. The view was spectacular. Far below were the twin diamond hulls of the *Dasheter,* connected by the thick joining piece. He could see Quintaglios moving about the deck. Even at this late date, it was easy to tell crewmembers from pilgrims, for only the former walked with complete steadiness across the swaying deck.

Afsan was amused by the dances of the individuals, how each changed course to give everyone else wide clearance as they passed. He had never seen it from this perspective before. The smaller—and therefore younger—Quintaglios always started to veer out of the way first, but even the oldest would also make at least a token effort to move aside as well. The pattern wasn't as smooth as that drawn by objects in the sky, but it seemed to be nearly as predictable.

Looking out to the horizon, there was nothing but water, an endless liquid vista, waves moving from east to west. There was something soothing about the unembellished vastness.

Afsan rotated slowly in the bucket, scanning the horizon through a complete circle. Nothing broke the waves anywhere. So simple, so uncomplicated.

And yet, as he looked, it seemed, perhaps, that the horizon fell off to his left and right. It didn't matter which direction he looked, the effect was the same. Perhaps, maybe, hard to say. But it *looked* like it curved away. *Or is that just me seeing what I want to see?* Afsan thought. Last night, he'd convinced himself of something new: that the world was round. Now he was even claiming that he could *see* the roundness.

And yet. And yet. The effect was persistent. No matter how hard he tried to force his eyes *not* to see the gentle sloping, it was always visible, always there just at the edge of certainty.

Overhead, though, was the most glorious sight of all. In the time it had taken Afsan to climb the mast, the Face of God had gone from almost half lit to a fat crescent, a vast sickle of orange and yellow and brown arcing across a fourth of the sky.

Afsan tilted his head back, his tail bowing under the shift in weight, and looked straight up.

What are you? he wondered.

Are you God?

The Prophet Larsk had certainly thought so. When he'd been a child, Afsan, like all his age, had memorized Larsk's original proclamations, the speeches the prophet had made in the central square of what is now Capital City. "I have gazed upon the Face of God," Larsk had said. "I have seen the very countenance of our creator . . . "

But the Face of God did not look like a Quintaglio face. It was orange and yellow and brown, not green; it was round, not drawn-out; it had many eyes, not just two; its mouth had no teeth—if that great spot, oval and white, sometimes visible on the Face was indeed the mouth.

And yet, why should God look like a Quintaglio? God is perfection; a Quintaglio is not. God is immortal, requiring no food, no air. Quintaglios have muzzles lined with teeth and terminated with nostrils precisely because they are *not* immortal, because they need material sustenance to live. And Afsan knew that two eyes were better than one, for with two came depth perception. Surely the ten or so that wandered across the Face were that much better than just two?

Even as the crescent waned, Afsan found himself spellbound by the play of colors across it.

But no! No. It is *not* the Face of God. It cannot be. Afsan's tail muscles twitched in frustration, there being too little room in the lookout's bucket for a proper slap.

He'd worked it all out. He *knew*.

The Face of God is a planet.

A planet.

Nothing more.

But if that is true, where is God? What is God?

There is no God.

Afsan flinched. His pulse quickened; his claws jumped from their sheaths. The idea frightened him.

There is no God.

Could that be so? No, no, no, of course not. Madness to even think such a thing. There must be a God. There must be!

But where? If not here, where? If not the swirling object above his head, where? If not looking down upon the pilgrims from high above, where?

Where?

Afsan's stomach knotted, and he knew it wasn't just from the constant swaying of the bucket.

Quintaglios exist, he thought.

And if we exist, then someone made us.

And that someone must be God.

Well, that was simple enough. All right, then. God existed.

But who created God?

The mast moved to and fro. A stiff breeze played over Afsan's features.

God just postpones the inevitable. If everything requires a creator, then God requires one, too.

He thought briefly of a children's astrology class he'd taken kilodays ago. His teacher had been trying to explain the rudiments of the universe—Land being a huge island floating down the endless River. But one of the other youngsters—a visitor from a Pack that normally roamed farther north in Arj'toolar province—had said no. The way she'd heard it, Land balanced on an armorback, the sturdy four-footed animal holding everything up on its thick bony carapace.

"Ah!" the instructor had said. "But what does the armorback rest upon?"

The girl had replied immediately. "Why, another armorback, of course."

The instructor's tail had swished with delight. "And what does that armorback rest upon?"

"A third armorback," said the girl.

"And that armorback?"

"A fourth."

"And *that* armorback?"

But here the girl had held up her hand. "I see where you're trying to go with this, teacher, but you can't fool me. It's armorbacks all the way down."

Back then, Afsan had clicked his teeth quietly in amusement. But it wasn't funny now. Was God just like that girl's armorbacks? A way of postponing the final question? A way of endlessly putting off dealing with—with—with *first causes*?

And Afsan, smug back then in his superior knowledge, was guilty of the same self-delusion, the same acceptance of easy answers. Either God was created by something else, and that something else was created by yet some greater something, and on and on to infinity, or it was possible to exist *without* a creator. Well, the former case was patently ridiculous. And if the latter case was true, then, well, then there was no need for a God.

No need for a God.

But what of all he had been taught? What of the great religion of the people?

The mast swayed.

Afsan felt his faith crumbling around him, shattering like an egg. And what would burst forth from the shell shards? What was Afsan about to unleash on the world?

For a few heartbeats he tried to convince himself that this knowledge was a wonderful thing, a great liberator. For did one not live in fear of God? Did one not comport oneself so as to gain favorable standing in the afterlife, such standing decided at the sole discretion of the supreme being?

But then it hit Afsan with an unexpected forcefulness.

He was afraid.

If there was no God, there was just as likely no afterlife. There was no reason to behave properly, to put the interests of others ahead of one's own.

No God meant no meaning to it all, no higher standard by which everything was measured. No absolutes of goodness.

Below him, Afsan heard faint sounds. He looked down upon the twin diamond decks of the *Dasheter,* far below. Standing at one side was the ship's priest, Det-Bleen, moving his arms in graceful orchestration. The pilgrims were arranging themselves in a circle, each one facing out. Their tails all aimed in toward a central point directly beneath the Face of God. They tipped their heads back, looking straight up. And they sang.

Songs of hope.

Songs of prayer.

Songs of worship.

The music, when audible above the wind and the slapping

of waves, was beautiful, full of energy, of sincerity. Clearer and brighter than the other voices, Afsan could hear the magic of Prince Dybo's singing.

They're together, thought Afsan, *united in worship.* For it was only through the church, through the religion, that Quintaglios saw fit to join forces for anything beyond the hunt.

The sacred scrolls said that in heaven there was no territorial instinct; that there, in the calming presence of God Herself, being in the company of others did not bring out the animal within. The church taught that one must work together, hold one's instincts in check, that to do so was to bring oneself closer to God, to prepare oneself for the unending bliss of the afterlife.

Without a church, there would be no such teachings. Without such teachings, there would be no working together, except, maybe, to fell the largest of beasts, the greatest of prey. Without working together, there'd be no cities, no culture.

Anarchy.

In one heady moment, Afsan realized that the church was the cornerstone of the culture, that the role of Det-Yenalb was more important than that played by Saleed or any scholar, that the cement that bound together a race of carnivores, a breed that had territorial imperatives fundamental to their being, was the *belief* in God.

Below him, the pilgrims rotated on the deck, their muzzles now facing in so that they looked straight at each other: together, conscious of their union, but calm, instincts in check, under the kindly influence of the Face of God. Slowly they lifted their muzzles again and began to chant the words of the Eleventh Scroll.

The Eleventh Scroll, thought Afsan. *The one about working together to rebuild, about how God sends landquakes not out of spite or anger, but to give us yet another reason to hold our instincts at bay and cooperate.*

But Afsan knew the truth.

He could not lie. Anyone could *see* that he was lying, for only an *aug-ta-rot,* a demon, could lie in the light of day.

Science must always advance.

The mast swung far to port, paused for an instant, then swung far to starboard. Afsan looked down again. Directly beneath him was open water.

In a horrible flash it was clear to him.

There was a way.

A way to keep it all secret.

To keep the dangerous truth unknown.

He could jump. He could put an end to himself.

Not just now, of course. Not with water below. Assuming he wasn't knocked unconscious breaking through the surface, Afsan could swim alongside the ship for days.

But if he jumped—*now!*—with nothing but hard wooden deck to break his fall, he'd be finished, instantly. There'd be no prolonged death, just a snuffing out like a lamp being extinguished.

He'd never have to let the world know what he knew, never have to share what he'd discovered, never risk dissolving the glue holding civilization together.

It would be for the best. Besides, no one would miss him.

Afsan stared down over the edge of the bucket, watching the ship move back and forth beneath him.

No.

No, of course not.

What he'd discovered was the truth. And he would tell that truth to all who would listen.

He had to. He was a scholar.

Quintaglios are rational beings. Perhaps there was a time, in the distant past, when we needed a God. But not in these enlightened days. Not now. Not anymore.

Not anymore.

His resolve hardened. He was still too cramped to slap his tail properly, but he gave it a good try.

The truth, then. And to the darkest pits with the consequences.

Nodding to himself, he scanned the horizon.

Say, there's something—

No. Nothing. For an instant, he'd thought he'd seen something far, far off, splitting the waters. But it was gone now. He rotated slowly, looking in each direction for anything out of the ordinary.

As the day wore on, the sun moved higher and higher into the sky. The narrow crescent of the Face of God waned into nothingness. The vast dim circular bulk of its unilluminated side hung above Afsan's head, a pale ghost of its former glory.

Chapter 15

Afsan had been thinking of how to get an appointment to see Captain Var-Keenir. There was no doubt in the young astrologer's mind that a hierarchy operated aboard the ship, that each member of the crew had specific responsibilities, and reported in turn to a designated individual. But, as to what that order was, Afsan had been unable to tell. Back at the palace grounds, Afsan had come up with a simple rule. If it wore a sash, call it "learned one." If it sported robes, call it "holy one." And if in any doubt, simply bob concession and get out of the way.

But the routine of the ship baffled Afsan. One day, an officer might be the lookout atop the foremast. On the next day, that same person might be working in the galley, pounding salted meats to tenderize them, and then carefully soaking them in the ship's limited stock of blood to make the meat at least appear fresh. It was as if they rotated duties, but if there was a pattern to the rotation, Afsan had yet to perceive it.

Finally he gave up and simply decided to approach the captain directly. The *Dasheter* had been designed to appear sparsely populated even when carrying a full complement. That meant Afsan had to wind his way to the captain's cabin through a maze of walls that seemed to serve no purpose except to shield one Quintaglio from another's view. These walls seemed to creak the most as the *Dasheter* tossed upon the waves, as if protesting their lot in life.

At Keenir's door, Afsan hesitated. What he had to ask was critical, and the captain's mood had not been good of late. Afsan had overheard the captain mumbling to Nor-Gampar about how much he disliked holding station here beneath the Face of God. Not that Keenir didn't revel in the spectacle—no, his heart was not so hard as not to be moved by the swirling maelstrom covering a quarter of the sky. But, said Keenir, a ship should sail! It should struggle into the wind, or fly like a wingfinger with a strong breeze at its back. It should *move*.

Well, if Keenir said yes to Afsan's plan, he'd get all the movement he could want.

Afsan watched his own shadow flickering on the door in the lamplight, a quavering silhouette, a palsied specter. He lifted his claws to the copper plate.

Keenir's voice was so deep as to be almost lost among the groans of the ship's lumber. "Who's there?"

Afsan swallowed, then spoke his own name aloud.

There was no verbal reply—did Keenir know how difficult it was to discern his voice over the sounds of the ship? Or did he simply choose to ignore a passenger—a child—invading his privacy? No, there was that ticking, the sound of Keenir's walking stick. After a moment, the door swung open. "Well?"

Afsan bowed. "I cast a shadow in your presence."

Keenir made a grumbling sound and Afsan's eyes were drawn to the scar on the captain's face, still inflamed although it was fading with time. It seemed to dance in the lamplight. "What do you want?"

Afsan found himself stammering. "I need to talk to you, sir."

Keenir looked down his muzzle. Finally: "Very well. Come in." The old captain walked back into his cabin. His tail had almost completely regenerated. It was as long now as one of the captain's grizzled arms, but still not long enough to reach the floor, and therefore of only limited aid in balancing the oldster's tremendous bulk. The tickings of his stick marked each pace back to his worktable. Afsan marveled at how the twisted length of wood managed to support Keenir.

On the walls of the cabin hung a variety of brass instruments, including several sets of articulated arms with scales marked on them. The captain's worktable reminded Afsan of Saleed's, back in the basement of the palace office building. Strewn across it were charts of the planets and moons. Indeed, although it was hard to tell viewing them upside down, some of them seemed to be in Saleed's own hand.

Keenir lowered himself onto his dayslab, the wood groaning. "What is it, eggling?"

Eggling. The word seemed destined to haunt Afsan for the rest of his days. The captain had to take him seriously—he had to!

"Captain, when do we head back?"

"You know the schedule as well as I do. A pilgrimage ship must hold directly beneath the Face for ten even-days and ten odd, unless weather or other circumstances prevent that. We've held this spot"—Afsan detected a certain weariness in the captain's tone—"for seventeen of the required twenty."

"And how will we head back?"

"What do you mean, how? We'll hoist the sails, and the steady wind—that same wind we tacked against all the way here—will blow us back." Keenir clicked his teeth in satisfaction. "You'll see this ship move then, lad! Nothing moves faster than the good ship *Dasheter* when the wind is at its back!"

"And what if we went the other way?"

"What other way?"

"You know, continued on, into the wind. Continued east."

From Afsan's vantage point, perpendicular to the crowded desk, he could see Keenir's tail jerk behind his stool. Keenir had tried to thump it against the floor, but it didn't reach.

"Continue on, lad? Continue on? That's madness. We'd end up sailing upriver forever."

"How do you know that?"

Keenir puffed his muzzle in exasperation. "It's in the books, eggling. Surely you've read the books!"

Afsan bowed slightly. "Of course, sir. Believe me, an apprentice does little but read. Perhaps I should try my question another way. How did the authors of the books know that the River continued on endlessly?"

Keenir blinked twice. He had obviously never thought about this. "Why, from other books, I'd warrant."

Afsan opened his mouth to speak, but Keenir raised his left hand, claws slightly extended. "Hold your tongue, boy. Grant me some intelligence. Your next question was going to be, 'And how did the authors of these earlier books know the truth?' " Keenir clicked his teeth in satisfaction. "Well, they knew it through divine revelation. They knew it directly from God."

Through force of will, Afsan kept his own tail from thumping the deck in frustration. "And all knowledge is gained thus? By divine revelation?"

"Of course."

"But what of the discovery by the Prophet Larsk of the Face of God itself? That was only a hundred and fifty kilodays ago, long after the end of the age of prophecy told of in the holy writings."

"Prophets come when they are needed, lad. Obviously God beckoned Larsk on, to sail farther and farther until he came upon the Face."

"There's no chance Larsk simply stumbled onto the Face by accident? That he sailed so far east out of—out of curiosity?"

"Eggling! You will not speak thus of the prophet."

Afsan bowed quickly. "My apologies. I meant no blasphemy."

Keenir nodded. "Saleed said you were prone to speaking without thinking, lad."

Speaking without thinking! Afsan felt the muscles of his chest knot. *Speaking without thinking! Why, I speak* because *I am thinking. If only others would do the same—* "Honorable Captain, did you ever eat plants as a child?"

Keenir scowled. "Of course. Gave me a monstrous bellyache, too. I imagine every youngster tries to eat things he or she shouldn't."

"Exactly. You were doing a different kind of thinking, sir. You had seen some animal—a hornface, perhaps, or an armorback, or maybe a turtle—munch away on some plant. You said to yourself, 'I wonder what would happen if I ate some plants myself.' And you found out—you got sick. We, and the other carnivores, such as the terrorclaws and even the wingfingers, can't eat plants. We can't digest them."

"So?"

"So, that's a way of looking at the world that scholars use. You make an observation: some animals eat plants and some do not. You propose an idea, a pre-fact, shall we say, a statement that might be a fact or might not: I can eat plants, too. Then you perform a test: you eat a plant. You note the results: you get sick. And you draw a conclusion: my pre-fact was in error; it is not a true fact. I cannot eat plants."

"Afsan, you credit youngsters with too much thought. Observations! Pre-facts! What nonsense. I just stuck some leaves in my mouth and swallowed. I'd done the same thing with dirt, with pieces of wood, and so on. It wasn't some grand test. It was just the silliness of childhood."

"Good Captain, forgive me, but I don't think so. I believe you *did* go through every one of the steps I described, but so quickly, so seamlessly, that you might not have been aware of it."

Keenir's tone was hard. "You are presuming a great deal, eggling."

"I meant no presumption, but surely—" Afsan thought better of what he was about to say, stopped, swallowed, and tried again. "Scholars have found that there is value in this method of inquiry."

"Well, if it got you to stop eating plants, I suppose there is." Keenir clicked his teeth in self-satisfied amusement.

"May I tell you of some other observations I've made?" asked Afsan.

"Lad, I've got chores to perform." He looked pointedly down his muzzle. "I suspect you do, too."

"I will be brief, sir. I promise."

"By the prophet's claws, lad, I don't know why people put up with so much from you. Somehow, even Saleed takes you seriously. And you've got the ear of the crown prince." Keenir was silent for a moment, and Afsan thought about what he'd said. *Saleed takes me seriously? Ha!* At last, the old captain spoke again. "Very well, Afsan. But I'll hold you to your promise of brevity. There's only a few days until we set sail again, after all."

Afsan decided that it would be politic to click his teeth in appreciation of Keenir's joke. Then: "I've been making observations with the far-seer and with my own unaided eyes. I've seen that the Face of God rose into the sky as we moved east, until, as now, it's at its highest point. It can rise no farther into the sky, for it sits directly overhead. I've seen, too, that it goes through phases, just as the moons do, and just—as I've learned by looking upon them through the far-seer—as some of the planets do."

Keenir raised his muzzle, exposing the underside of his neck, a gesture of mild concession. "I've used the far-seer myself to have a peek at the planets. I was mildly intrigued by that. Told Saleed about it, but he dismissed what I'd seen."

"Indeed?" said Afsan, grateful that Keenir had been curious enough to make some observations himself. "I think it's significant."

"Well," said Keenir, his voice a low rumble, "I did wonder how what previously had seemed only a point of light could show phases."

"I'm sure you saw through the far-seer that some of the planets show visible disks, Captain. They appear as points of light only because they are so far away."

"Far away? The planets are no more distant than the stars, no farther than the moons. All the objects in the sky move across the same celestial sphere, just sliding along it at different rates."

"Uh, no, sir, they don't. I've made models and I've done figuring on writing sheets." Afsan paused, took a deep breath. "Captain, my observations lead me to propose a pre-fact: the world is spherical, just as the moons are spherical, just as the sun is spherical, just as the Face of God is spherical."

"The world spherical? How can that be?"

"Well, sir, surely you have stood on the docks at Capital City and seen the tops of masts of ships appear at the horizon before the rest of the ship does." Afsan held up his right fist and moved a finger of his left hand over its curving surface. "That's the ship coming over the curve of the world."

"Oh, don't be silly, boy. There are waves in the great River—you can feel them tossing this boat right now. Well, some waves are so big and so gentle that ships move over the crests and troughs without us being aware of it. That's what causes the effect you've described."

Can he really believe that? thought Afsan. *Does he accept everything he reads so easily, without question?* "Sir, there's a lot of evidence to make me believe that the world is round. It must be! A sphere, a ball, whatever you want to call it." Keenir's tail was swishing in disbelief, but Afsan pressed on. "Further, this round world is mostly covered with water. We, here in the *Dasheter*, are sailing not on a River but rather on the watery surface of our spherical world, as if almost the entire surface was a—a—super-lake."

"You're saying we're a ball of water?"

"No, I'm sure the rocky floor we see beneath the coastal waters continues all the way around, even here, out where it's far too deep for us to see the bottom. No, our world is a sphere of rock, but mostly covered by water."

"Like a *raloodoo*?"

"Like a what?"

"Eggling, they don't feed you apprentices well enough at the palace. A *raloodoo* is a delicacy from Chu'toolar province. You take the eye of a shovelmouth, remove it carefully, and dip it in the sugary sap of a *raladaja* tree. The sugar hardens into a crunchy coating over the surface of the eyeball."

"Yes, then, you're right. Except that the eyeball is the rocky sphere of our world, and the thin coat of sugar is the water that covers almost all of the surface."

"All right," said Keenir. "I don't accept this for an instant, you understand, but at least I can picture what you're talking about."

Afsan nodded concession, then went on. "Now, then, how big is our world?"

"Surely that's impossible to tell."

"No, Captain. Forgive me, but we have all the information we need to make the calculation. As you remarked earlier, we are sitting still beneath the Face of God. If we don't move the ship, the Face doesn't appear to move at all. It is *only* the movement of this vessel that causes the Face to apparently rise or set. Therefore, we can use the speed of the *Dasheter* as our measuring stick to calculate how far we've sailed around the world. You yourself told us it was a four-thousand-kilopace journey from the point at which the Face of God was just below the horizon to when it was just above."

"Aye, I did say that. Thirty-two days sailing."

"Well, if it takes thirty-two days for the Face to rise by its own height, we must in those thirty-two days have sailed one-eighth of the circumference of the world."

"How do you figure that?"

"Well, the Face covers a quarter of the sky, and the sky is a hemisphere—a half circle."

"Oh, right. Of course. If the Face covers a quarter of a half, it therefore covers an eighth of the whole. Yes, I see that."

"And the angles subtended by the Face—"

"I said I saw it, eggling. I'm a mariner; I know all about measuring sky angles for navigation."

Afsan cringed, bowed quickly, then pressed on. "Now, it took thirty-two days to sail the four thousand kilopaces needed for the Face to rise by its own height. Thus, in thirty-two days we sailed one-eighth of the way around the world. Therefore the circumference of the world is eight times four thousand kilopaces, or thirty-two thousand kilopaces."

Keenir nodded dubiously.

Afsan continued. "And it took us 113 days to get from Capital City to the point at which we first saw the leading edge of the Face on the horizon." Afsan blinked once, doing the math. "That's 3.53 times as long as it took to sail one-eighth of the world's circumference. So, in that part of the voyage, we must have sailed 3.53 times one-eighth of the way around the world." Afsan blinked again. "That's just under halfway around; 44.125 percent, to be precise." He clicked his teeth lightly. "Of course, that's too many places of accuracy."

Keenir was deadpan. "Of course."

"And we've sailed even farther now—enough to let the Face rise all the way to the zenith."

"So you would have me believe that we've sailed about halfway around the world," said Keenir.

"Just about halfway, yes. Land is on the other side of the world from here, permanently facing away from the Face of God."

"The other side of the world," Keenir said slowly.

"That's right. And, good Captain, consider this: we could continue sailing eastward from here and reach Land again by coming right around the world, in no more time than it took to get here in the first place."

Afsan beamed triumphantly, but Keenir just shook his head. "What nonsense."

Afsan forgot his manners. "It is *not* nonsense! It is the only answer that fits the observations!"

"A pre-fact? Is that what you called it? Your pre-fact is that the world is round, and that we've sailed halfway around it?"

"Yes! Exactly!"

"And you now want to test your pre-fact by having me order us to continue on to the east?"

"Yes!"

Keenir shook his head again. "Lad, first, I don't agree with your interpretation. Second, the journey out is hard; we've been constantly sailing into the wind. It will be a lot easier going home by simply turning around and scooting directly back, so, even if you are right—and I don't believe you are—we gain nothing by going your way. Third, we don't have enough supplies to last for more than a few extra days. We can't risk that you are wrong."

"Ah, but if I am right, we do gain, Captain. We gain knowledge—"

Keenir made an unpleasant sound.

"And—" Suddenly Afsan saw a new angle. "And we vastly simplify future pilgrimages. For if the world is round, and the winds run in the same direction around the entire sphere, as I suspect they do, at least here in the band farthest from the sphere's northern and southern poles, then one could sail to the *west* to reach the Face, with the wind at your back the entire way. And, to return, one could continue on to the west, again with the wind at your back. Think of the savings!"

"A pilgrimage is not about saving time, eggling. Our goal is to retrace the prophet's journey, to see the spectacle as he saw it. And, beyond that, consider what you're asking, lad! God lives upriver from Land, watching out for obstacles and dangers ahead. She protects us. You're suggesting that we sail ahead, moving *in front* of God, into waters that She has not first observed. We'd be without Her protection, without Her blessing."

"But—"

"Enough!" Keenir raised his hand again, and this time the claws were fully extended. "Enough, eggling! I've been more than patient. We will head home as planned."

"But, Captain—"

The deck shook as Keenir slammed his walking stick into the floorboards. "I said enough! Eggling, you are lucky I'm not a priest; I'd have you doing penances for the rest of your life. You're talking not just nonsense, but sacrilege. I've got a mind to turn you over to Det-Bleen for some remedial training."

Afsan bowed his head. "I meant no disrespect."

"Perhaps you didn't." Keenir's tone softened. "I'm not a particularly religious person, Afsan. Most sailors aren't, you know. It's just not in our blood. Superstitious, perhaps—we've seen things out here that would chill a regular person to the soul. But not religious, not in a formal way. But the kind of silliness you're spouting just doesn't make sense. Keep it to yourself, boy. You'll have an easier life."

"I'm not looking for an easy way out," said Afsan, but softly. "I just—"

But suddenly Keenir's head snapped up.

"What is it?"

The captain hissed Afsan into silence. Barely audible over the creaking of the ship, over the slapping of the waves, came a cry. "Kal!"

And, moments later, the same cry in another voice, louder, nearer: "Kal!"

Then again and again, as if being passed along: "Kal!" "Kal!" "Kal!" And the sound of heavy footfalls thundering along the deck.

Keenir jumped to his feet, fumbling with his walking stick.

There was the sound of claws on copper from outside his door. "Yes!" shouted Keenir.

A breathless mate appeared, her face haggard. "Permission to—"

"Yes, yes," Keenir snapped.

"Sir, Paldook up in the lookout bucket has spotted Kal-ta-goot!"

Keenir brought his hands together. "At last! At last it'll pay for what it did! Unfurl the sails, Tardlo. Give chase!"

The old captain hurried from his quarters up onto the deck, leaving Afsan standing there, mouth agape.

Chapter 16

After a moment's hesitation, Afsan raced up on deck, following Keenir, the clicking of the oldster's walking stick a staccato rhythm on the planking. They were on the foredeck of the *Dasheter*. Ahead, along the angle of the bow, were most of the crew, their red leather caps like a line of bright berries against the horizon. Keenir looked up, the Face of God a vast crescent above his head, and shouted, "Where?"

From high on the observation platform, Officer Paldook pointed. "Dead ahead, sir!"

All eyes peered out into the vast watery distance, ignoring the beige and red and ocher highlights on the wave caps caused by the reflection of the Face.

Somewhat out of breath, Afsan, too, made it to the carved *keetaja*-wood railing around the edge of the bow. He was only a short distance from Keenir. The captain was intent, staring, searching. His claws were unsheathed, his black eyes wide. The crew was spread out along the pointed bow, almost like a hunting line.

"There!" shouted a sailor farther along the bow.

"Yes!" chimed another. "There!"

Afsan tried to sight in the direction the two were pointing. Way, way out, almost to the horizon, he saw *something* silhouetted against the azure sky—a crooked shape, like a bent finger, but thinner, more delicate.

Afsan looked at the captain. "What is it?"

Keenir glanced at the young astrologer. "A demon. A demon out of the deepest volcanic pits."

Afsan turned his gaze back onto the distant waters. It took him several heartbeats to find the object again—faster than normal heartbeats, he realized, as his nostrils picked up pheromones passing down the line of Quintaglios. There it was, a crooked curving shape, a— By the prophet! Look at how it moves! Like a snapping whip, it shot forward, then recoiled.

Keenir's muzzle was pinched in rage; his tail stub twitched openly. "Give chase!" he shouted.

"Give chase!" repeated an officer on his right, and others passed the command along. "Give chase!" "Give chase!" "Give chase!"

The crew began to run, tails flying, to various stations around the deck. Some climbed the webbing of ropes that led up the naked masts. Shouting instructions to each other, they pulled on ropes at the tops of the masts. The four great sheets of red cloth unrolled and, weighed down by dowels as thick as Afsan's waist, came crashing toward the deck. The sheets, each with its own tribute to the Prophet Larsk, billowed outward and soon began to snap. The deck lurched as the ship, having been still all these days, heaved into motion.

Crewmembers were swinging on ropes, pulling on cables. Spray in his face, Afsan watched booms swing around. The sails cracked in protest as they were brought against the wind. The booms groaned and howled; the wooden deck creaked under the stress.

But the *Dasheter* moved! By the very Face of God, it moved with speed and power, harnessing the wind, tacking toward the strange object far, far ahead.

"What's going on?"

Afsan turned, surprised at the voice. Prince Dybo had appeared at his elbow. "Ho, Dybo. I cast a shadow—"

"Yes, yes. What's going on?"

"We're pursuing something."

"But what?"

"Put a knot in my tail if I know."

Dybo made a gruff sound. A sailor was approaching, carrying a coiled rope. Dybo stepped into her path.

"What are we chasing?"

The sailor wasn't looking where she was going. "Get out of my way, child."

Dybo thumped his tail against the deck and bobbed his torso in a territorial display.

The sailor looked up. "What the—Oh, Prince Dybo. I'm sorry—" She bowed deeply.

Afsan thought his friend played the role well. Measured, with a distinct pause between each word, he said again, "What are we chasing?"

The sailor looked terrified. She realized that she'd insulted a member of The Family. Tail swishing nervously, she stammered, "Kal-ta-goot. The serpent."

"Which serpent?"

"Why, the one that attacked the *Dasheter* on our last pilgrimage. At least, we're assuming it's the same one. Keenir wants it."

Dybo's eyes went wide. "His injuries. His face, his tail . . ."

The sailor bobbed agreement. "Yes, yes. He fought bravely, of course. He's a hunter at heart, the captain. He wanted fresh meat for the passengers and crew, real bones to gnaw on. He took a hunting party out in one of the little landing boats, thinking to swarm the creature's back when it surfaced, to dispatch it quickly, and have a feast for all. But that beast is a monster, a killer. We almost lost Keenir." The sailor fell silent, then, timidly, "Good Prince, they need this cable up front to lock off the boom. May I go?"

"Yes." Dybo stood out of her way, and she scurried on up the deck.

Afsan, who'd been marveling at how well his friend assumed the mantle of authority when it suited him to do so, edged closer to Dybo. "So we're to give chase? If it almost killed him once, what's to say that this won't be a dangerous pursuit?"

Dybo looked at Afsan. "The hunt is always dangerous. But it purges our anger. Keenir certainly needs some purging."

Afsan clicked his teeth. "That much is certain."

At that moment, Keenir's voice went up over the sounds of the ship. "Faster! Faster! It's getting away."

The *Dasheter* cut through the waves, foam and spit flying in its path.

From high overhead, Paldook shouted, "It's moving east."

"Then east we go!" Keenir's rumbling voice had a dangerous edge.

A sailor near Keenir said, "But, Captain, if we continue east, we will move ahead of the Face of God."

And then Keenir did something a Quintaglio almost never does. He stepped directly into the personal space of the sailor, and, with a violent sweep of his cane, knocked the hapless crewmember to the deck. "*I said east!*"

Afsan's nictitating membranes blinked. Ahead, at the eastern horizon, barely visible, a strange curving neck darted back and forth. The *Dasheter* surged forward into unknown waters.

Chapter 17

Prince Dybo was surprised by the scratching of claws on the copper plate outside his cabin door.

"Who's there?" he asked.

"Var-Keenir. May I come in?"

"*Hahat dan.*"

Dybo had been leaning on his dayslab, snacking on a strip of salted meat. He looked up at the doorway, at the grizzled captain leaning on his walking stick.

"Yes, Keenir, what is it?"

Keenir's tail swished. "Good Prince Dybo, I—I'm ashamed." He looked at the planks making up the deck. "I have not given proper thought to your safety. We are heading into uncharted waters; we are pursuing a dangerous serpent. My first thought should have been for your welfare."

"Yes," agreed Dybo amiably. "It probably should have."

"This beast has preyed on my mind ever since our last encounter. It's an ungodly creature, Prince, and we'd be doing a service to all mariners by getting rid of it."

"How long do you anticipate chasing it?"

Keenir shifted his weight. It was clear that he wanted to say, "For as long as it takes." Instead, he said nothing.

"My friend Afsan is pleased that we're sailing this way."

"What?" said Keenir. "Um, yes, I suppose he is."

"Can you kill this creature? This Kal-ta-goot?"

"Yes. Of that I'm certain."

"You did not succeed before."

"No," said Keenir, "I didn't."

"But you're sure you can this time?" Dybo pushed off the dayslab and stood up, leaning back on his tail.

"Yes. The first time I took a handful of sailors out in a small shore boat. That was my error. We tried to overwhelm the creature, but it tossed the boat with one of its flippers. This time, I'll go right up to it with the *Dasheter* itself. It's no match for this great vessel, I assure you."

"I am a member of The Family; I am needed back in Capital City."

"I know."

Dybo looked at the tough, salted strip of meat he had been eating. Finally: "We would have fresh meat if you killed this serpent?"

"That we would, good Prince."

"How much time do you need?"

"Surely no more than forty days—"

"Forty days! An eternity."

"It's not easy to close the distance; Kal-ta-goot is swift. But I beseech you, Prince. I want this monster."

"It's just a dumb animal," said Dybo gently. "To be enraged with a dumb thing seems, well, pointless."

Keenir looked up. "I'd strike the sun if it insulted me. *I want this monster.*"

Dybo looked Keenir up and down. Scarred face, bitten-off tail. He thought of the hunt against the thunderbeast and how, when worked up for that battle, he had wanted the thing dead. And he thought of the sun. At last he said, "I might strike it, too." A pause. "Forty days. No more."

Keenir bowed deeply.

"God hunt us all, if we do not hunt Kal-ta-Goot to its death!" Keenir's words, presumably meant to inspire, seemed to have the opposite effect. The crew, although fiercely loyal to him, was visibly nervous. The passengers were terrified. But the *Dasheter* pressed on, Keenir and his walking stick ticking across the deck.

No ship had ever sailed this way before, heading eastward, past the pilgrimage point where the Face of God had hung at the zenith. At each daytenth, Afsan took careful note of the Face's position as it slipped slowly toward the western horizon, astern of the ship.

Kal-ta-goot stayed maddeningly out of reach. Afsan had only one chance to glimpse it through the far-seer before Keenir demanded it back. He had seen a snake-like neck, and, intermittently, a round hump of a body moving among the waves. At the end of the neck was a long head with—it was difficult to be sure at this distance—dagger-like teeth that stuck out and overlapped even when the thing's mouth was closed.

Keenir stood constantly at the ship's bow, occasionally barking an order, but mostly just staring through the far-seer at his elusive quarry, and muttering swear words under his breath.

Afsan spent most of his time up on deck, all but unaware of the chill spray, the biting wind, as he watched the sky with a fascinated intensity that matched Keenir's own. As day gave way to the ever-so-brief twilight, Det-Bleen, the ship's priest, approached Keenir within earshot of Afsan. Afsan understood that although Keenir had known Bleen for kilodays, the captain never really liked the priest, considering him a necessary part of the baggage for such journeys, but certainly not a colleague or friend.

"Good Captain," said Bleen, bowing deeply, "our vigil beneath the Face was not yet over. We had three days of prayers and rapture left."

Keenir kept his eye scrunched to the lens of the far-seer, the yellow scar on the side of his head a close match in color for the brass tube. "Does not God hear all?" said Keenir.

Bleen looked perplexed. "Of course."

"Then She will hear your prayers whether we are directly beneath her or not."

"Yes, but, Var-Keenir, for many aboard this is their first pilgrimage. It's important they stay the twenty days, do the thirty-seven penances, read and understand the nine scrolls of the prophet."

"There will be other trips."

"My fear is that there will not be. You take us into unknown waters. You take us into parts of the River that God Herself has not checked for us."

The ship rocked as it moved against a large wave. "I will have that monster, Bleen. I will have it!"

"Please, Keenir, I beg you to turn back."

The captain swung the far-seer around, trying to refocus on the distant serpent. "I have the authority of Prince Dybo for this journey."

"So Dybo tells me. You've got forty days."

"Then talk to me again at the end of that period."

"Keenir, please, it's blasphemy."

"Talk not to me of blasphemy. Before I'm done, these waters will be red with blood."

Bleen reached out to Keenir, bridging the territorial space between them, and touched the captain on the shoulder. Keenir, startled, at last lowered the eyepiece and looked at the priest.

"But whose blood shall it be, Keenir?" said Bleen.

The captain squinted at the holy one, and for a moment Afsan thought that Bleen had finally gotten through to Keenir. But Keenir shouted out, "Onward!" and went back to peering through the far-seer. One of the officers ran to sound the ship's beacon of loud and soft bells and drums, and Bleen, tail swishing in despair, moved to the aft deck, turned toward the setting Face of God, and began chanting prayers for mercy.

The *Dasheter* had chased the serpent for thirty-nine days now. Keenir was more agitated than ever. Sometimes they would lose sight of it for daytenths at a time, but whether because it had dived beneath the water or simply had slipped over the horizon, Afsan couldn't say. The lookout in the perch high atop the foremast always managed to catch sight of the beast again, and the chase continued. It occurred to Afsan that perhaps the monster was toying with Keenir, that it was deliberately staying out of reach. Regardless, the *Dasheter* continued its eastward journey, until eventually the Face of God touched the westward horizon behind the ship, a huge striped ball sitting on the water.

At last a cry went up from the lookout officer: Kal-ta-goot had turned around and—no mistake—was barreling toward the *Dasheter*.

Afsan and Dybo ran to the foredeck, looked out through

the choppy waters toward the eastern horizon. Without the far-seer, it was difficult to tell, but, by the prophet's claws, yes, the long gray neck looked closer.

Keenir, nearby, did have the benefit of the magnifying tube. "Here it comes," he muttered in his gravelly voice. "Here it comes."

Afsan's first thought was that the *Dasheter* should turn around, should run from the approaching serpent. But Keenir, perhaps sensing the fear rippling through the passengers and crew, shouted out, "Stay the course!"

Soon the beast was close enough that details could be seen with the unaided eye. The long neck, something like a thunderbeast's but more flexible, did indeed end in a drawn-out flattened head filled with incredible teeth, teeth that stuck out and overlapped like a spilled drawer full of knives, even when the creature's mouth was closed.

The monster's body, round and gray, striped with green, was only partially visible. The bulk of it seemed to be beneath the waves. Periodically, though, Afsan saw parts of four diamond-shaped fins or flippers clearing the water, churning it into foam with their powerful strokes. The tail, only glimpsed occasionally as the creature weaved left and right, was short and stubby, and seemed to have little to do with the beast's locomotion. The long, sinewy neck and the round, flippered body made Afsan think of a snake threaded through the shell of a turtle, but the thing's torso seemed unarmored and its head, with those terrible interlocking teeth, was more horrible, more deadly looking, than the head of any snake Afsan had ever seen.

The monster was easily as long as the *Dasheter* itself, although better than half its length was its protracted neck.

Closer and closer it came, a dynamo charging through the water, a wake of foam trailing behind it almost to the horizon.

And then, suddenly, it disappeared, diving beneath the waves, the tip of its short tail the last thing Afsan saw before it was gone completely from view.

Afsan tried to calculate the thing's speed and trajectory. At the rate it had been moving, it would only be twenty heartbeats or so before it would reach the ship. He grabbed the railing around the edge of the deck, bent his knees, leaned back on his tail, stabilizing himself with five points of support, waiting, waiting . . .

Ten heartbeats. Fifteen. Afsan looked left and right. Those who had surmised the same thing he had were similarly bracing themselves for impact. Dybo hugged the foremast. Dath-Katood grabbed the climbing web at the base of that same mast. Bog-Tardlo simply fell prone to the deck.

Twenty heartbeats. Twenty-five.

Keenir was leaning against the railing, too, his extended claws digging into the wood.

Thirty. Thirty-five.

Where was the creature? Where was it?

Keenir let go of the railing, swung around. "It's trying to get away!" he shouted into the wind. "Paldook, bring us about—"

But then Afsan felt the *Dasheter* rising as if on the swell of a huge wave. The upward movement continued, higher, higher still, the ship leaning wildly to port, the side railing dipping beneath the water. It was like being in a landquake, *above* and *below* no longer the same as *up* and *down*. Afsan saw one crewmember go flying, saw a passenger sliding across the deck, sliding toward the submerged side of the boat.

And then the lifting stopped. The *Dasheter* rocked back in the other direction, water washing across the deck, spilling against Afsan's legs. The ship crashed down, and, on the port side, rising out of the churning water like a vision from a nightmare, was the great gray neck, water rolling off it. It rose up and up until it stretched half as high as the *Dasheter*'s own masts, the mouth now opened wide, screaming a slick and wet reptilian scream, the razor teeth jutting out in all directions.

And then the neck lashed out like a whip, moving with blinding speed, and Tardlo was gone, scooped from the deck. Afsan briefly saw her bloodied form in the thing's mouth, limbs and tail as askew as the creature's pointed dentition. The serpent turned its head up toward the sky, tossed the body into the air with a snap of its neck, then caught it again, this time headfirst. The jaw labored, chomping and biting, and Afsan felt his stomach turn as he saw a thick bulge work its way down the serpent's elongated neck.

Everybody scrambled to the opposite side of the deck, out of the thing's whiplash reach.

Afsan thought how useful it would be to have a long pointed shaft of wood, or some other implement that could be used to ward off the creature. But such tools had been forbidden by the cult of the Five Hunters, and even in these enlightened days of the prophet, that stricture remained.

A Quintaglio kills with tooth and claw, said the First Edict of Lubal. *Only such killing makes us strong and pure.*

And, Afsan thought, not for the first time, only such killing releases our inner furies, keeps us from killing each other . . .

The ship rocked as it hit the waves made by Kal-ta-goot's flippers slapping the water. The beast maneuvered toward the bow, rushing around in front of the ship, trying to make it to the starboard side where ten tasty Quintaglios were lined up against the railing.

As Kal-ta-goot hurried along, the passengers and crew ran to the port side, their feet and tails slapping the deck in unison like a roll of thunder.

It seemed to be *gadkortakdt,* the point in a game of *lastoontal* in which neither player can force a win. But then something happened to destabilize the situation. Captain Keenir let out a massive roar and charged across the deck. Without a tail to balance his torso, he could not lean forward into the horizontal running posture, but still, with the aid of his cane, he managed a respectable clip. Shouts went up from the rest of the crew, begging him to stop, but to no avail. Kal began to swing its long neck around to face the captain, mouth open.

Loyalty runs deep aboard a sailing ship. Simultaneously two crewmembers, Paldook and Nor-Gampar, ran out onto the deck, jumping up and down, waving their arms, hoping to make a more tempting target than their captain did. They succeeded in getting Kal's attention, for the long tubular neck started to swing toward them.

Afsan turned to look at Dybo, but his vision quickly focused on what was going on farther along the deck. Katood and another mate, Biltog, were madly working the ropes that tied off the boom of the foresail. Afsan caught sight of them just in time to see them finish loosening the knots, and suddenly the great corded lines were flying freely through the pulleys, the boom swinging around and across. Passengers and crew hit the deck to avoid the massive log swiveling through the air.

Afsan snapped his eyes back to Kal. The serpent was drawing its neck into a tight curve as if ready to strike. But the boom, barreling with great speed, slammed into the side of Kal's neck. The beast, taken by surprise, made a sound like "oomph" as its neck bent against the impact. The creature seemed momentarily stunned, and Afsan hoped the crew would somehow get the ship moving again.

But no! Before anyone could react, Keenir leapt over the gunwale onto the creature's shoulders. Immediately, the old captain brought his jaws to bear, chomping into the thing's flesh.

Kal's neck swung as far as it could to the right and tried to curve back upon itself so that its horribly toothed mouth could reach Keenir, but its anatomy wouldn't allow such a tight coiling of the neck. As Afsan watched, three other sailors leapt over the side of the boat into the water. They swam toward Kal with powerful side-to-side strokes of their long tails.

All of the action was taking place on the side of the ship opposite Afsan. He wanted to better see what was going on, but wasn't foolish enough to rush out into the open, making himself an easy target for that dexterous neck. Instead, he hurried to the base of the mast, where the climbing web began. He fought to keep his claws shielded: they would hinder climbing. Afsan scrambled up the webbing, its interlocking network of ropes between him and Kal. The ropes didn't provide much protection but he doubted that even Kal could bite through them, and the little open squares formed by their crisscrossing were much too small for Kal's massive head to poke through.

By the time Afsan had climbed high enough to see clearly what was going on over on the far side of the boat, the three sailors who had followed Keenir overboard had reached Kal. Two were clawing their way into the beast's flank just above its right front flipper. The third had his jaws dug into the trailing edge of that same diamond-shaped fin. Kal began to flap it against the surface in an effort to dislodge the sailor, and Afsan tried to imagine the body slams the Quintaglio must be enduring.

And then Kal dived. Its sleek form cut through the water so smoothly that it was gone beneath the waves in the blink of an outer eyelid, the choppy surface leaving no sign that the beast had ever been there.

Gone, too, were Keenir and his three sailors.

Afsan fought down a wave of panic. Kal was a reptile like himself—an air-breathing creature. It would have to come up for air soon . . .

Indeed, although Afsan expected that the great and hideous beast could dive for long periods when it had prepared to do so, perhaps by hyperventilating first, perhaps by simply gulping massive amounts of air, this dive had not been premeditated. Rather, it had been a desperate attempt to dislodge the puny creatures clawing and biting into its hide.

Afsan thought he could make out the outline of the beast just beneath the surface, but the bluish-white light from the sun and the red and orange reflection of the crescent Face of God to the stern cast odd tones across the wave caps, making it difficult to be sure.

After a few heartbeats, there was a commotion in the water. Irb-Hadzig, the sailor who had chomped onto Kal's flipper, had broken to the surface, and was now swimming toward the boat. Afsan, with his vantage point high on the climbing web, realized that he was probably the only one except the lookout at the top of the mast who could see Hadzig, a female perhaps twice Afsan's age, as she approached the hull. Afsan tried to call out to the sailors below, but there was too much of a ruckus on deck, too much shouting going on. He scrambled down the webbing and, grabbing a lifeline, hurried to the railing around the boat's edge. Hadzig was still twelve of her body-lengths away from the ship when Afsan tossed the line toward her.

Hadzig's tail whipped back and forth, sliding her through the waves. She made it to the side of the *Dasheter* and slipped the lifeline, which ended in a wide loop, over her head and shoulders, then pulled it up under her armpits so that Afsan could haul her aboard.

But from behind her, Kal's head ascended from the waves, the neck streaming water, the maw gaping. The serpent rose enough that its shoulders were exposed, and Afsan saw Keenir, his claws still dug into the base of his foe's neck, gasping for air. The other two sailors, who had been farther down Kal's flank, on the part still submerged, were nowhere to be seen.

Kal's neck darted, moving with the speed of a snake's flicking tongue. The mouth, with its horrible splayed daggers, gulped, and Hadzig was caught, her body from tail to waist already within the demon's gullet. Just as the jaw came down, Hadzig yanked on the lifeline wrapped around her body. Afsan tried with all his might to pull her forward, to reel the line in, but Kal had her firmly, and with a recoil of its neck yanked the rope hard enough to slam Afsan forward into the railing.

Afsan looked up and saw again that hideous sight of a great bulge working its way down the monster's endless neck.

It was moving slowly down the long expanse, and suddenly Afsan realized that Hadzig's death might not be in vain. Kal was an air-breather, and Hadzig was quite a mouthful. The serpent couldn't possibly gulp much air while in the process of the long, horrible swallowing of Afsan's shipmate.

The rope that Afsan was holding, although it looked more like a thread in comparison to the neck, was still dangling from Kal's mouth. If it had stopped to chew, it would easily have severed the fibers, but the lump about a quarter of the way down the long neck made clear that Hadzig's body had moved past the serpent's teeth—at least Afsan hoped it was her dead form; he shuddered to think that she might still be alive, sliding down that dark gullet toward the acid bath of Kal's stomach—

Kal's neck was raised high, held almost straight up, presumably to aid the swallowing. The rope hung down, drawing a line from the creature's mouth to Afsan. He climbed onto the railing that ran around the edge of the ship, the choppy waves beneath him, and pushed off.

Afsan swung through the air, the waves dizzyingly far below, Kal's neck, huge and thick and gray, apparently hurtling toward him as the arc of his leap brought him closer and closer.

Afsan felt the air go out of his own lungs as he slammed into the neck. Four of Afsan's body-lengths below, half submerged, but biting away like a wild animal, was Keenir. Although he'd taken many chunks out of Kal's muscular shoulder, the bites were insignificant compared to the creature's great bulk, and each wave that washed over Kal's back left Keenir gasping and cleared the blood away.

As soon as he hit Kal's neck, smooth and sticky and wet, Afsan kicked off again, as though he were rappelling down the ragged face of one of the Ch'mar volcanoes. His body swung through the air and then came crashing back toward the neck, but this time Afsan twisted wildly in flight, using his tail held straight out to change his center of gravity, so that he landed on the other side of the neck. He immediately slid around and kicked off again. Kal, alarmed by this creature slamming into it, craned to see what was happening. Perfect: the craning made it easy for Afsan to land this third time near the spot that he'd originally hit. He swung over once more and began to shimmy down the rope toward the waves. Kal was probably too stupid to realize what was going on, but in anger it snapped its jaws shut, the splayed teeth interlocking, the rope shearing.

But it was too late for that. Afsan had effectively wrapped the rope around Kal's neck, about halfway down its length. Above he could see the bulge of Hadzig's body still making its way down the throat. The body fit so tightly that Afsan could make out Hadzig's legs, her torso, and the small depression made by her long, drawn-out face.

Afsan hit the water gasping for air. Keenir looked up briefly and saw him. The other two sailors, missing for some time now, appeared bobbing on the surface. They, too, spotted Afsan. Suddenly they realized what he was up to and began swimming toward him. Keenir, too, slid down Kal's side and swam in Afsan's direction as fast as he could with his abbreviated tail. Others jumped off the side of the ship, sending up great splashes where they hit. Everybody grabbed the rope, claws extended, and swam with lashing tails toward the *Dasheter*.

More and more hands joined in, and the strength and weight of now ten, now twelve, now fifteen Quintaglios, pulled on the rope, dragging Kal's neck down toward the water.

Afsan looked up, hoping that whoever was left on deck would know what to do. There, against the glare of the sun, a round silhouette: Dybo.

The prince was just standing there, stunned like one whose shell had been too thick.

Afsan called out to his friend, but Kal was crashing its flippers into the waves with such force that the splashing drowned out the words.

Then, at last, Dybo moved, and Afsan could see that he was shouting—but not to him. No, the prince was summoning others on the deck of the *Dasheter*.

Kal was yanking back on its neck, and Afsan felt himself coming to a halt in the water, then beginning to be pulled backwards.

Come on, Dybo . . .

Afsan looked up into the glare again. There, the angular shape he'd been waiting for, coming down over the side, black metal, five splayed arms, the anchor.

Dybo and the others were paying out the chain as fast as they could, but still the anchor moved slowly, the ratchet sound of its pulley mechanism like a symphony of cracking bones.

Suddenly Afsan was completely submerged, pulled down by the fighting Kal. He gulped water. His eyes were wide open, but all he could see were sheets of bubbles. He felt as though his lungs would burst, and his vision seemed to be fading.

Then, at last, the anchor broke through from above, coming beneath the surface. Afsan fought the need to breathe and he and the others wrapped the rope around the anchor chain. Finally, when he was sure it was secure, Afsan let go of the rope and swam madly toward the surface. When he broke through into the air, he opened his muzzle wide and gulped and gulped and gulped.

Suddenly he felt an arm about his waist and then another supporting his elbow. A lifeline snaked down from the *Dasheter*. Afsan looked over his shoulder. Kal was madly attempting to bend its neck around enough to reach the rope tying it to the anchor chain, but it couldn't. The chain continued to lower, pulling the great beast down beneath the waves. It fought with its diamond flippers and stubby tail to keep at the surface, but it wasn't strong enough—especially now, unable to breathe easily with Hadzig's body lodged above the constriction in its neck where Afsan had tied the rope. The anchor continued to descend as Dybo and the others released more and more chain.

At last the thing's wicked head, with its jaws full of angled teeth snapping as it tried to draw breath, was pulled beneath the waves. Afsan watched as, for a time, its flippers flailed even more, splashing sheets of water onto him and the others. Then, quite suddenly, Kal's flippers stopped moving at all.

Afsan, who had finally recovered his breath, let out a deep and long sigh. Dybo and the others pulled on the lifeline to hoist him back aboard the *Dasheter*.

Chapter 18

The ship's priest, Det-Bleen, had opined that he might be unable to bless the meat of Kal-ta-goot because tools—rope and anchor—had been used to aid in the kill. It was a weak point, though, and the hungry sailors and pilgrims didn't seem keen on debating the issue. Keenir quickly settled it with a quotation from the Twenty-third Scroll: "That which is at hand is there by the grace of God; use it if need be, but take not a weapon with you on the hunt, for that is the coward's way." Well, the anchor and lifeline were simply at hand—they'd never been intended for killing—so Afsan's use was quite acceptable, Keenir insisted. "It's a variation on the same precept that allows us to use nets to haul aboard fish, mollusks, and aquatic lizards," he said, seemingly taking some joy in catching Bleen in an indefensible interpretation of the scriptures. "Those animals are at hand, just waiting to be picked up. No hunt is involved, since no stalking is required. God put them there for us." Bleen relented—somewhat reluctantly, Afsan thought—and said some words over the bobbing carcass.

The body of Kal-ta-goot had to be butchered in the water, since it was much too large to haul aboard. Once disentangled from the anchor, the corpse had floated back to the surface. Although Keenir and others had taken bites out of it, it did not bleed much. Still, enough blood had spilled to attract various aquatic predators. Mollusks, able to rise and fall in the water by adjusting the pressure in their spiral shells, used the beaks at the center of their clusters of tentacles to nip bites out of Kal's tail and flippers.

Afsan himself, joining one of the parties in the water carving away at Kal's body, was firmly bit on the leg by a coiled mollusk. It took much yanking by Paldook and Dybo to get the tentacles off Afsan's leg. When they did release, the sound of the thousands of suction cups popping was like the breaking wind of a herd of plant-eaters. The bite was not severe, though: the lost flesh would regenerate within a dekaday.

They sawed through Kal's neck at two places, severing it from the body just above the beast's shoulders, then cutting off the horrid head, with its vicious teeth, as a trophy for Keenir.

The neck was slit horizontally to allow the removal of the body of Hadzig. Det-Bleen insisted it be brought aboard. An aquatic burial was acceptable, he said, but not here, not up ahead of the Face of God. Her corpse would have to be stowed until the ship returned to safe waters.

After that, the neck, spilling blood from both ends, was set adrift. Tentacled mollusks latched onto it immediately and soon aquatic lizards converged on it as well, their needle snouts ripping off gobbets of meat.

Afsan even saw one of the large wingfingers land on the long tubular neck, something he thought such a flyer would never do. But, after nipping off several choice hunks, the creature had no trouble regaining flight by running the length of the neck and flapping its massive furred wings a couple of times.

Much to everyone's disappointment, Kal's giant flippers were so full of disk-shaped bones as to be inedible. They were cut loose and floated like four flatboats toward the western horizon and the setting Face of God.

But the main body, round and sleek, was delicious. Huge sections of it were hauled aboard the *Dasheter*'s fore and aft hulls. Everyone was tired of the daily catch from the nets—that was mere sustenance, but this, *this* was hunter's food! Meat you could sink your teeth into, flesh you could tear with your jaw. Real food, hot and bloody.

Eating such a meal did much to release pent-up frustrations, to counteract the effects of the prolonged confinement aboard the ship. When it was done, everyone was torpid, and most slept where they were, on the ship's deck, lying down on their bulging bellies.

An even-night passed thus, as did most of the following odd-day. But, finally, it was time for the ship to move on, and, Afsan knew, it was time for him to once again seek a meeting with Captain Var-Keenir.

Keenir had been in a strange mood since Kal had been killed. Afsan had tried to catch the oldster's eye once or twice, but Keenir had always turned his muzzle away. Afsan had hoped to get in a private word with Keenir in the captain's office, but when he found him on the aft deck, the opportunity was too good to pass up.

"Captain, a moment of your time, please."

Keenir looked down at Afsan for several heartbeats, his shiny black eyes seeming to stare. Afsan tried to puzzle out where the captain's gaze was falling. At last he realized that it was on the hunter's tattoo over Afsan's left ear, a tattoo obtained the night all of Capital City had feasted on the thunderbeast Afsan had killed. Self-consciously Afsan brought his hand, claws sheathed, to the side of his head.

Keenir nodded at last. "When we met in Saleed's office, you didn't have that tattoo."

Afsan looked down at the three claws on his feet, at the swirling grain of the wooden deck. "No, sir, I did not."

"So, in the short time between then and when we left on this voyage, you went on your first hunt."

"That's right."

"I heard a story one night while I was staying in Capital City at The Orange Wingfinger. It was a story of an apprentice at the palace being the hero of a hunt for a giant thunder-beast."

Afsan lifted his head, looking now over the stern of the *Dasheter* at the Face of God, its top half brightly lit, the dark bottom just touching the western horizon. "Stories are often exaggerated."

"So I thought at the time. But you were also the hero of the hunt for Kal-ta-goot, or so I've been told by those who saw the events unfold from a more stable position than my own."

"The hunting party is as creche-mates, Captain."

"That's what they say, yes. Afsan, your heroism saved my life."

"It was nothing."

"My life? Or your deed?" Keenir clicked his teeth. "I'd like to think that in either case, that's not true. You can be sure Saleed and the Empress herself will hear of what happened. I am in your debt."

The wind, as always, was blowing steadily; the ship rolled port and starboard. Afsan steeled his courage. "Then do as I requested, Captain. Continue sailing east. Chasing Kal has brought us farther than any ship has ever gone. If my calculations are right, it will actually now take us less time to continue on this way to Land than it would to turn around—to turn tail—and head back."

Keenir looked like he was about to speak. Afsan pushed ahead. "You can't cite food as a problem. The leftover meat of Kal is being salted now; the kill has released the hunting urge for dekadays to come. And you can't claim that the waters here are unsafe because we are beyond the Face of God. We met the worst demon imaginable, a monster from the darkest nightmares, and we beat it. We—" Afsan almost said, *We don't need God to look out for us,* but he knew that would be pressing his luck. He closed his mouth and looked intently up at the captain.

Keenir's own gaze had wandered off to the water, spreading out in all directions to all horizons. The *Dasheter*'s great red sails snapped in the breeze. Afsan felt his heart racing, felt an itching at the base of his claws, as he waited for the answer.

Suddenly Keenir's eyes went wide. He turned to Afsan and lifted his left hand with claws out on the two fingers closest to his thumb, the remaining two fingers spread but with claws sheathed, the thumb across his palm.

Afsan recognized the gesture. He'd seen it every day on his cabin door in the carvings of the Original Five Hunters and had even practiced it a bit, wondering what it meant. With a shrug, he raised his own left hand and duplicated the hand sign.

And then the inexplicable happened. Var-Keenir, Master Mariner, Captain of the *Dasheter,* bent low from the waist, balancing his bulk with his stubby tail and his walking stick, and nodded total concession to Afsan. "I'll order the course change," he said, and left.

Chapter 19

"We'll all die!" shouted priest Det-Bleen, the ship's identifying bells and drums a peal of thunder beneath his words. Every day, he tried some variation on the same argument with Keenir.

"No doubt," said the captain, lowering his bulk onto his dayslab, angled above his worktable. His tail had grown enough to just touch the deck now. "Eventually."

"But this is madness," said Bleen. "Absolute madness. No ship has ever sailed this far past the Face of God. Soon the Face will set completely—then we really will be without God's protection."

"How do you know that?"

Bleen's mouth dropped open in surprise at the audacity of the question. After a moment, he spluttered, "Why, it is written!"

Keenir rearranged some sheets of leather on his worktable. "Young Afsan tells me that just because something is written doesn't mean it's so."

"Afsan? Who's that?"

"The boy who led the killing of Kal-ta-goot. The apprentice astrologer."

"A boy? Who cares what a boy thinks? I am a priest; I carry the authority of Det-Yenalb."

"And Det-Yenalb told you we shouldn't continue to the east?"

"No one told me that. I read it in the scriptures; you'd know it, too, if you'd read the holy words."

Keenir decided lying down wasn't the right posture for this debate. Waiting for the ship now rolling on a wave to steady, he brought himself back to his feet and groped for his walking stick. "Oh, I know the holy words, Bleen. 'And the water of the River is like unto a path; yea, it is the path to God. But go ye not beyond God's purview, for there lies only God knows what.' Doesn't say anything about danger; just that what's there is unknown."

"The unknown is always to be feared."

"Well, why not ask your God?"

Bleen's tail swished left and right. "What?"

"Ask your God. That's Her, isn't it? Mostly submerged below the horizon?" Keenir gestured at the aft bulkhead. "Go up on deck and ask for a sign that we should not continue."

"Surely the arrival of the sea-serpent was a sign. Two Quintaglios are dead because of it."

"But I'd encountered Kal-ta-goot once before, back on the other side of this line you draw, back when the Face of God was still rising in the sky. What was that monster a sign of then?"

"How should I know?" said Bleen.

"How should you know? Portents and omens are your stock-in-trade. How can the serpent be a warning not to enter these waters if when I first encountered it, when it did this"—Keenir gestured at his tail—"it was in waters you consider safe, waters your whole religion *insists* that we travel?"

"*My* God, Keenir? *My* religion? It's your religion, too, I believe. Unless—you're not a disciple of the Five Hunters, are you?"

"There's much to admire in that ancient system."

"It was a false system, one that didn't acknowledge the true God."

Keenir shook his head. "The Lubalite religion puts *personal* excellence foremost. Skill at the hunt, purging violence through killing one's own food, the camaraderie of the pack. Even your religion makes much of that camaraderie. Isn't it what we're all waiting to get into heaven for? Well, the Lubalites had it every day, here in this life."

"How dare you compare the one true religion to that ancient cult!"

Keenir walked across the room, cane ticking. "I meant no disrespect."

Bleen shook his head. "This Afsan is a powerful force, it seems. I've never heard you talk like this before."

"We all change with the passing of the days."

Bleen narrowed his eyes, and sought some insight in the dark orbs of the captain. "But, Keenir, what if you're wrong?"

"Then I'm wrong."

"And we're dead."

"A ship is a dangerous place. I make life-and-death decisions every day."

"But never one so foolhardy as this."

They were interrupted by the clicking of claws against copper sheeting. "Permission to enter your territory?" asked a voice muffled by thick wood.

"*Hahat dan,*" barked Keenir.

The door swung open and in came Nor-Gampar, commander of the current deck watch. He glanced nervously at the priest, then said to Keenir: "You wanted to be told . . . just before it was going to happen."

Keenir bowed in gratitude. "Come along, Bleen." The captain shouldered through the doorway, following Gampar up the ramp and onto the deck.

It was early night, the breeze cool and steady, the sky illuminated by six bright moons, ranging from thick crescents to almost full. Keenir looked to the rear, across the wide aft deck of the *Dasheter*. The trailing edge of the Face of God, an unilluminated dome, sat on the western horizon, far, far away.

Prince Dybo, Afsan, and several others were on deck, watching. Anticipation or apprehension was running high. Young Afsan's claws were extending and retracting in spasms; Dybo's were fully unsheathed on his left hand but somehow kept in check on his right.

Keenir looked at Bleen. The priest was tipped over from the waist, balancing his horizontally held torso with his stiff tail: the posture of penance, of one walking the replica River that bisected a Hall of Worship. *Asking forgiveness already,* Keenir thought. But then he looked more closely at Bleen, saw that his glistening dark orbs were reflecting the six moons oddly—ah, his eyes were tracking left and right, scanning the horizon, as if looking for the sign Keenir had suggested he seek, some proof that God really did disapprove of this journey.

But Bleen remained silent, presumably not finding what he wanted so desperately to see. Keenir turned back to the tiny remaining part of the Face of God, slipping slowly, ever so slowly, beneath the distant waves.

And at last it was gone. Keenir suspected that since the Face had been mostly unilluminated when it sank beneath the waves, the Godglow would not last long, and indeed it did not. After a short time there was no sign that the Face of God had ever been there.

Dasheter sailed on into the night.

Chapter 20

Afsan and Dybo lay on their bellies on the deck on the *Dash-eter,* their bodies warming under the tiny but oh-so-bright sun. The wooden planks rolled gently beneath them, but here, below the railings that ran around the edge of the deck, no breeze played over them. There was a body-length between them, that being as close as two males, even friends as good as the prince and the apprentice, could lie without getting on each other's nerves if they hadn't recently eaten.

"I understood chasing Kal-ta-goot," said Dybo. "Well, I *sort* of understood it—I don't think I could ever get quite so obsessed about anything as Keenir did. But I don't understand why we're continuing to the east now that the serpent is dead."

Afsan, sleepy in the hot afternoon, was listening as much to the crashing of the waves and the barking of the sails as he was to his friend's voice. "It will get us home faster," he said at last.

"That's what Keenir claimed, too, when I asked him about it." Dybo yawned. "It still doesn't make sense to me."

"It was my idea," Afsan said. "The world is round."

"Suck eggs," said Dybo.

"No, it really is."

Dybo's dark eyes rolled. "You're getting too much sun."

Afsan clicked his teeth. "No, I'm not. The whole world is a ball, a sphere."

Dybo's tail, sticking up like a rubbery mast, bounced with glee. "A ball? Be serious."

"I am serious. I'm convinced of it, and Keenir is convinced of it now, too."

"What makes you think the world is round?"

"The things I've seen on this voyage, both with my own eyes and through the far-seer."

"And what have you seen?"

"The moons are worlds, too—with mountains and valleys. The planets are more than just points of light in the night sky. They, too, are spheres, and at least some of them go through phases just as the moons do. Some of the planets are accompanied by their own moons. The Face of God is a sphere, and it does not glow on its own but shines by reflected light from the sun."

Dybo looked dubious. "All of that is true?"

"All of it. I'll show you tonight, if you like."

"And you've made sense of this jumble of observations?"

"I think so, yes. Look, discounting the stars, which are dim and far away—"

"The stars are far away? I thought everything in the sky moved across the same celestial sphere."

"Forget what you think you know, my friend. Hear me out. Discounting the stars, which are dim and far away, there is only one true source of light in the sky." Afsan flicked his tail toward the hot white orb near the zenith, although neither he nor Dybo could actually see the gesture from their recumbent positions. "The sun."

Dybo's tone conveyed a willingness to go along with the joke. "All right."

"And moving around the sun in circular paths are the planets. The ones that appear to never get far from the sun in the sky are in fact the closest to it. In order out from the sun, we have Carpel, Patpel, Davpel, Kevpel, Bripel, and Gefpel." He paused. "Although having seen so many additional points of light in the night sky with the far-seer, I wouldn't be surprised if there are other planets so dim that we've yet to observe them. Anyway, of these planets, the four innermost—Carpel,

Patpel, Davpel, and Kevpel—go through phases, just as the moons do."

"Wait a beat," said Dybo. "You can't know that; even I know that Patpel hasn't been visible during our voyage."

"You're right; I'm assuming it goes through phases. I know from my astrology books that it gets farther from the sun than Carpel does, but not as far as Davpel. From my observations, all of the inner planets that I have seen do go through phases, so it makes sense that the one I can't see does, too."

"Why does that make sense?"

"Can't you see?" said Afsan. "It just does."

"It doesn't make sense to me."

"Can I finish what I was saying?"

Dybo's stomach rumbled softly. "Very well," he said, but his tone was weary, as though to convey that the punch line of the joke better be awfully good.

"Now, the outer two, Bripel and Gefpel, don't go through phases"—Afsan held up a hand to forestall Dybo's objection. "Yes, I know Gefpel hasn't been visible during our voyage, either, but again I'm assuming."

Dybo *harumphed*.

"So you see," said Afsan, "that makes sense. The objects closer to the sun than we are show phases; those farther away do not."

"I don't see that at all."

Mist washed over Afsan's back as the *Dasheter* rolled on a large wave. "Well, look, you've sat around a fire at night, no? To keep warm?"

"Of course."

"Well, you must at some time have sat somewhere neither near nor far from the fire. Some people were sitting closer; others, farther away."

"I'm the prince," said Dybo. "I usually sit in front."

"Of course, of course. But you can imagine what I'm describing. Now, I'm not saying you're all lined up on one side of the fire. Rather, simply that the distance between you and the fire is, say, five paces. The distance between someone else and the fire, partway around a circle from you, is four paces, and another person, at a different angle to you, is six paces from the fire. Well, if you look at the person closer to the fire than you, he or she will only be partially illuminated. Depending on where they are sitting, perhaps just half their muzzle will be in the light from your perspective. But the fellow farther away from the flames than you, no matter where he's sitting, will seem to be entirely illuminated."

"But he can't be—obviously half of his head must be in darkness, too."

"Exactly! But from your point of view, he's fully lit up—it doesn't matter whether he's behind you or opposite you; he's still completely illuminated—unless of course he is in your own shadow."

"Yes," said Dybo, who had closed his eyes for a moment. "I can picture that."

"All right, then. The planets and the sun are the same way. Those planets that are closer to the sun than we are will sometimes appear less than completely illuminated—will go through phases. Those farther away will always seem fully lit."

"So you're saying we're partway out from the sun. Some planets are closer to the sun than we; others, farther away."

"That's right!"

"I suppose that might make sense," said the prince. "So you hold that the world—*our* world—is like a planet, neither nearest to nor farthest from the sun."

"I'm afraid it's more complex than that." Afsan took a deep breath. "The Face of God is a planet."

"What?"

"You heard me. The Face of God is a planet."

"It can't be a planet. You said planets either are fully illuminated or go through phases. The Face of God does both."

"That's right. When it's nearer to the sun than we are, it goes through phases. When it's farther away, we see it as full."

"Well, then, what are we? What is our world?"

"A moon."

"A moon?!"

"That's right. Our home moves around the Face of God, and the Face of God moves around the sun."

"That's ridiculous. Land floats down the River."

"Land does not. The River is just a vast shoreless lake covering the entire surface of the ball-shaped world we live on."

"Oh, come on!"

"Really. Our home is a moon, revolving around the Face of God. Indeed, when we are between the sun and the Face, you can see the shadow we cast moving as a small black circle across the Face."

"You mean God eyes? Those dots are shadows?"

"Oh, yes. I've charted them quite precisely. I can even tell you which shadow is cast by which moon, including which one is cast by us."

Dybo shook his head. "Incredible. Well, you can show me what you mean when we turn around and head back."

"We are *not* going to turn around. We're going to continue on to the east until we reach Land again."

"You're not yanking my tail, are you?"

"No."

Dybo lifted his muzzle from the deck, brought in a hand to scratch his dewlap. "Well, then, what moves around us?"

"What do you mean?"

"I mean," said Dybo, "that the planets move around the sun, and the moons move around the planets, and we're on a moon. What moves around us?"

"Nothing."

"*Nothing?* You mean we're at the end of the chain? The bottom? Like plants in the food cycle?"

"Umm, yes, I guess you could put it that way."

"Like plants? That's not an appealing thought."

Afsan had never worried about how appealing any given idea was, only about how accurate it might be. He was surprised to hear Dybo concerned about the aesthetics of this notion. "But it's the truth," is all Afsan said.

Dybo shook his head. "It can't be true. I mean, the Face of God is only visible if you travel way upriver. And it hangs there, motionless in the sky. It's not moving at all."

"It only appears to not be moving. And as for the Face only being visible after a long voyage by boat, our world is a great ball, and Land happens to be on the side of it that faces away from the Face of God."

Dybo's teeth clicked in derision. "Remarkable coincidence, that: Land happening to be on the side that never faces the Face of God."

"Not really. Our world is lopsided, because of Land—it's heavier on one side because of the huge mass we live on.

Obviously if something is lopsided like that, there are only two positions it can take that are stable—with the heavier part facing directly toward the object it's revolving around, or with the heavier part facing directly away. Anything else would cause a wobble."

"Really?"

"Sure. You can see that for yourself. Get a rock ground into a torus shape—"

"With a hole in the middle, you mean? Like a bead?"

"Yes, but much bigger. More like a *guvdok* stone. Tie a length of twine through the hole, and then put a lump of clay on one side of the outer edge of the disk. Spin the whole thing around by swinging the twine over your head. You'll see that the clay lump orients itself either pointing directly toward or away from you."

"What happens if the string breaks?"

"Eh?"

"What happens if the string breaks?"

"Well," said Afsan, "I imagine the rock goes flying off and—"

"—and hits someone in the head. Which is what I think must have happened to you."

Afsan did not deign to click his teeth.

"But," continued Dybo, "why then does the Face of God hang steadily in the sky?"

"The rate at which we revolve around the Face is the same as the rate at which we rotate around our own axis."

"We rotate?"

"Of course. That's what makes the stars appear to spin through the course of a night."

"And you're saying the two rates—rotation and revolution—match."

"Precisely."

"That sounds like another remarkable coincidence."

"No, it's not. I've been watching the moons, both the ones that revolve around the Face and the ones that revolve around the other planets. For those around other planets, there's only one that I can see any detail on. It's darker on one side than the other—not because of phases, but because of its constitution, I think. Anyway, it always faces the same side toward its planet. And in our—*system,* I guess you'd call it—in our system, the nine innermost moons all constantly show the same side toward the Face of God."

"And we are one of the innermost moons?"

"We are, in fact, *the* innermost moon."

"Ah hah! You may save my faith yet: of all the objects in the sky, you're saying we are the closest to the Face of God."

"Yes, that's right."

"All right; I'll listen further. If you were going to undermine the special relationship between Quintaglio and God, I would have had to leave." Dybo's tone had become deadly serious. Afsan hadn't realized quite how important faith was to his friend.

"Don't worry, Dybo," Afsan said. "In fact, we're closer to the Face of God than any other moon is to its planet, from what I've been able to see. And we're much closer than the next nearest moon in this system, the Big One."

"Hmmm," said Dybo, and he stretched his chubby body, reveling in the warm sun, already now well past the zenith. "But the sun rises and sets. Why does it do that, but the Face hangs stationary, only rising or setting if you sail toward or away from it?"

"The sun *appears* to rise and set as we swing around the Face of God, just as objects come in and out of your field of vision if you rotate your own body."

"You've got all the angles figured out, eh?" said Dybo. "And you told this to Keenir, and he listened?"

There was no point in emphasizing Keenir's stubbornness. "He listened," Afsan said simply.

"Wow. And you really believe this, Afsan?"

"I really do."

Dybo grunted. "Someday, my friend, I will be Emperor. And, if your studies go well, someday you will be my court astrologer. Perhaps an Emperor *should* be open to new things. You say you can show me proof of this?"

"The calculations and charts are in my cabin; the planets and moons will reveal their truth to you tonight, if the sky is clear."

"It's hard to believe."

"No," said Afsan. "It's the truth."

The ship rolled with a wave. "The truth," echoed Dybo. But after the wave, the planks of the deck did not stop creaking.

Afsan lifted his head. A mid-sized male was moving toward them, his feet stamping. There was lots of room between where Afsan and Dybo lay and the mast supporting the red sail with the crest of Larsk's Pilgrimage Guild, so Afsan felt sure he would avoid them. But the male—he was close enough that Afsan could now see that it was Nor-Gampar, a member of the crew—seemed to be heading straight at them. Dybo, too, lifted his head in astonishment, as the deck planks bounced with each thunderous footfall. And then, incredibly, the crewmember charged right between Afsan and Dybo, violating both of their territories, a three-clawed foot impacting the deck less than a handspan from Afsan's muzzle, the chitinous points splintering the wooden planks.

Afsan pushed himself upright with his forearms and swung around to look at the intruder. Dybo, too, rose to his feet, claws unsheathed. There, standing now a few paces behind them, was Gampar, his torso tilted from the waist, bobbing up and down in territorial challenge.

Chapter 21

It happened from time to time. That didn't make it any easier. Afsan leaned back on his tail, a solid tripod of lean muscle, the wind now steady on his back. For a moment, Afsan blamed himself: perhaps Nor-Gampar would have been able to contain his feelings if he'd really believed they were well on the way home, instead of still outward bound. But the thought passed quickly: this was a dangerous situation, and a wandering mind could cost Afsan his life.

He glanced to his left: Dybo had folded his arms across his chest, hands carefully tucked out of view so that Gampar could not see his claws, extended in reflex. No need to provoke the crewmember. Afsan realized that Dybo was right. He balled his own fists, the points of his fingerclaws digging into his palms.

Gampar's whole body was bobbing up and down, a lever tipping on the fulcrum of his hips. His tail, rigid and still, stuck out almost horizontally behind him, his torso parallel to the deck, his neck, head, and muzzle pointed forward, tipping up and down, up and down.

Afsan then stole a look over his shoulder. The aft deck, where he and Dybo were, was empty. So was the connecting piece that led to the foredeck. Five Quintaglios were at the far end of the foredeck, looking out over the pointed bow, their backs to the tableau of which Afsan was part. And high above, in the lookout's bucket atop the foremast, someone—it looked like Biltog again—was scanning the surrounding waters, but paying no attention to what was happening on the twin diamond hulls of the *Dasheter*.

Afsan took a few steps sideways, distancing himself from Dybo. That way, Gampar couldn't rush them both simultaneously—he'd have to choose his target. Afsan leaned back on his tail and watched the crewmember.

Gampar's movements were slow, deliberate. He tilted his head toward Dybo, then toward Afsan. His eyes seemed glazed over. His body continued to bob.

"Take it easy, Gampar," said Afsan, his voice soft, the gentle hiss an adult uses when talking to an eggling. "Take it easy."

Gampar's arms dangled at the side of his horizontally held torso, claws extended, fingers dancing.

"Yes," said Dybo, trying to match Afsan's tone, but a tremulous note encroaching. "Remain calm."

Afsan looked over at Dybo. Was that fear he had heard? He hoped so, but the prince was swinging forward from his hips, too, his round body held now at an angle halfway between horizontal and vertical. He had moved his unsheathed claws into view.

Afsan's mind echoed with the words of Len-Lends, Dybo's mother, the Empress, who had ticked off each part of the sentence with another extended claw: "*I will allow him to go with you, but you will be responsible for his safe return.*"

Dybo was reacting instinctively to the challenge from Gampar. If they fought, there was no doubt that the crewmember—a good eight kilodays older than Dybo, and correspondingly taller, although probably no more massive—would kill the prince.

Afsan tried again. "Just relax, Gampar," he said. "We're all friends here."

For a few heartbeats, they held their positions and Afsan thought his words were calming Gampar. But then Gampar bent his knees, crouched low, opened his jaws to expose sharp teeth, and sprang at Dybo. Afsan reacted as quickly as he could, leaping into the air himself.

It was all a blur. Gampar hit Dybo, knocking him down. Afsan heard the breath go out of the prince with an "oomph."

Gampar's jaws snapped, trying to dig into Dybo's throat, but succeeding only in taking a hunk of fatty meat the size of a fist out of Dybo's shoulder.

Afsan's leap, with which he had meant to intercept Gampar, had been miscalculated. He landed with a sound of reverberating wood on the deck just in front of the ball of limbs that represented the fighting Dybo and Gampar. Afsan spun around, his tail *whooshing* through the air, and jumped on Gampar's back.

The crewmember hissed. Afsan felt his own instinctive urges coming to the fore, felt his intellect ebbing, knew that he must end this soon before it degenerated into a brawl to the death, blood washing the decks of the *Dasheter*.

Over the crashing of the waves, the snapping of the sails, Afsan heard the thunder of feet as the five Quintaglios who had been up at the bow rushed now to the scene of the fight. A quick glance showed that Biltog, the lookout, was clambering like a giant green spider down the rope webbing that led to his perch.

Gampar's jaws slammed shut again. Dybo had managed to bring an arm up, and his assailant bit into it, several teeth popping out upon hitting bone. The smell of the blood, driven into Afsan's face by the steady breeze, was getting to him, bringing him to a boil.

Ticking on the deck. Without looking up, Afsan knew it was Keenir approaching. He did not care, did not think about anything except the fight—

No.

By God Herself, no! *Think clearly.* His vision was blurred. *Intellect can win out over instinct.* Afsan fought not to lose himself in the frenzy. Dybo's jaws were snapping now, trying to take a piece out of Gampar. Afsan raked his claws across the side of Gampar's face, digging into the soft flesh of his muzzle, the fibrous construction of the salt gland. Gampar flinched, screamed, turned his head toward Afsan. That was the moment, the chance: Afsan brought his jaws together in a terrible, wonderful, shearing bite, rending through the sack of Gampar's dewlap and slicing through the underside of his neck. The crewmember's body twitched a few times, and Afsan felt hot wind billowing out of Gampar's lungs through the great rent in his neck, his final breath escaping.

Blood was everywhere. Afsan felt his own neck pulling back, readying for another strike, readying now to attack Prince Dybo—

"Afsan, no!"

A voice as deep as the bottom of a cave, as rough as rocks clacking together.

"No!"

Blind rage. The urge to kill—

"*No!*" shouted Keenir again.

Afsan's vision cleared. He saw, at last, his friend, bloodied and hurt. Afsan forced his jaw closed, rolled off the corpse of Gampar, and, heart pounding, breath ragged, lay on his side on the deck, staring into the rapidly setting sun.

Chapter 22

"Land ho!"

The shout went up from one of the other pilgrims, doing her turn in the lookout's bucket, high atop the forward mast.

At that instant, Afsan's teeth clicked together in self-satisfied amusement. It was a moment as if out of a work of fiction, like one of those improbable stories that Gat-Tagleeb was known for, when something happened at the most propitious instant.

Ship's priest Det-Bleen had cornered Afsan on the aft deck. Afsan had been keeping to himself these last few dekadays. Partly it was because of what had happened with the mad Nor-Gampar. No one blamed Afsan for Gampar's death—it was the only way to resolve such a frenzied challenge when there was nowhere to retreat—but, still, no one liked to be reminded of the violence that they all were capable of, that they held in check just below the surface. And partly it was because of the whispers, the askance glances, that seemed to follow him, people wondering at the folly of sailing east, ever east.

But Afsan needed to see violet sky overhead as much as anyone else, and when the decks were mostly empty he'd come topside and pace, enjoying the steady wind.

But Bleen had approached him, anger plain in his stiff,

nonswishing tail, in his extended claws, in his posture, fully erect, as far from a concessional bow as possible.

Because of Afsan, Bleen had said, all aboard the *Dasheter* were doomed. The flesh from Kal-ta-goot was turning rancid; more individuals would soon go wildly territorial, as Gampar had. Their only hope, said Bleen, was for Afsan to recant, to convince Captain Keenir that he had been wrong, that nothing but endless River lay ahead.

"Turn us back!" Bleen had just finished saying. "For the sake of God and the prophet, get Keenir to turn us back!"

But then the pilgrim's cry rang out, faint but distinct over the snapping sails, the crashing waves.

"Land ho! Land ho!"

Afsan's mouth closed, his teeth clacking with glee. Priest Bleen's mouth dropped open, his face a portrait of surprise. Afsan didn't wait for the elder to give him leave to go. He ran down the aft deck, across the connecting piece, onto the foredeck, and up to the point of the bow. It was a long distance, the *Dasheter*'s length from stem to stern, and Afsan arrived out of breath, his dewlap waggling in the breeze to dissipate heat.

Afsan didn't have the advantage afforded by the lookout's greater height; he could see nothing except blue water right out to the horizon. He swung to look up at her, high above. She was pointing. Afsan turned around, and, by God, there it was, rising slowly over the edge of the world, indistinct at this distance, but doubtless solid ground.

"What is it?" asked a gravelly voice from nearby. Afsan turned his head around and saw that Keenir had approached. Now that the captain's tail had completely healed, his arrival was no longer heralded by the ticking of his walking stick. "Is it our Land? Or some unknown island?"

That possibility hadn't occurred to Afsan. It *must* be Land, the place they all called home. Oh, there were some islands off Land's western shore, an archipelago trailing back like a tail off the mainland. Indeed, Afsan supposed that what he was now seeing was probably one of these, the island Boodskar.

But that it might be totally unfamiliar territory hadn't crossed his mind. *We must be back home,* he thought. *We must be!*

"Look!" shouted another voice, and Afsan realized that

Prince Dybo had also drawn near. "It's covered with trees!"

How could he tell that? Afsan turned to face his friend—who had a brass tube held to his eye. Of course, the far-seer! Dybo had become quite a fan of it since Afsan had shown him the wonders of the night sky through its lenses.

"Give me that," said Keenir. Afsan thought the language a bit curt for addressing a prince, but Dybo immediately handed over the instrument.

Keenir put it to his eye. Obviously he'd been thinking the same thing as Afsan. "Trees, all right," he said, "but if that's Boodskar, there should be an oddly shaped volcanic cone, and I don't see—wait a beat, wait a beat, yes, by the Hunter's claws, yes, there it is!"

Keenir's great paw slapped down on Afsan's shoulder, and the young apprentice staggered forward under the impact. "By God, lad!" shouted the captain. "You were right. You were absolutely right!"

Keenir turned to look out on the deck. Afsan did likewise. He then realized that all thirty people aboard were here, crowded together, the wonder and relief at being at the end of their journey enough to quell the territorial imperative, at least for a short time.

Keenir's voice went up. "We're home!"

Afsan scanned the ranks around him. One after another, the Quintaglios bowed in concession to him. Tails thumped the deck in thunderous applause.

"Home!"

"Finally!"

"The eggling was right!"

It took the better part of six days for the *Dasheter* to make it into the mainland, passing in turn each of the volcanic islands that made up the archipelago. They briefly saw another sailing ship, but it was far out to the north and, although everyone aboard was desperate to see some new faces, Keenir pressed on toward the main shore. The inward voyage was accompanied by a more frequent ringing of the ship's bells, an increase in the pounding of the ship's drums.

Finding just where to put to shore was difficult, though. Capital City, clear on the other side of Land, was the only truly permanent settlement. The Packs tended not to stay put long. Rather, they followed the herds of animals. Afsan's home Pack of Carno migrated up and down the north bank of the Kreeb River; shovelmouths were the staple of their diet.

Buildings would be abandoned by one group, only to be picked up, a kiloday or two later, by another. That is, if they had remained intact despite the landquakes.

At last Keenir settled on a dock set in a small bay, which, judging from his charts, seemed to be the Bay of Three Forests in the southernmost part of Jam'toolar province. The buildings visible from the shore seemed currently unoccupied but mostly intact. Keenir brought the ship in slowly, majestically. The waters were too shallow for the *Dasheter* to go in all the way, though, so the anchor was put down and everyone rowed ashore in smaller landing boats.

Each shore boat was designed to hold six people, but the *Dasheter* had only four, not five, the one lost in Keenir's original battle with Kal-ta-goot having not yet been replaced. Still, everyone crowded into the remaining boats, their joy enough to keep instinct in check for the brief trip to the beach.

At last! After 304 days, Afsan stepped back on solid land. It felt strange not to be rocking back and forth, not to feel the waves, not to hear the snapping of the sails. He took a few steps onto the shore, then collapsed to the sand, delighted, oh so delighted, to be on firm ground.

Others ran off into the forests, perhaps just for the joy of running, perhaps to catch something fresh to eat.

Most of the passengers wanted to be returned to Capital City, so they could get on with their lives. But Capital City was still twenty-five days or so away, sailing along the coastline of Land, and Keenir knew that his passengers and crew needed some time off the ship before they headed back. Indeed, Keenir seemed not the least surprised when two passengers and one crewmember said that they had decided to consider this the end of their voyage. They would make their way inland on their own, catching food as they went.

Soon, small search parties were organized to try to find other Quintaglios. The hope was to find a newsrider, one of those who rode from Pack to Pack on a bipedal mount, bringing the latest word from Capital City to the outlying provinces.

Afsan and Dybo formed one such search party. They

headed directly into the interior, looking for the telltale signs that a hunting group or a hornface caravan had passed by recently.

Their skills weren't really up to the task, but after a half day of searching, Dybo noticed three large wingfingers circling endlessly in the distance. This, they agreed, likely meant a fresh kill. The pair hiked through the forest, occasionally sighting the wingfingers again through breaks in the canopy of trees.

At last they came across eight Quintaglios working over the recently felled carcass of a shovelmouth, bloody muzzles dipping in and out of the torn flesh for gobbets of meat.

The hunters looked up as Afsan and Dybo approached. Sated with food, their territorial imperatives were well in check. They waved for the two youngsters to join them.

"Plenty to go around!" shouted a large female, whom Afsan guessed was leader of the hunt.

The meat, red and runny with blood, did look awfully good after the endless dekadays of bland water creatures hauled aboard the *Dasheter* and the increasingly gamy flesh of the great serpent Kal-ta-goot. Afsan and Dybo both eagerly bowed concession and helped themselves to fresh flesh, Afsan shearing a large hunk off the tail and Dybo digging into the beast's haunch with tooth and claw.

"Where are you from?" the hunt leader asked after the boys had eaten their fill.

"We've just landed with the *Dasheter,*" said Afsan. There were a few appreciative murmurs: Keenir's ship was well-known all over Land.

"I am Lub-Kaden," said the hunt leader, crouched on the ground. "What are your names?"

"I'm Afsan and this is Prince Dybo."

Heads that had been buried in the flesh of the shovelmouth lifted themselves clear into the sunlight. Other hunters, already stuffed and lying on their bellies, stirred to face Afsan.

Kaden looked directly at Afsan. "Say that again."

"My name is Afsan. This is Prince Dybo."

She appeared to watch Afsan carefully, but his muzzle did not flush blue. A Quintaglio can get away with telling a lie only in the dark.

Kaden rose to her feet. "You are Dybo?" she said to Afsan's friend.

"I am."

No change in his muzzle color, either. One of the other hunters nodded and whispered to a companion, "I had heard the prince was of a mighty girth."

"And you've been away on a water voyage, you say? Aboard the *Dasheter*?"

"That's right," both Afsan and Dybo said in unison. "A pilgrimage."

"Then you don't know, do you?" said Kaden.

"Know what?" asked Dybo.

"It pains me to have to tell you, good sir," said the hunt leader, "but we were visited by a newsrider only last evennight. Her Luminance, Empress Len-Lends, died a short time ago."

"My mother?" said Dybo. "Dead?"

"Yes," said Kaden. "A landquake in Capital City, apparently. Part of a roof collapsed. I understand it was a swift death."

Dybo's tail twitched. Afsan, too, felt pangs of sadness. He'd been too much in awe of his friend's mother to really say that he had liked her, but he had certainly admired all she had done for the people.

"It also means," said Kaden, bowing low, her tail lifting from the ground as she did so, "that you, good Dybo, are now Emperor of the Land, ruler of all eight provinces and of the Fifty Packs."

Even gorged as they were, other members of the hunting party managed to make it to their feet, bowing their respect. "Long live Emperor Dybo!" shouted one, and soon, the same cry went up from every throat. "Long live Emperor Dybo!"

Chapter 23

Lub-Kaden and a couple of her hunters returned with Afsan and Dybo to the beach near where the *Dasheter* was anchored. Afsan could see two shore boats, one heading out to the mighty sailing ship, the other coming from it back to the beach. It seemed that the *Dasheter* was not yet ready to depart.

On the beach were several passengers and crewmembers from the *Dasheter,* including Captain Var-Keenir. Keenir was obviously deep in thought. He'd been pacing back and forth along the beach, but with his regenerated tail swishing in such a wide arc behind him that it erased his footprints from the black basaltic sands.

Also present was a party of riders: a semi-ten of Quintaglios and their green bipedal running beasts. It quickly developed that Keenir and some of the others had run into this group out on the open lava plains that ran between the three forests that led away from this beach.

The running beasts had round bodies, lengthy necks, horizontally held tails, and legs that had elongated final segments to increase their strides. Their eyes were huge and round, and, rather than the solid black of Quintaglio orbs, they were a rippling gold with vertical oval pupils. The heads were tiny, making the eyes seem even bigger, and ended in drawn-out toothless beaks.

Hunter Kaden repeated her news about the Empress, and Dybo's ascendancy. It was quickly agreed that he should return to Capital City as soon as possible.

"The *Dasheter* won't be ready for another three or four days," said Keenir, whose pacing had stopped but whose tail, the regenerated part almost a chartreuse in the brilliant afternoon sun, still swished in the sand. "Katood has found a couple of leaks. I have a party collecting *gaolok* sap now so that we can seal the offending portions of the hull. And we'll need provisions. Plus, of course, the crew is fatigued after our long voyage. They need some more time to run and hunt before we set sail again." Keenir turned his head in a way that made it clear that his dark eyes couldn't possibly be looking at Afsan. "We've already had one mate go berserk. I won't risk losing another."

One of the hunters who had come with Kaden spoke up. "There's another ship, the *Nasfedeter,* moored not far from here, at Halporn, a port just over the border in Fra'toolar province. It's a cargo vessel, carrying a shipment of new fishing equipment, ordered by someone at the palace." Few Quintaglios were partial to fish, but they were often fed to domesticated animals. "It sets sail for the Capital next evenday."

"I'll go with it, then," said Dybo, already adopting a decisive nature. "Afsan, you'll come with me."

"With the Emperor's indulgence," said Afsan, bowing deeply, "there are some errands I wish to run here on the western shore. Would you give me leave to do so?"

Dybo wrinkled his muzzle. "Of course, friend. I'll see you in the Capital . . . when?"

"Two or three hundred days. I'll probably take a land caravan back, perhaps meet up with my old Pack, Carno, for a visit." He paused. "I'm sure you'll have plenty to keep you busy at court."

"Very well," said Dybo, and he bowed the bow of friendship at Afsan.

"It'll be tight getting to Halporn before the *Nasfedeter* sails," said Kaden, looking up at the sun to gauge the time of day. "You had best leave now, Emperor Dybo."

"My things—"

"I'll see to it that they get packed up, Dybo," said Keenir, "and returned to you when the *Dasheter* arrives back at Capital City."

"Well, then, I guess I'm off," said Dybo. "Keenir, a most fascinating voyage; I thank you. See me at court when you return; you'll be rewarded well. Afsan, any message for Saleed?"

"I think I'd better save what I've got to say until I see the old fellow in person." He shuddered. "It's going to be a tough fight, I know."

Dybo clicked his teeth in sympathy. Then, turning to immediate concerns, he surveyed the assembled group. "And how should I get to Halporn?"

One of the riders stepped forward. "Val-Toron, at your service, Emperor," she said. "I'd be honored if you rode my mount; the rest of my party will be glad to escort you to where the *Nasfedeter* is docked."

"Right, then; let's go." Dybo moved toward the running beast Toron had indicated. The two-legged creature turned its long neck right around to look dubiously at the rotund Emperor. It then looked back at its handler, who was standing now in a relaxed tripod stance leaning back on her tail. The runner tilted its tiny head at her in a way that seemed to say, "You have *got* to be kidding."

Two of the other riders helped Dybo mount the beast and get comfortable in the saddle. Then they rode off with the traditional cry of "*Latark!*"

Afsan turned to Keenir. "Captain, Saleed told me that the far-seer was made for you by an artisan on the west coast of Land."

"Did he? Yes, that's true."

"Well, sir, we're on the west coast now. I'd like to meet this glassworker. Does he or she live here, in Jam'toolar?"

Keenir wrinkled his muzzle and looked away. For a moment it seemed to have flushed blue, as if he'd been contemplating telling a lie. But then, when he looked back, his face was composed and its normal deep green.

"Yes, she does. Her name is Wab-Novato. But her Pack is Gelbo, and their home base is still a five-day hike from here, or so. It's a long way, and I really don't think—"

"Wab-Novato?" said a voice. Keenir turned. Kaden was standing within earshot. "I know her well," said the hunter.

"We're from Gelbo; she's a member of our base group. Quite a talent, that one."

Afsan's tail swished in delight. "Will you take me to see her?"

"Of course," said Kaden.

"But—" Keenir stammered a couple of times, then looked away, his breath coming out in a long, hissing sigh. "Oh, all right. Have a good trip, Afsan. Just—just don't mention to Saleed that I had anything to do with this."

"Why should Saleed care?" asked Afsan.

But Keenir did not seem moved to answer.

Chapter 24

The base group of Kaden's Pack Gelbo was like most mid-sized villages: many temporary wooden structures and a handful of stone buildings. In the dim past, Quintaglios had built many stone temples and houses, but, so the stories went, landquakes had been few and far between then. These days, it didn't make sense to lavish too much care on a building, for it would not be too many kilodays before tremors would crack its foundations or topple its walls.

The Packs had to move about, lest they hunt all the meat in an area. Soon enough, Kaden's people would abandon this village and move to another. Likewise, after this territory had been unhunted for several kilodays, another Pack would come here.

Kaden and Afsan arrived at the village shortly after even-dawn. Both were dusty after their long hike. They'd killed well on the way, though, so Afsan sought only a brief swim in a stream before going off to see where Wab-Novato plied her craft.

Novato's workshop was in what used to be a temple to Hoog, one of the Five Original Hunters. Although most of the temple's rooms were no longer inhabitable, their roofs having caved in or their supporting walls buckled, several were still usable.

Kaden's instructions had been no more precise than that—

one of the rooms in the temple—and Afsan had to poke his muzzle through the entrances of three chambers before he found the one he wanted. The first housed a massive old female who worked metal into surgical instruments that were traded, so Afsan was told, throughout Land. The second was a small movable-type shop, apparently setting up documents for printing. They had worktables covered with thousands of tiny metal slugs, each one with a different glyph on it. The third was a bizarre place in which two young males had thousands of lizards in open-mouth glass jars. Something about trying to understand why some bred with certain characteristics, apparently.

These two fellows gave Afsan directions to Novato's room—"last one on your right after you pass the sacrificial pit"—and Afsan headed down the corridor, sunlight streaking through cracks in the ceiling.

On his way, he noted that on some of the walls faded murals were still visible, depicting ancient hunting rituals and—Afsan shuddered—what seemed to be a cannibalistic feast.

Novato was nowhere to be seen, but her office turned out to be quite small, far smaller than that occupied by the lizard-breeding operation, for instance. In the foreground was a round flat basin that reminded Afsan of some he'd seen used by lapidarists to polish stones. Leaning against one wall were big sheets of the clearest glass Afsan had ever seen. Another wall was crowded with shelves containing books, carefully organized, Afsan saw, in The Sequence.

Most of the titles were recent, printed on the new presses, but a few were older hand-copied volumes. As Afsan scanned the titles, one discipline flowing smoothly into the next, his tail did an involuntary jump. Novato had a complete set of Saleed's *Treatise on the Planets,* bound in rarest *kurpa* leather.

Suddenly Afsan heard a low growling from behind him. His claws automatically extended and he turned quickly around. There, in the doorway arch—whatever actual door the ancients had used was long since gone—stood a female five or six kilodays older than Afsan, her skin mottled with those yellow flecks sometimes seen on people from the mountains.

Afsan immediately realized what he had done. Having spotted the books, he had walked clear into the room, violating every territorial rule. Quickly he bowed low from the waist.

"Forgive me," he said at once. "Your room fascinated me so I—" Afsan thought briefly about trying to explain how he'd assumed that an ancient discarded temple was open territory, but he realized that would simply get him in worse trouble. He swallowed hard. "I'm sorry; I meant no disrespect. You are Wab-Novato, aren't you? The glassworker?"

The female's claws were still at full extension and her mouth hung loosely open, showing serrated teeth. "I'm her," she said after a moment. "What do you want of me?"

"I've traveled a long way—"

"Where are you from?"

"From Carno, originally—"

"Carno's not so far."

"But my home now is in Capital City." He bobbed his muzzle toward the bookshelf. "I am Tak-Saleed's apprentice."

Novato's claws retracted so quickly that they seemed to just disappear. "Saleed's apprentice! By the eggs of creation, come in!"

Afsan clicked his teeth weakly. "I am in."

"Of course, of course. I've read your master's works a great many times. He's a genius, you know—a complete genius! What a treat it must be to study under him."

Afsan knew his muzzle would give away any polite lie, so he simply bobbed his head slightly.

"What brings you here, good fellow? You *are* a long way from home."

"I've been on my pilgrimage. Our ship is docked near here."

"Pilgrimage boats don't come to the west side of Land."

"This was, ah, a most unusual pilgrimage. That's part of what I want to talk to you about. But the main thing is your far-seers."

"What do you know about my instruments?"

"I sailed with Var-Keenir—"

"Keenir! That gruff old beast! By the prophet's claws, he was fascinated with my work."

"A boon to navigation, he said."

"That it is."

"But it has other uses," said Afsan.

"Aye, that it does. If the hunters ever get over their silly prejudice against it, it could revolutionize tracking. And—"

"And astrology."

Novato clicked her teeth loudly in delight. "You've tried it, then? To look at the objects in the sky?" Her tail pranced with joy. "Glorious, isn't it?"

Afsan was actually slightly disappointed. He thought he'd been the first to use it for serious night-sky observations. "Indeed. I saw many things on my journey."

"You were using that far-seer I'd made for Keenir? The brass one about this long, with an ornate crest just below the eyepiece?"

He nodded.

"Ah, not a bad effort. Exceptionally good lenses, but not all that powerful. The one I used to have up on the Osbkay volcano is much bigger. It showed a lot more detail."

"More detail? That would be wonderful! Please, you must let me see."

"I'm sorry, Afsan, but it's broken." She indicated a tube about as thick around as Afsan's leg lying on a nearby bench. "The lens cracked—I have that problem a lot with the bigger ones. I've been meaning to repair it, but we've been getting more and more black clouds belching from the volcano. I'm afraid we're going to have to move the village again, and my equipment does not travel well. It seemed better to wait until we get to our new location before making another lens that size."

Afsan was disappointed. "I've seen some amazing sights through Keenir's far-seer," he said. "But with a larger instrument, you must have seen even more."

"Oh, indeed. Wondrous things. But there is much I can't explain."

Afsan clicked his teeth in empathy. "Me, too."

"Come," said Novato. "Let me show you the sketches I've made. Perhaps you've got some ideas."

They moved across the room, Afsan needing three steps for every two of hers. At the far side, she had a couple of wooden stools. He straddled one while Novato fetched a leather-bound book from a nearby bench. She swung a leg over her stool, too, and sat not far from Afsan, proffering the book. Afsan opened it, the stiff leather creaking slightly as he did so. At first he thought that she'd acquired the book full of empty pages, but then he saw the gut ties that pulled the spine together and he realized that she added each new leaf as the sketch on it was done. The leaves were large and square and the sketches seemed to have been created with a combination of graphite and charcoal.

And what sketches they were! Novato had a keen eye and a steady, practiced hand. Add to that the fact that she had done most of her observations through a more powerful far-seer and the results were breathtaking. At the bottom of each page she had noted the name of the object depicted and the date and time she had made the observation.

The first page showed Slowpoke, Afsan's favorite moon, as a thin crescent with a ragged edge—mountains like predator teeth—along the demarcation between lit and unlit parts.

The next showed another moon, Swift Runner. Its surface, seen in a gibbous view, looked like spilled entrails, fresh from a kill. Lumpy forms covered its face, each shaded a little differently with charcoal smudges or graphite cross-hatchings.

Several more views of moons followed, and then Novato showed Afsan her sketches of the planets. She had devoted five pages to Kevpel, the planet Afsan believed, although he hadn't yet told Novato this, to be the next closest to the sun from the Face of God.

The first sketch showed Kevpel with a diagonal line through it, almost as if Novato had meant to strike out the sketch, unhappy with the result. But why add it to the bound collection if that were so? The next showed Kevpel with handles coming out of each side, like a drinking bowl, similar to the handles Afsan had observed on Bripel during the voyage of the *Dasheter*. The third page also showed Kevpel with handles, but they seemed larger, more open. The fourth showed another view, with the handles oriented differently again. And the fifth, like the first, seemed to have a line through Kevpel, although this line was canted at an opposite angle to the one on the first page.

"What do you make of those?" asked Novato.

Afsan looked up. "The ones with handles are like what I saw on Bripel when I observed it with the far-seer."

"Yes, I've got a similar set of studies of Bripel. It's much like Kevpel."

"But," said Afsan, "I don't understand the ones with the lines through them."

"They are the same thing. The handles seem to be thin indeed. When seen edge on, they all but disappear. In fact," and here Novato lowered her voice, somewhat embarrassed, "I have to admit that in that last sketch what I drew as a continuous line really looked like a few broken line segments. But I *knew* it must be continuous; I knew it."

Afsan's mind raced ahead. "It's almost like a torus, or a ring, around the planet."

"Yes."

"A solid ring. Incredible. It would be like a gigantic *guvdok* stone. Or like those great lava flows that harden into flat pathways, only in the sky, floating. Imagine walking on such a thing!"

Novato lifted the book from Afsan's lap, thumbed it to find a particular page near the back, and returned the volume to him.

"Look at that," she said.

"Yes?" Afsan said blankly.

"See the planet in the foreground?"

"Yes," said Afsan. "It's Kevpel again, isn't it?"

"That's right. Do you recognize the pattern of stars in the background?"

"It's the Skull of Katoon, isn't it?"

"That's right. Look at the star representing Katoon's right eye."

Afsan scanned the page, noting the silvery-gray marks that Novato had used to indicate stars. "It's behind the ring around Kevpel."

"Say that again," said Novato.

"I said, it's behind the ring around Kevpel—by the prophet's claws, it's behind the ring, but still visible! The ring must be glass. No, that can't be right; we'd never see it. It must be—it must *not* be solid; maybe it's made up of pieces of—what?—rock? It *looks* solid—"

"From this distance, yes. But up close," said Novato, "I bet it's made up of countless tiny fragments."

"Amazing."

"And Bripel has such a ring, too," said Novato.

"Yes." Afsan wrinkled his muzzle in thought. "Then why doesn't the Face of God have a ring?"

This took Novato completely by surprise. Her jaw dropped

open, showing teeth, something one never did in polite company. "What do you mean?"

"The Face of God is a planet, too." And then he told her everything he'd come to believe during his voyage with Var-Keenir aboard the *Dasheter,* told her how the *Dasheter* had sailed around the world at his suggestion, proving that the story of Land being an island floating down an endless River was just silly myth, proving that the world they called home was nothing more than one of the moons that moved in circular paths around the planet known as the Face of God.

Novato knew at a glance that Afsan was relaying what he believed to be the truth. Yet her expression made it clear that she was having trouble digesting it all. But at last she nodded slowly. "It's incredible," she said, "but it explains much." She wrinkled her muzzle. "Our world a moon . . . "

"That's the easy part," Afsan said softly.

Novato nodded. "Indeed. The other part—"

"God merely another planet."

"It frightens me to even hear those words," she said.

"It frightened me, as well."

"How can it be thus?"

"How can it be anything *but* thus?" Afsan gestured at her sketches. "You've seen that what's in the sky often isn't what it first appears to be. I didn't set out to disprove the existence of God. I was simply looking at things to make sense of what I saw."

"But for there to be no God . . . "

Afsan's voice was softer still. "There may still be a God."

"But you said the Face was nothing supernatural."

"That proves only that what we call the Face is *not* really God. There may still be a God."

Novato looked excited. "You've seen something else, then, something that could be God?"

Afsan dipped his muzzle. "No. No, I haven't."

"Then . . . ?"

"I'm not sure. People believed in God long before Larsk returned with his story of having seen Her directly."

"That's true," said Novato.

"Perhaps Larsk was wrong. Perhaps no one has ever seen the real face of God."

"But She may still exist." Novato's voice gained strength. "She *must* still exist."

"I don't know," said Afsan. "I just don't know. Have you read the ancient philosophers? Dolgar? Keladax? People like that?"

"I read a little Keladax, kilodays ago."

"You know his dictum: nothing is anything unless it is something. That is, a concept without material reality is meaningless."

Novato bobbed. "So he said. But Spooltar disagreed. She stated, 'A true belief is stronger than the mightiest hunter, for nothing can bring it down.' " She paused, looked at the ground. At last she said, "I still believe in God, Afsan. Nothing can bring that down."

"I'm sure of what I said about the Face, though," Afsan said gently. "I've been sure for over a hundred days, but your sketches have made me even more sure." He leafed through the pages, steering the conversation back to matters of observation and deduction. "Look at the way you drew Kevpel and Bripel, which are the closest other planets to us. You've got them both striped horizontally. Like the banded clouds that cross the Face of God."

Novato shook her head. "I never thought of that." Then she looked up, bringing her mind back to practical matters, as well. "But you say the Face is a sibling to Kevpel and Bripel, right? Similar to them in structure and each with a large entourage of moons. Then why do Kevpel and Bripel each have rings around them and the Face does not?"

"Exactly," said Afsan. "Why not, indeed?" He scratched the underside of his muzzle. "Have you mapped the circular paths of the moons around Kevpel and Bripel?"

Novato looked blank. "I don't know what you mean."

"I mean, have you examined how far to the left and the right each of the moons appears to get from the disk of the planet? Do any of them move less far left or right than the outermost edge of the planet's ring?"

"No. They all extend farther than the ring—much, much farther in most cases."

"Then the moons move outside the ring; they travel beyond it."

"If you say so."

"They must; they move in circular paths. The farthest apparent distance from the planet indicates the radius of that circular path."

Novato was quick. She nodded. "And the rings are circular, too; the particles within them must be moving in their own circular paths."

Afsan thumped his tail over the back of the bench. "Eggshells! Think about it: I know from my observations that the farther out a moon is from a planet, the slower it moves in its circular path."

"All right."

"And the farther out a planet is from the sun, the slower it moves in *its* circular path. Kevpel revolves around the sun faster than our planet, the Face, does, and the Face revolves around the sun faster than more distant Bripel does."

"All right."

"So: the particles on the inside of the ring must travel faster than the particles on the outside. It *couldn't* be a solid ring: the stress between the inside parts wanting to move quickly and the outside parts wanting to move slowly would tear it apart."

Novato closed her eyes, struggling with the concept. "I'm still not sure I understand."

"Do you have more paper?" Afsan asked.

"Yes. There." She pointed across the room. Afsan got up, retrieved a leaf and a piece of charcoal, and returned to the bench, sitting even closer to Novato than he had been before.

"See," he said, sketching a solid circle in the middle of the page. "This is a planet." Novato nodded. He made a dot. "Well, here's an object moving around it in a tight circle. That object could be a particle in a ring, or it could be a moon, like the one we live on. Well, let's say it takes one day to rotate around the planet." She nodded again. "Now, here's an object farther out, moving around the planet in a looser circle. Again, it could be a more distant moon, or it could be a particle in the ring that's farther out. Say this more distant one takes *two* days to move around the central planet." He drew in the paths of the two objects, so that his planet now had two concentric circles around it.

"So there's a difference in the, the force, that makes the object swing around the planet, right?" said Novato. "The closer the object, the faster it wants to move in its path."

"Exactly."

She reached over, took the charcoal stick from his hand. "But a moon isn't a point; not when seen through a far-seer, that's for sure. It's a sphere."

Afsan's turn to look somewhat lost. "Yes?"

"Well, don't you see?" She drew overtop of the two dots Afsan had made to represent his two different particles, making them into fat circles. Then she pointed with an extended claw. "The inner edge of a moon is closer to the planet that it rotates around than the outer edge is. The inner edge wants to move quickly; the outer edge wants to move slowly."

"But a moon is a solid object."

"Right," said Novato.

"So it can only move at one speed."

"Perhaps it splits the difference," said Novato. "If the inner edge wants to take one day to revolve around the planet and the outer edge wants to take two, then the whole thing does it in one and a half days."

"That makes sense," said Afsan. "Really, for most moons it wouldn't be any big deal. Take a distant moon, say one like Slowpoke that takes a hundred days or so to revolve around its planet. Well, maybe the inner side wants to take ninety-nine days and the outer side wants to take a hundred and one. That's only a one percent variation, nothing major."

"True," said Novato.

"And, of course, those moons that are farther out rotate on their own axes at different rates than they revolve around the planet. So it's not like the same side is always going slower. The stress of going too fast or too slow is evened out over the whole thing."

"What's this about rotation rates?" said Novato.

"Well, the moon we're on always keeps the same side toward the Face of God. That's why the Face of God is never visible from Land. So the part with Land on it is always moving around the Face of God faster than it really wants to. And the pilgrimage point, directly beneath the Face, and on the other side of our world from Land, is always moving slower than it wants to."

"Ah, okay," said Novato. "So the stress does not get evened out."

"No," said Afsan. "I guess not. Not really. Yes, over the

whole sphere, the difference is split. But some parts are always rotating faster than they want to, and others are always rotating slower than they want to."

"Is this normal? For a moon to always keep the same side toward the planet it revolves around?"

"It's normal for moons that are close to their planet, yes. In our system, nine of the thirteen moons seem to always keep the same side facing in. Excuse me: ten of the *fourteen* moons; I keep forgetting to count us."

Novato looked puzzled. "But the stress must be significant if you are close to your planet. I mean, we don't take long at all to rotate around the Face of God."

"We take exactly one day, of course."

"Of course," she said. "That's not long. And the world's a big place."

"Indeed," said Afsan. "Based on how long it took the *Dasheter* to make its voyage, I'd say the world has a diameter of about ten or eleven thousand kilopaces."

"Well, doesn't that mean that there's a big difference between the speeds that the Land side and the pilgrimage-point side want to move at?"

"Yes, I guess it does." Silence for a few moments while both thought. Then Afsan continued. "In fact, I bet there's a point at which a moon would be so close to the planet it revolves around that the stress between inside and outside would be too much. The difference in the desired speeds of movement would be enough to tear the moon apart."

"Leaving rubble," said Novato. "Wait a beat." She turned, staring off into space. "Wait a beat. How about this? The particles that make up a ring are the rubble left behind from a moon that moved too close to the planet it revolved around. What we see now as the ring around Kevpel might once have been the innermost moon of Kevpel. And the ring around Bripel might have once been the innermost moon of Bripel."

Afsan's jaw dropped open; his tail swished in agitation. "But the Face of God has no ring around it."

"True."

"And *we* are the innermost moon of the Face of God."

"We are?"

"We are."

"*Vegetables.* That doesn't sound good." But a moment

later she brightened. "But look, not every planet has a ring. I've seen no signs of one around Davpel—and I can clearly see its phases—or around Gefpel. Now, Carpel and Patpel are too small and dim to show any detail, even in my big far-seer, but there's no reason to think they might have rings, either."

"No."

"Besides, Afsan, Land isn't breaking up. It's as solid as can be."

Afsan gestured at the cracks in the temple walls. "Is it? The ancients used to find it worth their while to build temples such as this. Now we're lucky if a building will stand for a few tens of kilodays."

"Yes, but—"

"And the volcanism, the landquakes, the riverquakes—"

"You're jumping to conclusions, Afsan. Look, Land has been here since time began. It'll be here for a long time to come. Besides, if we're right about the origin of the rings around Kevpel and Bripel—*if*—well, then, there are moons that travel in tight circles around them, as well. I'm sure we could work out how close a moon has to be before it's in danger of breaking up."

Afsan nodded mild concession. "You're right, of course." The intellectual stimulation of being here with Novato had excited him. Such a lively mind she had! He looked at her and clicked his teeth in a good-natured gesture. She clicked back, and he realized that Novato must have been thinking much the same thing about him. For it *was* a heady atmosphere, full of startling revelations and incredible discoveries.

And in that moment, Afsan understood that although he'd already been through a series of rites of passage—leaving his home Pack of Carno, starting a profession, undertaking his first hunt, receiving his hunter's tattoo, completing his pilgrimage to the Face of God—there was still one rite of passage he had not yet completed.

It was unusual for a female to go into estrus outside of the mating season, but great excitement could cause it. Afsan's nostrils flared slightly at the first whiff of the scent coming off Novato, the chemical that unlocked the drive in the male. His claws extended in response to the unexpected stimulus, then slowly relaxed into their pockets at the tips of his fingers as his own body recognized what the pheromones were signaling.

His dewlap went from being a flaccid sack waggling beneath his muzzle to a puffed ruby balloon, almost as big as the dome of his cranium.

Novato turned and looked at Afsan, sitting closer than normal territorial instinct would allow.

Afsan was embarrassed. His body was reacting in unexpected and, he feared, inappropriate ways. But Novato, sweet, beautiful Novato, bobbed her head twice, slowly, deliberately, in concession.

Energy surged through Afsan and he rose. At the same time, Novato fell to her knees, propping up her torso with her arms.

She lifted her tail . . .

And Afsan mounted her from the rear, his penis slipping out of the folds that normally protected it, feeling cool and hard in the open air.

He worked his hips, maneuvering by instinct.

She was perhaps as much as half again his age; half again his size, but the union worked—oh, how it worked!—as Afsan and she moved in a rhythm that matched the pounding of their hearts, the pulsing of his sex organ, the puffing of his dewlap—

Until . . .

Until . . .

Until his seed was released within her, his mind exploding with a delight only previously imagined, a delight held for heartbeat after heartbeat, Novato beneath him hissing quietly in pleasure . . .

And then, finally, he withdrew, his energy spent, her pheromones shifting to a more neutral character, his dewlap deflating, but hanging loosely open to help dissipate his body heat.

He climbed off her, stepped back into a relaxed tripod stance, catching his breath. She stretched out, belly down on the stone floor of her workshop, her eyes half closed, each breath taking longer to come than the one before.

Afsan slid to the floor beside her, his tail loosely wrapping around hers. He was exhausted; soon they both slept.

The world might be coming to an end.

But they'd worry about that tomorrow.

Chapter 25

And, indeed, tomorrow did come—too soon for Afsan's tastes, even though he woke well after dawn. Wab-Novato had already risen, apparently some time ago, and was hard at work adjusting the lenses on another far-seer.

He lay there, eyes open, watching her across the room. She was not that much older than him, really. Only a few kilodays. Still, she had her work here; Afsan's job required him to return to Capital City.

Finally Afsan pushed off his belly, rising to his feet.

Novato dipped her muzzle in his direction. "Good morning."

Afsan returned the gesture. "Good morning."

And then there was silence. Did she know it had been his first coupling? Did she regret having done it? Think about it? He swallowed. Did she want to do it again?

I'll miss her, Afsan thought. And with that, he realized there was no need for discussion. Their roles—hers here, his there—were immutable.

"I'm expected back in Capital City," Afsan said. "I've got to head out this morning."

Novato looked up. "Of course."

Afsan started for the door. He hesitated, though, after a step or two. "Novato?"

"Yes?"

"I cast a shadow in your presence."

She looked up. "We cast shadows in each other's presence, Afsan. And when we're together, there is light everywhere and no shadows fall at all."

Afsan felt his heart soar. He bowed deeply, warmed to every corner of his body.

"I have a present for you," said Novato. She picked up the far-seer she'd been working on and brought it over to him.

Afsan's tail swished in delight. "I'll treasure it," he said.

"As I will always treasure our time together," she replied.

If he'd had to walk the entire way, allowing time for sleeping and hunting and a little sight-seeing, it would have taken Afsan forty days to reach Carno. He managed it in twenty-three. For the first seven days, he rode with a caravan of traders whose wares included brass buttons, needles for sewing leather, and equipment for tanning hides. But Afsan had to take his leave of them when their path diverged from his intended course.

The next ten days, he walked alone, thinking. His mind was constantly full of calculations. He stopped every few kilopaces and pulled out his writing leather and strings of beads to work through the more complex math.

Each evening, he used his new far-seer to observe the other moons, the rings around Kevpel, the secrets of the night.

It became clear that what he and Novato had feared was the truth. The world they were on was much, much closer to the Face of God than was any other moon in this system or any other moon around any other planet Afsan could see.

He felt a small temblor one night and an aftershock the next day.

The numbers suggested it; the quaking ground confirmed it. The world was indeed unstable, would indeed break up at some point in the not too distant future. He'd have to consult the palace library to check records of increasing landquake frequency and severity and to confirm his memory of the strength of rocks, but it seemed as though the differential forces acting on the near and far sides of this moon would tear it asunder within perhaps twenty generations.

It did not make for a pleasant journey.

On the eighteenth day, he walked across a new bridge of cut

stone that spanned the river marking the border between Jam'toolar and Arj'toolar.

That evening, he came upon a tributary of the Kreeb and was able to join up with a troupe of musicians traveling by raft down its winding course. They had many instruments, some with strings and intricate gold inlays, others with brass tubes and keys made from spikefrill horns. The musicians agreed to let Afsan ride with them in exchange for sharing tales of the Capital, but after the first day, the deal was modified: Afsan could ride with them so long as he didn't try to sing along when they practiced. They took him straight to Carno, the Pack in which he was born. The rafters continued on, and Afsan bade them a safe trip.

There would be reunions here: happy meetings with his creche-mates; tales told in the merchants' square; a time to recover from the long voyage aboard the *Dasheter;* a time to decide how best to deal with Tak-Saleed upon his return to still-distant Capital City.

In modern times, since the rise of the religion of Larsk, the world had been divided into eight provinces, each under its own governor. But the ancient Lubalite grouping of the Pack was still the principal social unit.

According to legend, there had been five original hunt leaders, each with her own pack. Just as Tetex had done during Afsan's first hunt, Lubal, Belbar, Katoon, Hoog, and Mekt had each used sign language to designate the members of their hunting parties. Ten fingers, ten hunters to a pack.

Eventually each of the ten hunters in their packs had founded his or her own pack. Five original packs each with ten hunters thus gave rise to the Fifty Packs that now roamed Land.

Actually there were many more than the fifty traditional packs these days, since subgroupings had formed, but each group knew its lineage. Carno, for instance, traced itself back to Mar-Seenuk, one of the hunters comprising Belbar's original pack of ten.

The term "pack" was still used to refer to any group of hunters. But "Pack," emphasized with an expansive swish of the tail, written in left-facing glyphs instead of right, referred to the whole social unit: hunters and those who plied a craft, healers and teachers and scholars, priests and administrators, the young and the old.

Carno was Afsan's home Pack. His parents probably lived there still, although he did not know who they were. He suspected Pahs-Drawo was his father, for they both had something of the same look about them: earholes slightly lower than the norm (or perhaps foreheads that were slightly higher) and an unusual freckling on the underside of their tails.

But it didn't matter. Drawo's loyalty was to Carno as a whole. Afsan had never given much thought to the issue until after he had left and gotten to be friends with Dybo. The prince actually knew his mother (and father, although Ter-Reegree had been killed in a hunt long before Afsan's arrival in Capital City). The Family! The one group in all the world that knew its lineage, that recognized son or daughter, father and mother, grandfather and grandmother. The Family: the direct descendants of the Prophet Larsk.

Saleed had once sarcastically referred to Afsan as "the proudest son of far Carno," but it was true, in a sense: the children were the children of the Pack, not of any individual. Old Tep-Terdog, whom Afsan obviously was not closely related to at all—he had much lighter skin than Afsan's and eyes closer together—considered Afsan as much his son, as much his responsibility to guard and protect and educate, as did Drawo (or Rej-Serkob, the other likely candidate for being Afsan's biological father).

Carno, like all villages, had been based on this principle of protecting the young: at its center, farthest removed from the roaming beasts, was the creche, the communal nursery.

In loose bands around the creche were the tents and buildings used by those who hunted only occasionally: the scholars and artisans and merchants. And at the perimeter, constantly on the move, were the Pack's principal hunters, those responsible for the defense and feeding of everyone else.

If Afsan had still been part of Carno when preparing to take his first hunt, his lessons would have included a tour of the creche to remind him of why Quintaglios went out and sometimes died on the hunt: to protect the future, to feed the young.

And, if his preparations had not been so rushed back in Capital City, he would have been shown the creche there.

Actually *both* creches there, the public one off the central town square and the royal one, used exclusively by The Family, where the eggshells of past Emperors were on display.

But even if that had happened, it wouldn't have been the same. The creche here in Carno was the one he had been born in, the one he had spent his early days in. He had, at best, dim memories of it. It bothered him that he'd never seen it as an adult.

He thought about asking for someone to show him the creche, but one of the rules of survival he'd picked up back at the palace, where bureaucracy seemed to slow everything, was that it is easier to apologize later than to get permission now.

Besides, he *was* an adult: he'd had his first hunt, he'd taken the pilgrimage. He'd been through all the rites of passage. There seemed no reason why he couldn't simply walk into the creche and have a look-see for himself.

Carno's creche, at the center of the band's roving area, was a building near the north shore of the Kreeb River. It was shaped like the shell of a *gabo* nut, three rounded sections joined together. Although the main entrance was on one side of the middle section, there were doors scattered along the perimeter, some for emergency exit in case of fire, some for use by food-bearers, and some for the priests.

Since his approach down the Path of Children had brought him closest to one of the food-bearers' entrances, Afsan decided to go in that way.

The door was the kind used in service areas: balanced to swing open with a simple push from one's muzzle, making entrance easy even with laden arms. Afsan, with nothing to carry, used his left hand instead. He'd half expected the door to squeak on its hinges, but they were well oiled. Of course: a hinge that awoke sleeping children would be a high priority for fixing.

He found himself in a curving corridor. A dim memory came back to him: the creche had a double wall, the space between the inner and outer walls being where adults walked who did not want to disturb the egglings.

He moved down the curving perimeter corridor, light from outside entering through windows along its length. About ten paces along he found another doorway, this one in the inner wall. The planks making up the door were carved with a cartouche Afsan hadn't seen before, depicting whole eggs, jawbones, and what seemed to be broken pieces of shell. There was an unusual locking mechanism: the kind that only worked from one side. Fortunately it was the side Afsan happened to be on. He pressed the metal bar and the door opened.

Hot air hit his face. Inside it was much darker than where he had been, and it took a while for his eyes to adjust.

The room was circular, perhaps thirty paces across. The floor was covered with sand. No, Afsan realized after drawing his heel claw back and forth across the brown grains, no, that wasn't right. There was no floor. Rather, the walls rose directly out of the flank of the Kreeb River.

There were fires arrayed in a pattern around the room. He could tell by the smell that they were burning *kadapaja* logs, a wood prized for its even flames and slow consumption. Above each fire was a hole in the roof, allowing most of the smoke to escape. The whole thing could have been heated more efficiently with coal furnaces and aired out with brick chimneys, Afsan thought, but creches were places of ancient traditions.

Suddenly Afsan noticed the eggs: beige, elongated, laid in circles of eight, the long axis of each pointing outward, sand partially covering the shells. The clutch he spotted first was halfway between two of the fires, but he soon realized that there were five—no, six—clutches around the room, each consisting of eight eggs.

However, halfway between many of the fires, there were no eggs at all. Well, it was the hatching season. It looked like most of the eggs had already opened, but a few clutches remained.

Afsan moved partway along the wall until he found a wooden stool. He swung his legs over it, letting his tail drape off the back, and sat, marveling at the wondrous room. His dewlap swung freely in the heat. He could hear his own breathing, the soft crackling of the fires, and, yes, something else, something faint. A ticking, like stones touching together. Where was it coming from?

There! By the prophet's claws, right in front of him. In the nearest clutch, one of the eggs was cracking from within. He saw the shell bulge out, fragmenting into little segments, a tough white membrane holding them together. The egg was still for several moments, then it quivered again and more cracks appeared in the shell. Afsan watched, fascinated. Finally a large piece of shell dropped from the membrane, falling to the sand. It was followed by another and another and another. A little head was visible now, slick and yellow and wet, with giant eyes closed. Afsan could see the tiny white birthing horn on the upper surface of the baby's muzzle, a horn that would be lost within a few dekadays of the hatching.

A crack was now visible all the way around the egg. Afsan could see the head and shoulders of the baby. It seemed to stretch its body and the egg split along this crack, the two halves falling away from each other. The baby—its head oversized, its body scrawny and pale, its tail only half the length of its body—stumbled forward, then began to crawl from the nest on its hands and knees.

Two other eggs had begun to hatch, as well. One of them split open cleanly, and its little Quintaglio waddled away. But the other seemed to be having trouble. The shell was too thick, or the baby within too weak. Afsan was horrified. After watching the egg rock back and forth without cracking further for as long as he could bear, he walked over to the nest. In the flickering light of the fires, one on either side, Afsan bent over and, extending the claw on his fifth finger, tapped on the egg until it was cracked in a semi-ten of places. At last, the little one within was able to break the shell apart, and as Afsan beamed down on it, the baby began to crawl away.

The three babies made little peeping sounds as they wandered about. Another one of the eggs started to hatch.

"What are you doing here?"

Afsan's claws extended. He calmed himself and turned around. There was a female of middle age standing in the main doorway, hands on hips. The fires reflected in her eyes.

"Hello," said Afsan. "I just came in to watch."

"How did you get in?"

"Through one of the side doors."

"That's not the proper way. Who are you?"

"Afsan."

"Afsan?" The female's voice was suddenly warm. "By the Face of God, you've grown! How long have you been away?"

"Just shy of a kiloday."

"You're still a skinny thing, though."

Afsan peered at the female. "Do I know you?"

"I'm Cat-Julor. I work here."

"I don't remember you."

"I don't often leave the creche. But I remember you. I was here when you were born. That would have been, what, twelve kilodays ago?"

"Thirteen thousand five hundred."

"That long!" Her muzzle moved up and down as she looked him over. "You were always a clever one. I'd love to talk to you some more, but I've got work to do. You may watch if you wish."

Afsan nodded concession. "Thank you."

Julor lay on her stomach, arms stretched out in front of her forming a wide angle. After a moment, her body convulsed, and she opened her jaws wide. Lying on her broad tongue and spilling over into the sides of her mouth was a brown-gray lumpy mass. Afsan reeled slightly from the smell of partially digested meat. But the newborns reacted more positively. They lifted their tiny muzzles, sniffed the air, and half crawled, half walked toward Julor, then stumbled into her gaping maw, first one, then another, and, at last, the little fellow Afsan had helped out of his shell. Tiny heads with giant still-closed eyes lapped at the regurgitated food.

Julor obviously couldn't carry on a conversation in this position, so Afsan went back to his stool. He watched for the better part of the afternoon as the remaining eggs opened. It was the most beautiful thing he had ever seen that wasn't in the sky.

The next day, Afsan decided to go back to the nursery and see how the hatchlings were doing. He was particularly interested in his little friend who'd had trouble getting out of his shell.

It was a fine day. The sun shone down from a cloudless purple sky. Pale moons were visible. Most everyone was in a good mood, judging by how little room they left between themselves on the paths of Carno. Afsan bowed cheery concession to those who passed him, and others reciprocated. The walk to the bank of the Kreeb was invigorating.

Although Julor had seemed surprised that Afsan had used the food-bearers' entrance, she hadn't really rebuked him for it. Since it was the closest door, he decided to use it again, this time, just for fun, pushing it open with his muzzle. Once more he was in the corridor between the inner and outer walls.

Suddenly all cheeriness drained from him. His claws burst from their sheaths. Something was very wrong. He heard thundering feet and the peeping of egglings. Afsan hurried down the curving hall and opened the inner door he had gone through the day before.

A large male was running around the room, his purple robe flying about him, his tail lifted high off the sand. Peeping loudly and running and stumbling and crawling with all their might, the babies, their obsidian eyes now open wide with fear, were trying to get away from him.

The figures danced in the flames from the heating fires. The male tipped his body low, bringing his head down parallel to the ground. His jaws swung open. There was a baby a single pace in front of him. With a darting motion of his head, the adult's mouth slammed shut around the infant. Afsan heard a slurping sound and saw a slight distension of the male's throat as the young one slid down his gullet.

"No!"

The robed male looked up at Afsan's call, startled to see him there in the doorway. He made a swiping motion with one clawed hand. "*K'ata halpataars,*" he grumbled from low in his throat. *I am a bloodpriest.* The voice was deep, ragged, as if forced to the surface. "*Get out!*"

Suddenly Cat-Julor appeared behind Afsan, obviously brought running by his scream. "Afsan, what are you doing here?"

"He's eating the babies!"

"He's Pal-Donat, a bloodpriest. It's his job."

"But—"

"Come with me."

"But he's *eating*—"

"Come!" She, head-and-neck taller than Afsan, put an arm around his shoulders and propelled him from the room. Afsan looked back, horrified, and saw the robed one scoop up another infant, this one smaller than the rest—likely the one Afsan had helped out of the egg.

Afsan felt sick.

Julor took him down the inner hallway and through the main door, out into the harsh light of day.

"He killed two of the babies," said Afsan.

Julor looked out at the rest of Carno. "He'll kill seven from each clutch before he's done."

"Seven! But that will leave—"

"Only one," said Julor.

"I don't understand," said Afsan.

"Don't you?"

"No."

Julor's tail swished in indifference. "It's to control the population. We need space and we need food. There's only so much of either to go around. A female lays eight eggs in each clutch. Only one is ever permitted to survive."

"That's horrible."

"That's necessity. I'm no scholar, Afsan, but even I know that if you increase your population eightfold with every generation, it won't be long before you're out of room. Somebody told me that in just five generations, one Quintaglio would have tens of thousands of descendants."

"Thirty-two thousand seven hundred and sixty-eight," said Afsan automatically. "Eight to the fifth."

Julor's tail swished in amazement. "I don't know what 'eight to the fifth means,' but—"

"It's a new way of expressing big numbers—"

"*But* I think there are more important things to know in life than fancy counting. Surely you knew something about the bloodpriests?"

Afsan bowed his head. "No."

"But you knew eggs were laid in clutches of eight?"

"I'd never thought about it before."

Julor's teeth touched. "You who can read always amuse me. You bury your muzzles in dusty old pages, but you seem at a loss for dealing with day-to-day life. It's hardly a secret that most egglings are dispatched. By God's tail, how could it be kept a secret, after all? I bet you could recite facts to me endlessly about your profession, but you never bothered to wonder about babies."

"Most people know this?"

"Many do. There are unpleasant aspects to life; we accept them, but don't dwell on them." Julor looked down her muzzle at Afsan. "Of course, most people learn about it in an abstract way, not by actually stumbling on a *halpataars* at work. Even the bloodpriests must force themselves into a trance before they can do their jobs. It's a distasteful task."

Afsan thought for an instant that Julor was making a pun with her last sentence. But of course she wasn't; she couldn't be—could she? Perhaps she *was*. Perhaps having to deal constantly with such issues, one did develop a callousness about them.

"I didn't know," Afsan said simply.

"Well, now you do." She nodded concession to him. "And now you have something to think about. Go."

She gave him a little push that was not unkind—only a creche mother would touch another without thinking. Afsan began to amble away, the sun, which earlier had seemed joyous, now hot and uncomfortable and harsh.

He found a tree to lie under and closed his eyes. He realized, horribly, what that final panel in the intricate carving on his cabin door aboard the *Dasheter* had really depicted. Mekt, one of the Original Five, clad in priestly robes, a whip of tiny tail hanging out of her mouth; Mekt, a bloodpriest. The cannibalistic rite of devouring children went right back to the ancient religion of the Five Hunters, indeed, was probably the only rite from that religion that was still widely practiced, the only role Lubalites had in the modern worship of the Prophet Larsk.

Afsan sat there and thought. About the dead egglings. About the harshness of existence. And, longest and most of all, about his own seven long-dead brothers and sisters, whom he had never known.

In the middle of the night, Afsan woke with a start. As every learned person knew, Land was divided into eight provinces: Capital, Kev'toolar, Chu'toolar, Mar'toolar, Edz'toolar, Arj'toolar, Jam'toolar, and Fra'toolar. Beside being head of state for all of Land, the Emperor or Empress was also governor of Capital province. But the governors of the other seven were always fiercely loyal to whoever lay on the throne of Capital City. It had hit Afsan that the other governors, from Len-Quelban in distant Fra'toolar to Len-Haktood in Carno's own province of Arj'toolar, all of whom he'd seen at processions in Capital City, were about the same height, and therefore the same age, as the late Len-Lends, Dybo's mother.

It was all so obvious. *Of course* these seven governors had been loyal to the Empress. They were her *siblings,* her—Afsan ran down the list of governors—her five sisters and two brothers.

Imperial hatchlings weren't gobbled by bloodpriests. Rather, the fastest was selected to become Emperor or Empress, and the other seven would become provincial governors. Their loyalty was assured, since they owed their lives to the institution of the monarchy. Without it, without the special dispensation for imperial hatchlings, they would have been swallowed whole.

Lends's brothers and sisters now ran the seven outlying provinces. Dybo's seven siblings would have been spirited away shortly after hatching, and they would become provincial governors when their—Afsan had to search for the words, they were so rarely used—their *aunts* and *uncles* passed on.

The descendants of Larsk ran the entire world.

Perhaps this, too, was common knowledge. Perhaps Afsan had, indeed, spent too long removed from the concerns of real life. But he *understood* now, and maybe this was the greatest rite of passage of all: the movements of celestial bodies were simple and predictable, but the machinations of politics were more complex and more subtle than anything to be found in nature.

Afsan lay on his belly in the dark, but never managed to get back to sleep.

Chapter 26

It was time, Afsan knew, to return to Capital City. For one thing, Saleed would doubtless be angry that he had taken any time off at all. For another, Dybo was now Emperor—and that would be something to see!

When Afsan had first made the journey from Carno to Capital City, it was via hornface caravan, a slow way to travel. But each Pack had to send a tribute to the new Emperor, and so a group from Carno was heading out on the fastest running beasts to make the journey. After liberally mentioning his friendship with Dybo, Afsan was invited to join the party. He was delighted: this would cut his travel time by two-thirds.

The runners were similar to those used by Kaden's hunting pack: round bodies; stiff tails; legs built for great strides; long necks; tiny heads; giant eyes. But these were the inland variety, an unattractive pinkish beige, with eyes that were green rather than golden, and beaks of shiny black.

Afsan climbed atop his mount and settled into the saddle, his own flexible tail wrapping around the runner's stiff one. Afsan could steer the beast simply by moving his tail to indicate the direction he wanted to go, and the interlocking of their tails would help Afsan stay on the creature's back even at the fastest speeds.

Three others were in the riding party: Tar-Dordool, leader of Pack Carno; Det-Zamar, one of Carno's senior priests; and

Pahs-Drawo, the individual Afsan idly speculated might be his father. Drawo was one of the most skilled hunters in Carno, and he would be responsible for seeing to it that the group ate well on the trip.

With cries of "*Latark!*" they left at first light. Afsan snapped his tail to spur his runner into motion. The horizon jumped up and down as the runner's two long legs came into their stride, and Afsan, who had survived the voyage aboard the *Dasheter* without feeling sick, realized that if it were not for the cooling wind created by the beast's great velocity, he would be nauseous from the bouncing. He placed his arms around the base of the creature's long neck to steady himself, taking care not to unsheathe his claws even though they wanted to pop out in fright, lest he dig into the runner's flesh.

By noon that day, Afsan's stomach had quelled. Priest Zamar, whose beast was running alongside Afsan's own, taught him the trick of matching his own breathing to the beast's stride: sucking air in as it lifted its left foot, pushing it out as the right one kicked into the dirt. Eventually the rhythm of the beast became transparent to Afsan, and when they dismounted to let the runners rest, he found himself feeling as though his body was still rushing through the air.

They continued through the day without eating, and slept under the stars that night. Afsan looked up at the great sky river, wondering what it really was, and watched the moons go through their motions. His mind raced, still trying to comprehend all the secrets of the sky, but at last he grew tired, and simply drank in the beauty of the night until he fell into a dreamless, pleasant sleep.

The runners, voracious beasts, had been turned loose to hunt. With their swiftness, there was no doubt that the four of them, operating as a pack, would bring down something large enough to satisfy themselves.

No time was wasted in the morning. The mounts had indeed eaten well, judging by their torpor, but after a few false starts they were goaded back into action.

The party followed the Kreeb River for days. It meandered a lot and Afsan marveled at how he'd ever believed that the great body of water that covered the moon he lived on was simply a giant river, how anybody had ever believed that.

Eventually they left Arj'toolar for the plains of Mar'toolar.

After several days, Pahs-Drawo announced that he wanted to catch something special for dinner: a fangjaw.

Afsan had openly clicked his teeth. "A fangjaw? No Quintaglio can catch one of those. They're much too fast."

"Ah," said Drawo, "but the runners can catch them."

Afsan's stomach churned. Eat an animal killed by another animal? Drawo must have read the revulsion on Afsan's face. He clicked his teeth, and Afsan noticed that the way he did that, a loud click then a soft, was much like his own laughter. "Don't worry, eggling. We will do the killing, but we'll give chase upon the backs of the runners."

And so they did. A fangjaw was one of the few four-footed carnivores in all of Land. It hunted in the tall grasses, bringing down thunderbeasts and shovelmouths, running silently on padded feet. Its narrow face had two long curving teeth growing upward from the lower jaw. Afsan had heard their meat was sweet: he'd now find out for himself.

Zamar and Dordool declined to participate. Drawo picked up the trail of a fangjaw in short order, and he and Afsan mounted their bipedal racing animals and set off in the direction the fangjaw must have gone.

It took the better part of the morning to track the creature, but at last they caught sight of it, scaly brown shoulders rising and falling behind the grass. Drawo used the hunters' sign language to indicate it was time to charge, and their mounts rushed toward the fangjaw. Their quarry looked up, let out a sticky hiss, and bolted into the distance.

The fangjaw was a natural predator for the running beast, and Drawo said it had taken much training to get them to chase fangjaws instead of galloping away. But chase they did! Afsan's mount surged beneath him, and he held on for dear life, wrapping his tail tightly around the runner's. The wind in his face was incredible.

The fangjaw was low in the grass, its passage mostly visible only by ripples through the blades.

They were closing.

The fangjaw made a sharp turn. Afsan didn't know why it had done so, but he trusted its instincts. With a yank of his tail, he commanded his runner to copy the fangjaw's maneuver. As he passed the spot where the carnivore had turned, Afsan saw a crevice in the ground. If he hadn't changed direction, his runner would have stumbled into it, probably breaking both legs.

Drawo's runner moved off at an angle, so that he was approaching the fangjaw on the left, while Afsan barreled in from the right. Suddenly Drawo leapt from his mount. Afsan did the same, the ground rushing by beneath him at a dizzying rate. His claws sprang out. He landed on the fangjaw's shoulders. Drawo missed, smashing into the dirt. Afsan was alone on the creature's back.

It was twice Afsan's body-length, but his weight was slowing it down. He felt the thing's muscles ripple as it moved its shoulders, trying to buck him.

Afsan dug in.

One bite should do it . . .

The fangjaw arched its neck, trying again to throw Afsan. Afsan brought his jaws together with a crunching sound where the fangjaw's head joined its body. He twisted, cracking the quadruped's vertebrae.

In mid-stride, the fangjaw stopped moving of its own volition. But momentum carried it forward, smashing it into the ground. Afsan bounced, but did not fall off his kill. Drawo, brushing dirt from his body, ran over to where Afsan and the fangjaw lay.

"Such skill from an eggling!" shouted Drawo, apparently genuinely pleased, and not disappointed to have been left out of the kill himself. "I've never seen the like."

He stared at Afsan for a moment, as if wondering something, then made a strange gesture with his left hand: claws exposed on the second and third fingers, the fourth and fifth fingers spread, thumb pressed against his palm.

Afsan recognized the gesture. It was the same one he'd seen on his *Dasheter* cabin door and elsewhere. But the double impacts, first into the fangjaw's hide, then as the beast had slammed into the ground, had left him slightly dazed. Not sure quite what he was doing, he made a halfhearted stab at duplicating the sign, still wondering what the silly thing meant.

Drawo looked delighted. "I'll summon the others," he said, bowing deeply.

Afsan saw no reason to wait for the rest of the party. He

tore a large chunk off the beast's flank. The meat was very sweet indeed . . .

The rest of the journey was uneventful. Afsan slept under the stars when the sky was clear; in one of the tents Det-Zamar had brought on those nights it rained. Finally they made it through the pass between the two largest of the Ch'mar volcanoes, and spreading out before them were the stone and adobe structures of Capital City.

Home at last, thought Afsan. Then he clicked his teeth, realizing how he'd changed. As much as he'd enjoyed his visit to Carno, it was no longer his home. The Capital was, and he was glad to be back. But he wondered if he'd still be glad after he'd seen his master, chief palace astrologer Tak-Saleed.

Chapter 27

Afsan descended the spiral ramp to the basement of the palace office building. He knew he'd have to endure Saleed's wrath: anger that he was late in returning from his pilgrimage and fury that Afsan had the temerity to question his teachings. In no hurry to face this, he tarried to look at the Tapestries of the Prophet, peering at them through the reflections of lamp flames dancing on their thin glass covering. There had been many parts of these images he'd not understood the last time he'd seen them, 372 days ago. But now everything was plain. That strange bucket atop the mast of Larsk's sailing ship: that was the lookout's perch, just like the one aboard the *Dasheter*. Those black spots on the Face of God—"God eyes"—were the shadows of moons. Afsan was surprised to see them scattered all over the Face here, instead of just concentrated along its widest part, but then he realized that the artist—the famed Hel-Vleetnav—simply hadn't been a skilled observer of such things, or had made the painting from fallible memory long after her own pilgrimage. Indeed, she'd depicted the Face fully illuminated even though the sun was also visible in the picture, an impossible arrangement.

Around the edges of the tapestry were the twisted, loathsome demons, those who supposedly told lies about the prophet in the light of day. Afsan had always been horrified by their appearance, but now he looked at them differently.

Surely they hadn't been monsters, hadn't been demons masquerading as Quintaglios.

And Larsk himself, the prophet. Had Vleetnav ever met Larsk? Did she really know what he had looked like? She had painted him with a serene expression, eyes half closed. Afsan clicked his teeth. That was *exactly* right.

After looking his fill, Afsan continued slowly down the corridor to the *keetaja*-wood door that led into Saleed's office. Steeling his strength, Afsan drummed on the copper plate in the doorjamb and called out, "Permission to enter your territory?" He heard a tremulous note in his voice.

He waited for a gruff and low *hahat dan,* but no sound came from within. After several beats, Afsan called out again. When there was still no answer, he pressed his palm against the fluted bar, and the door swung wide.

There was no one in Saleed's office. Afsan crossed the room to the old astrologer's workbench. There were many papers and sheets of leather on it, arranged in neat stacks, but they were covered with dust.

Scanning the room, Afsan noticed that a few of Saleed's favorite things were missing: his great porcelain drinking bowl, always half filled with scented water; his metal drawing tools, used to make star charts; his leather-bound copy of the book of mathematical tables; his *guvdok* stone, the torus inscribed with the astrologer's many awards for scholarship.

Afsan left the room and continued down the corridor to the office of Irb-Falpom, the palace land surveyor. Again, Afsan called out for permission to enter. Falpom replied, and Afsan pushed open the door.

Falpom, much younger than Saleed, but still many kilodays Afsan's senior, was bent over a table, adjusting an intricate metal device that had several calibrated wheels attached to it. "Adkab?" she said. "By the prophet's claws, is that you?"

Adkab had been two apprentice astrologers before Afsan. Falpom often accidentally called Afsan by that name, and Afsan tried to keep a good humor about it. After all, she was one of the few palace officials who even attempted to remember the names of any of the underlings, and keeping Saleed's parade of apprentices straight was probably no easy task.

Afsan bowed low. "Hello, Falpom. It's good to see you again."

"And you! My, how you've grown!"

Afsan realized that, yes, in the time he'd been gone, he probably had increased in size noticeably. "Thank you," he said vaguely. "Falpom, I'm looking for Saleed."

The surveyor pushed off the dayslab and leaned back on her thick tail. "Haven't you heard?"

"Heard what?"

Falpom dipped her head. "Saleed took ill not too long after you left. He's been resting at home."

"What's wrong with him?"

The surveyor clicked her teeth once, a rueful sound. "He's *old,* Afsan." Falpom looked at the ground. "I'm frankly surprised that he's lasted this long."

Afsan's tail swished back and forth. "I will go see him at once." He took a step back toward the door, then a thought crossed his mind. "Has a successor been appointed?"

"Not yet. What with the loss of Empress Lends—you did hear about that at least, I hope—and the delay before the succession of Dybo, nothing much has been done. I think Dybo is reluctant to name a replacement. He doesn't want Saleed to think that he's given up hope of him recovering, but, really, there's no chance of that."

"I'll go see Saleed," said Afsan.

Falpom nodded. "He'll like that. Give him my good wishes."

Saleed lived in a small building a few hundred paces from the palace. It was an adobe structure, the commonest kind, easy to repair or replace after a landquake. The reddish-beige exterior was covered with a thin layer of glaze for waterproofing. Afsan had stopped by his own tiny quarters before heading to Saleed's. The slight detour had done nothing to help clear his mind. Saleed had been around forever. As much as the oldster terrified Afsan, he also inspired him. It was impossible to imagine the palace without Saleed.

The adobe structure was free-form in shape, having no right angles. But windows, although at first glance appearing equally free-form, had in fact been meticulously carved as miniature duplicates of the building's own melted profile. This unit contained the homes of several palace officials. Saleed's apartment was on the ground floor. Afsan had always known where it was, but he had never visited it before.

He made his way down the main hallway, lamps spluttering along its walls. He found Saleed's cartouche carved into a door at the end of the corridor, a rendition different from the one that appeared on his office door. With a start, Afsan recognized by the way certain characters were drawn that Saleed had made this cartouche himself. It wasn't a bad rendering, really, although clearly an amateur effort. *Saleed a hobbyist woodcarver?* thought Afsan. *What else don't I know about him?*

He clicked claws against the copper plate by the door, then called out for permission. He thought he heard a sound from within, but it was so low he couldn't be sure.

He opened the door. Inside was Saleed's living room, like its owner, stern and hard-edged. There were four ornate dayslabs, one in each corner of the room; shelves of books; an intricate *lastoontal* board with playing pieces made of gold and silver distributed across it, a game half finished. Afsan hurried through into the sleeping chamber. There, prone on a stone pallet, was Saleed. He looked old and weary, the skin hanging loosely on his face, the black orbs of his eyes shot with red. There were soft leather sheets piled on the sleeping pallet, and a blanket of what looked like thunderbeast hide covered most of his body. The room was dim, no lamp lit, the windows covered by curtains.

On a table next to the bed sat Saleed's favorite porcelain drinking bowl. Afsan noticed that it was cracked. It must have been dropped at some point after Afsan last saw it, then glued back together. Unfortunately not everything could be repaired so easily. He looked down at Saleed. "Master . . . "

The tired bulk stirred slowly. "Afsan?" The voice was dry, husky. "Afsan, is that you?"

Afsan bowed low. "It is I, master."

Saleed coughed, as if the effort of speech had disturbed his condition. His throat sounded raw, and his words were little more than protracted hisses. "You were long in returning."

"I'm sorry, master." Afsan felt a pain in his chest, a sadness. He realized now that he had missed Saleed—was going to miss Saleed. "But you taught me well. I discovered many things on my voyage."

Saleed coughed again, forcing his throat back to life. "I hear from Keenir that you sailed around the world."

"Yes, master. Not everyone believes that, though. They think we're confused. Or deluded."

Saleed's teeth clicked together weakly. "I'm sure they do." His breathing was labored, loud. "But I believe you."

"You do?"

"Of course. You saw the Face of God?"

"Yes, master."

"And—" Saleed's body racked with another cough. Afsan moved closer to the old astrologer, almost invading his territory. "And what did you discover?"

"Master, this isn't the time. When you're well—"

Saleed coughed once more. "I will never be well again, Afsan. I'm old, and I'm dying."

Afsan knew that Saleed was telling the truth, but he hoped that in the dim light of the room, the discoloration of his own muzzle would go unnoticed. "No, you'll be all right. You just need rest—"

"Tell me what you learned." For an instant, there was the sharp edge Afsan was used to hearing in Saleed's voice, the edge that demanded to be obeyed.

"Yes, master. I—you won't agree with me, I know—I've come to believe that the Face of God is—forgive me—a planet. Like Carpel or Patpel or any of the others."

Afsan prepared for Saleed's rebuke, but it did not come. "Good. That's good, Afsan." He coughed again, and when he was done, he said softly, "I knew you were bright enough."

Afsan was startled, felt his tail swish in a wide arc. "What? Then you already knew this?"

Saleed coughed several times. When the fit subsided, he spoke again, even more weakly. "Yes, I have known. But I was too old to do anything about it. You—you're young." Another cough. "You're young."

"But without the far-seer, how could you know?"

"Keenir brought me a far-seer kilodays ago, before you'd been summoned from Carno to Capital City."

"But I heard you reject it from him—"

"You don't survive as long at court as I have without learning how to put on appropriate performances. I wanted you to discover it all for yourself. I could not tell anyone what

I'd learned—even Keenir did not know the details, although he agreed to help me entice you." Saleed's tail moved slightly. "Creche-mates are as one."

Afsan stared into his master's eyes, eyes that were dark as night. He wondered where Saleed was looking. "I don't understand."

Saleed coughed again, and Afsan waited for the old one to gather enough strength to continue. "If the Face is a planet," said Saleed, "then the religion of Larsk is based on a misunderstanding." The sheets heaved as he drew in breath to push on. "It will take a young person to fight that battle, to tell the world the truth about itself. I combed the vocational test results from every Pack, and still I ended up going through six apprentices before I found you. I'd almost given up hope. I knew if you wouldn't dare to defy your master for the sake of finding out the truth, you couldn't possibly be expected to go against Yenalb. I needed to test the courage of your convictions." Saleed's muzzle turned toward Afsan. "I see now that this time I chose well."

Afsan dipped his head, accepting the compliment, although not yet quite understanding. "There's more, though, master," he said. "Do you know of the rings around some of the planets?"

"Rings?" Saleed's head moved slightly on the sleeping pallet. "So that's what they are. My old eyes weren't good enough, I'm afraid, or maybe my old mind was incapable of realizing what it was seeing. Rings. That makes sense, yes." Although still as attenuated as a pre-dawn wind, Saleed's voice had taken on a wondering tone. "Not solid, I'd warrant. Particulate?" Afsan nodded. "Particulate rings." The air escaped from him in a sigh. "Of course."

"They form when moons around other planets move too close to them."

"That makes sense."

"But, master, *our* world is too close to our planet to be stable."

Saleed tried to lift his head from the pallet, failed, and grunted weakly. After a moment, he said, "So the student has exceeded the master. Hmph. That's what every teacher wants. Congratulations, Afsan."

"Congratulations? Master, the world is coming to an end!"

"Whether it does or not, I won't be here to see it. It appears I've given you an even tougher job than I'd thought and for that, my boy, I do apologize."

Afsan felt his fingertips itching, a response to surprise. "What do you mean?"

"Well, Afsan"—and then, maddeningly, the old astrologer fell into a fit of coughs again. When it was done, he continued, "Well, Afsan, if the world is coming to an end, then we must—" and here Afsan saw in his master's wizened face some of the spark, the excitement he was used to seeing there, saw the brilliance of the mind that had written the definitive works on the stars and planets and the moons, saw his genius "—we must *get off this world.*" He found the strength to lift his head slightly. "And you must convince the people to do just that."

Afsan fell back on his tail, stunned by Saleed's words. "Get off the world? Master—"

But Saleed was coughing again. When he finished, he said, "I had to wait until you came back, Afsan. I had to know that you would be the one." And then his black eyes closed and Afsan saw his torso collapse beneath the leather sheet as the breath went out of him.

"Master?"

There was no reply. Afsan fished in his sash's pouch for the object he had stopped by his quarters to get, the traveler's crystal, hexagonal and ruby red, that Saleed had given to him before he had left on the *Dasheter*. He placed it on the sleeping pallet next to the senior astrologer's head. "Have a safe journey, Saleed."

Chapter 28

Afsan was heading from Saleed's home to the palace grounds, where he intended to inform the authorities of his master's demise. Clouds were gathering, and the sun appeared as nothing more than a mauve discoloration behind them. Afsan wasn't really paying attention to where he was going. He was lost in thought about what Saleed had said.

"Aren't you Afsan?"

The voice caught him off guard. He turned to face his inquisitor, a female just shy of middle age, perhaps twice his own weight.

"Yes, I'm Afsan." He peered up into her face. She made no move to bow concession. Afsan didn't recognize her. "And you are—?"

"Gerth-Palsab," she said. Gerth, derived from the miracle worker, Gerthalk, was a praenomen syllable often chosen by deeply religious females, just as Det, from Detoon the Righteous, was a frequent choice among males, especially those who had entered the priesthood.

"Hello, Palsab," said Afsan. "How do you come to know me?"

She placed hands on broad hips. "I've seen you around."

"Oh?"

"Yes. You work at the palace." She said it as though it were an accusation.

"I'm an apprentice astrologer, that's right."

"I hear they go through those the way I go through teeth." A rude thing to say, thought Afsan, but he made no reply. Palsab continued in a harsh tone. "You've recently returned from a pilgrimage."

Afsan felt wary. His tail swished through a partial arc before he quelled the gesture. "Yes, my first."

"I've heard stories about you."

Afsan clicked his teeth, feigning good humor. "At day or at night?"

She ignored his remark. "You blaspheme God!"

Two others were passing in the opposite direction. Afsan saw them stop short at Palsab's outburst, and one half turned to listen.

Afsan thought about simply walking away, but he'd been brought up to respect his elders. "I've said nothing that isn't true," he replied softly.

"You looked upon the Face of God, and called it a fraud."

The two passersby were making no effort to hide their eavesdropping now, and another couple who had been heading in the opposite direction had stopped, as well, startled by what Palsab had said. *Calthat'ch*—fraud—was a word rarely heard, since the very idea of a blatant deception lasting into the daylight was so difficult to believe.

"I suggested no deceit, good Palsab," said Afsan.

"But you said that the Face of God was not, well, the face of God."

Afsan looked at the ground, black sand strewn with pebbles. When he looked up again he saw that a fifth pedestrian had tarried to see what the commotion was about. "What I said," Afsan replied, "was simply that the Face of God is a planet. Like Carpel, Patpel, and the rest."

There was a buzz of conversation between two of the onlookers. "And you don't call that blasphemy?" demanded Palsab.

"I call it observation," said Afsan. "I call it truth."

A trio of young females joined the gathering, and, a moment later, a giant old male. Afsan heard one onlooker remark to the fellow standing next to him, "It sounds like blasphemy to me."

"The truth?" barked Palsab. "What does an eggling know of the truth?"

"I know what I see with my eyes." Afsan scanned the faces around him, then turned back to Palsab. "Look, this isn't the place to discuss it. I plan to do a paper on what I've seen; perhaps I can arrange for you to be loaned a copy."

One of the males stepped forward. "Do you mock her, boy?"

Afsan looked up. "Pardon?"

"She can't read." He turned to her. "Can you, Palsab?"

"Of course not. I'm a blacksmith; what use do I have for writing?"

Afsan had been with the palace for so long, he'd all but forgotten that most people were illiterate. He'd swished his tail right into a pile of dung. "I'm sorry; I didn't mean a slight. It's just—"

The male who had spoken up a moment ago said, "What gives you the right to say such things about God?"

"I claim no right," said Afsan quietly. "I'm just relaying what I've seen."

"What you believe you have seen," countered Palsab. "A pilgrimage is a time of visions and raptures. Many think they see things during them—especially during their first."

"I'm sure of what I saw."

"Keep your blasphemy to yourself!" said Palsab, tail slapping sand.

"No," called a new voice. Several more people had stopped to listen. "I want to hear. Tell us what you've seen."

Afsan didn't recognize anyone in the group, but coming down the street was someone wearing the red and black robe of a junior priest. He, too, came over to see what was going on.

"I saw," said Afsan, "that the Face of God goes through phases, just as the moons do."

Someone in the crowd nodded. "That's right; I've seen that."

Afsan sought out the speaker, looking for a friendly face. "Well, don't you see, then," said Afsan, "that this must mean that the Face of God is illuminated by the sun, just as the moons are."

"The moons are illuminated by the sun?" said the same fellow. This was clearly a new concept to him.

"Of course they are! Where do you think they get their light—from oil lamps?" Afsan realized in an instant that he'd spoken too harshly. "I'm sorry, I mean, yes—that's right. The sun is the only true source of light."

But it was too late. The fellow adopted a hostile posture. "Seems to me we could use a little more light around here," he grumbled.

Palsab spoke overtop of him. "See, you've already contradicted yourself. First you say the Face of God is a planet; now you're babbling about the moons."

At the edge of the crowd, the junior priest looked agitated. Afsan saw him take off for the Hall of Worship. He turned to look back at Palsab. "But some planets go through phases, just as the moons do."

"What nonsense!" said Palsab. "The planets are just points of light."

"No, they're not. They're balls, spheres. And they go through phases. I've seen it."

"How?" called a voice from the crowd. "How could you see something like that?"

"With a device called a far-seer," said Afsan. "It magnifies images."

"I've never heard of such a thing," said Palsab.

"It uses lenses. You know: like the way a drop of water can magnify what's beneath it."

Palsab sneered. "So this blasphemy was revealed to you in a drop of water?"

"What? No, no, no. The far-seer works on the same principle, that's all. Look, what I'm saying is the truth. I've seen it. Emperor Dybo has seen it. Many others have seen it, too."

"And where's this magic device that lets you see such things?" said Palsab.

"Well, I've got a far-seer of my own now, but I don't have the one through which I saw these things for the first time anymore. It didn't belong to me; it was Var-Keenir's, captain of the *Dasheter*."

"Oh, Var-Keenir! Of course!" Palsab sounded quite pleased with herself. "Well, you know what they say about *him*."

"That he's a master sailor?" said Afsan.

"That he's an apostate, eggling. That he practices the ancient rites."

Afsan had never heard that said, but, in any event, he couldn't see how it was relevant. He was about to point this out when a voice from the crowd said, "What's this got to do with the Face of God, anyway?"

Afsan turned to look at the speaker, a female much younger than the belligerent Palsab. He bowed politely, determined not to alienate yet another member of the crowd. "A very good question, indeed. The Face of God—the thing we see hanging there in the sky—is a planet, just seen from very close up. It's the planet that our world revolves around."

In the distance, Afsan saw the junior priest returning with Det-Yenalb, the Master of the Faith, in tow.

"I've never seen the Face of God," she said, and Afsan realized that she was indeed much too young to have taken the pilgrimage. "But I've seen paintings of it. My class went to see the Tapestries of the Prophet once. It doesn't look anything like a planet."

Afsan bent low, his tail lifting into the air as he did so. He scooped up a handful of black sand.

"See this sand?" he said, letting it sift between his fingers, falling back to the ground.

"Of course."

"It's basalt; ground volcanic rock." He pointed over his shoulder. "See the Ch'mar peaks there, off in the distance?"

"Yes."

"They're covered with the same sand. Can you see it?"

"Don't be silly," said the girl. "The peaks are too far away."

"Exactly. And the other planets are too far away to be seen in detail. But when seen close up, they would appear as great spheres, just as the Face of God does. And our world revolves around the Face of God."

Palsab made a hissing sound. The girl looked intrigued, though. "But I thought the world sails down the great River."

"No, it doesn't. That's just a story. I've sailed clear around the world—"

Palsab made another hissing sound. "You've seen this! You've done that! *Pah!*"

"The entire crew of the *Dasheter* sailed around the world," said Afsan, trying not to become angry. "And all its passengers, too."

The crowd had continued to grow. Each member was standing a polite distance from the next, so Afsan could easily see to the outmost circle of watchers, where Yenalb now stood. "Did you really sail around the world?" asked the young female.

"Yes. Absolutely."

She shook her head. "Someday, I'd like to sail around the world, too."

"Don't talk nonsense!" Palsab spat in the youngster's direction. "The world is flat."

The youngster looked at the ground, but muttered, "He says there are many witnesses."

Afsan was pleased to have found an ally. "That's right. Many witnesses." He looked at the crowd. Some, like Palsab, were openly hostile, claws exposed, mouth open to show teeth. Others seemed merely curious. He thought of Saleed, of what Saleed had asked him to do. Perhaps now was the time to begin; perhaps this was the place to start. Perhaps . . .

"But there's more," he said, the words tumbling out, his decision made for him. "So much more. That we're on a moon revolving around a planet—" He heard a sharp intake of breath from several people and realized he'd just laid another explosive egg. "Yes, that's right, our world is itself a moon, just like Swift Runner or Slowpoke or Sprinter. But that we're on a moon, and that this moon revolves around a planet, is perhaps only of academic interest. It excites me, and I hope that knowledge for knowledge's sake excites most of you. But I grant that the reality of the way the universe works is mostly of no consequence." He nodded at faces in turn, trying to connect individually with each member of the crowd. "You still have to sleep, you have to toil at your tasks, you must hunt, you must eat. None of what I've said affects any of that." He saw a few heads return his nods and felt encouraged to continue. "But I have discovered one fact that is of dire urgency, that will change everything."

A roll of thunder sounded from above. Afsan looked up at the leaden sky.

Palsab grunted. "I take it you're about to blaspheme

again," but even she recognized that the sound from the sky was coincidence. Teeth clicked around the circle.

But Afsan swallowed hard. This was important, vital. Those who hadn't believed what he'd told them so far certainly wouldn't accept what he was about to say. The weight upon him was almost palpable. At last, he forced out the words. "The world is coming to an end."

The reaction was as he'd expected: expressions of disbelief or derision, and, on a few faces, of fear. Afsan raised a hand, careful, despite his excitement, to keep his claws sheathed. "What I say is true. It's a consequence of the other discoveries I made. We're too close to the Face of God; our path around it is not stable. Our world will be torn apart."

"Nonsense!" shouted one voice.

"You're wrong!" called another.

"The eggling's insane," muttered a third.

"I am not insane. I am not imagining things." Afsan fought to keep his voice calm. "What I'm saying is the absolute truth—the *demonstrable* truth."

Palsab's claws extended. "You cannot prove what cannot be."

"No," said Afsan, "I cannot. But I can prove *this*."

Palsab wiggled her fingers, but the onlooker next to her—the same fellow who had taken offense when Afsan suggested that Palsab read his paper—spoke quietly to her. "Let him talk, Palsab. He'll put a knot in his tail, I'm sure."

Afsan had wanted to make his case in writing, to carefully set up each potential argument, then, piece by piece, show why his interpretation was correct. But here, on a public street, with the first spits of rain hitting his head, here, surrounded by a mob of illiterates, of people who didn't have the training or temperament to follow an intricate line of reasoning, here, facing those he was arguing with directly, instead of through the safe and neutral medium of an academic paper, a document that would be hand-copied by scribes and circulated quietly to a few hundred academics, here he was very much in trouble indeed.

Still, what choice did he have? Was that not Galbong, the newsrider, now at the back of the crowd? Wouldn't she spread the story that Afsan didn't have the courage of his convictions, that he had run rather than defend his wild ideas?

Afsan leaned back against his tail, a passive, nonthreatening posture. "To understand what I've come to believe, you have to understand some basic astrology."

"We all know about portents and omens," snapped Palsab.

"No, no. The symbolism of what's seen in the sky is a matter for priests to interpret, or at least for more senior astrologers than myself—"

"You see!" cried Palsab to the crowd. "He admits his own ignorance."

"I'm honest about which things I know and which things I don't know. Everything I've come to believe about the way our, our—*system*—works I can justify and demonstrate to anyone who cares to listen. I'll warrant those who claim to foretell your personal futures by reading the sky can't do the same." Afsan saw Yenalb, at the periphery of the group, scowl, and he realized that again he'd spoken rashly. But, by the prophet's claws—*by Saleed's claws*—it was the truth!

"Look," said Afsan, trying to remain calm. "It's a simple chain. *If* those of us who sailed aboard the good ship *Dasheter* managed to travel from the east coast of Land back to the west coast simply by continuously sailing east, *then* the world cannot be sailing down an endless river. It must be round." He tipped his muzzle from person to person in the inner concentric circle around him. "It must be."

"*If,*" said Palsab bitterly.

"It's true; it cannot be denied. I speak of it here in the light of day, and even if I'm confused—which I'm not—you can hardly believe that Var-Keenir, or the other sailors aboard his ship, could become mixed up about which direction they were sailing in."

Palsab opened her mouth as if to speak, but someone on the other side of her—presumably an intimate acquaintance, for he dared to lightly touch her shoulder—said, "Let him finish."

Afsan nodded politely at this new benefactor. "Thank you." He looked now not at Palsab, who seemed no longer to be the speaker for the group, but rather, by lifting his head slightly, he made it clear that he was addressing them all equally. "Now, if the world is round, then what is it? Well, we see many round objects in our sky. We see the sun. But our world is not like the sun. It does not burn with white flame. We see, when we take our pilgrimage, the Face of God. But our world is not like the Face of God. It is not covered with bands of swirling color. And, although our world seems big to us, I have sailed around it, so I know now its approximate dimensions. The Face of God is gigantic; our world is not. Finally we see the moons. Some have cloudy surfaces, some have rocky ones. All go through phases, meaning parts of their surfaces are alternately illuminated and in darkness, just as parts of our world are in night and parts are in daylight. Indeed, as I'm sure some of you know, if a daytenth glass is turned over immediately every time it runs out during a pilgrimage voyage—so that it always has sand flowing through it—you can see that when it's midnight here in Capital City it is high noon when one is observing the Face of God."

Thunder cracked the air again. The drops grew fatter. Afsan saw that some of those assembled were following what he was saying. "And I can provide similar chains to take you through to my other conclusions: that the Face of God is a planet, that we revolve around the Face of God, that we are in fact the closest moon to the Face of God." Afsan flashed back to his conversation with Dybo on the deck of the *Dasheter*. He looked directly at Palsab. "So, you see, what I'm saying isn't that bad. We're closer to the Face of God than anything else. Isn't that an appealing thought?"

"It would be," said Palsab, "if you didn't go on to say that the Face of God was nothing more than, than a natural object. 'The creator is inexplicable,' say the scriptures."

"And," Afsan said, pretending now to ignore Palsab, pressing on to the bitter conclusion, "my knowledge of the laws that govern the way things work tells me that because we are so close to the Face of God, this world is doomed. Our world will be torn asunder by the same stress that causes the volcanism and the landquakes."

"They *are* worse now than in the ancient past," said someone from the middle of the crowd. Palsab stared at the speaker. "Sorry," he said with a shrug, "but we're not all unable to read."

She turned, fuming, looking now neither at Afsan nor the fellow who had spoken of the history of landquakes.

"So you claim we are doomed," said another voice, female, sounding frightened.

This was the chance, Afsan realized, the opportunity to test the reception Saleed's ideas would have.

"No," said Afsan. "I claim only that our world is doomed."

"What's the difference?" said the girl whom he'd spoken with earlier. "If the world crumbles beneath us, then surely we will die."

"Not necessarily."

"What do you mean?" demanded Palsab's friend.

"Well, consider. We now build ships to ply the River—"

"You said it was *not* a River," said Palsab.

"No, it is not; it's more like a vast lake. But the name 'River' will endure, I'm sure, just as we still refer to the Fifty Packs, when there are many more than that number."

She nodded, conceding Afsan at least this much of his story.

"Well, we build ships for travel in water," continued Afsan. "We know travel by air is possible—"

"*What?*" said Palsab.

"Wingfingers do it," said Afsan simply. "So do many insects. There's no reason we cannot."

"They have wings, fool."

"Of course, of course. But we could build vessels to fly, like those toys children play with that float upon the air."

"And if we did so?" said a female from the middle of the crowd.

"Why, we could fly from this world to another. One of the other moons, perhaps. Or a moon around a different planet. Or maybe somewhere else entirely."

Afsan cringed at the sound of clicking teeth. "What nonsense!" said Palsab. A flash of lightning lit the group.

"No," said another voice. "I've read tales of such voyages. The fantasies of Gat-Tagleeb."

"Children's stories," sneered Palsab. "Worthless."

But the fan of Tagleeb spoke again. "I'd like to hear more of what this fellow has to say."

"And I'd love to tell more," said Afsan. The rain was growing heavier. He tipped his muzzle up at the clouds. "But this is not the time, I fear. Tomorrow, I'll be in the central square at noon. All those who wish to discuss this more, please join me there." As an afterthought, he did not know why, he added, "I have a friend named Pal-Cadool in the palace butchery. I'll arrange for a haunch of meat to be available."

This seemed to satisfy most of the crowd, although Palsab glowered at Afsan before moving on. Lightning jagged across the sky, and the people hurried to get out of the rain.

Afsan tried to catch Yenalb's attention, wanting to thank him for helping arrange his passage on the *Dasheter,* but he had already left.

Oh, well, thought Afsan, *I'm sure I'll be seeing him again soon.*

High Priest Det-Yenalb returned to the Hall of Worship, his claws flexing in agitation. What had gotten into the boy? Afsan hadn't been like this before his pilgrimage.

Before his time with Var-Keenir.

Yenalb slapped his tail.

He *should* have heeded the stories about that one. Yes, there were still Lubalites scattered throughout the eight provinces, but Yenalb had dismissed the grumblings about Keenir. Idle gossip, he'd thought, the kind you hear about any public figure, the kind that even circulated about himself.

But the boy's mind had been corrupted. He was talking heresy, blasphemy.

That could not be allowed. It could not.

Yenalb entered the main part of the Hall. Most of the lamps were off now, conserving thunderbeast oil. But in the flickering flames of those that were lit, he took stock of the room: circular, so that the domed roof could represent the Face of God, swirling and banded.

Yenalb had seen the Face many times, taken the pilgrimage over and over again, gone there with Empress Lends and her predecessor, Empress Sardon, would go there with the new Emperor, Dybo, on his next pilgrimage.

He had seen the Face, felt the rapture, heard the voice.

It was no lie. It could not be.

Shifting his weight onto his tail, he looked down the mock river, that channel of water between the planks through which the sinners walked. It was half empty, much of the water from the last service having evaporated.

But this was only a model. There *was* a real River, and Land did float down it, and the Face of God did look down upon the way ahead, to make sure it was safe.

It was true.

It must be.

It was his way of life.

It was the way of life for all the people.

He stared at the sinners' river for a long time. And, at last, Yenalb felt a calm come over him. The tranquillity of the room entered him, the peace that comes with faith relaxed him, comforted him, assured him.

He knew what he must do.

Chapter 29

Afsan had expected his reunion with Dybo to be a private affair. After all, he'd once met on his own with Dybo's mother, the late Empress Lends. Surely Dybo himself—Dy-Dybo, as he was apparently called now—would make time for his returning friend.

But when Afsan arrived at the main palace, the guards did not nod concession to him, as they had the first time he'd had an audience here. Instead, they turned and walked just behind Afsan, closer than protocol would normally allow. They were much larger than he, and Afsan had to step quickly to keep up with the speed they were imposing.

He was allowed no time to enjoy the Hall of Stone Eggs, with its myriad polished hemispheres of rock cut to reveal the crystal hollows within. The guards marched behind him wordlessly. The complex and uneven walls of the Hall deadened the echoes of their mighty footfalls.

They came out into the vast circular chamber with its red *telaja*-wood doors. Afsan was hustled along so quickly he barely had time to notice that the cartouche representing the Emperor was different: gone were the profiled heads of Tak-Saleed and Det-Yenalb. Instead, most of the cartouche was a carving of an outstretched hand spread over a flat map of Land in the great River. Odd choice, thought Afsan, since Dybo knew full well that such depictions were now obsolete.

One of the guards pushed ahead of Afsan and clicked heavy claws against the copper signaling plate by the door.

Afsan warmed at the sound of his friend's voice. "*Hahat dan.*"

The guard swung the door open, and Afsan and his burly escorts stepped into the ruling room.

Lying on the ornate throne slab, high on the polished basalt pedestal, was Dybo. His head sported several new tattoos, including an intricate web-like one fanning outward from his right eye and extending back to his earhole. On his left wrist he wore the three silver loops that signified his position. He'd lost weight, although it would take a charitable soul to think of him still as anything less than fat. And he'd grown—even recumbent, it was obvious that he was slightly older.

Afsan realized that Dybo was likely appraising him the same way. The Emperor's eyes were probably tracking up and down Afsan's body, but with those obsidian orbs, there was no way to be sure.

Dybo was not alone. Benches, perhaps ten paces long, with intricate gold inlays at the ends, extended from either side of the throne slab. On the left-hand one sat Det-Yenalb, Master of the Faith. On the right, a mid-sized fellow with a slightly concave chest. Afsan didn't know his name, but recognized him as a palace advisor—quite senior, obviously, if he was allowed to sit upon a *katadu* bench.

To the left and right of the benches stood more people, some wearing priestly robes, others sporting the orange and blue sashes of the Emperor's staff. Lends's worktable on wheels was nowhere to be seen.

Afsan bowed low. He half expected to be greeted by one of Dybo's usual barbs—a quip about Afsan's scrawniness, perhaps. But it was Det-Yenalb, not Dybo, who spoke.

"You are Afsan?" the priest said, his voice liquid and unpleasant.

Afsan blinked. "Yes."

"You took a pilgrimage aboard the *Dasheter*?"

"You know I did, Your Grace. You helped arrange it."

"Answer yes or no. You took a pilgrimage aboard the *Dasheter*, a sailing vessel captained by one Var-Keenir?"

"Yes." At the far right, one of those in the sash of a staff member was writing into a small leather booklet. A transcript of the proceedings?

"You claim to have made a discovery while on this voyage?"

"Yes. Several discoveries."

"And what were those discoveries?"

"That the world is round." There was a sharp hiss from several members of the assembly. "That the object we call the Face of God is really just a planet." Tails swished back and forth like snakes. Individuals exchanged worried glances.

"You really believe this?" said Yenalb.

"The world *is* round," said Afsan. "We did indeed sail continuously to the east, leaving from Capital City here on the east coast of Land and arriving back, simply by continuing in a straight line, at the Bay of Three Forests on the west coast."

"You are mistaken," Yenalb said flatly.

Afsan felt a tingling at the tips of his fingers. "I am *not* mistaken. Dybo was there. He knows."

Yenalb slapped his tail against the floor. The sharp cracking echoed throughout the chamber. "You will refer to the Emperor as His Luminance."

"Fine. His Luminance knows." Afsan moved his head so that there could be no doubt in anyone's mind: he was looking directly at Dybo. "Don't you?"

Dybo said nothing. Yenalb pointed at Afsan. "I say again, you are mistaken."

"No, Your Grace. I am not."

"Eggling, you risk—"

"A moment, please," said a wheezy voice. It was the senior advisor, seated on Dybo's right. He rose with a hiss. Every movement seemed to be an effort for him. His caved-in chest heaved constantly. He was not all that old, but his breathing was ragged—some respiratory ailment, Afsan guessed. The advisor nodded at the clerk who had been taking notes, and that one put down his book and held his inked claw at his side. The advisor's gait was slow, accompanied at every step by a hissing breath. At last he was close to Afsan. He looked Afsan in the face for several heartbeats, then spoke quietly in a protracted wheeze that only Afsan could hear. "Tell them you are mistaken, boy. It's your only hope."

"But I'm not—"

"*Shush!*"

Afsan tried again in a faint volume. "But I'm not mistaken!"

The advisor stared at him again, his breath noisy, ragged. At last he said quietly, "If you value your hide, you will be." He turned and headed back to his *katadu* bench, his steps slow and pained. One of those wearing an orange and blue sash helped him sit down.

Yenalb, looking irritated at this interruption, turned to face Afsan again. "As I said, you are mistaken."

Afsan was quiet for a moment, but then said softly, "I am not." He saw the wheezing advisor close his eyes.

"You are. We have heard how the *Dasheter* engaged a serpent, how the ship was tossed and turned. You, and the others, were simply confused by what had occurred. You are not a mariner, after all. You're not used to the tricks the open water can play on one's mind."

"I am not mistaken," Afsan said again, more firmly.

"You must be!"

"I am not."

One of the other priests spoke. "His muzzle shows no blue."

Afsan clicked his teeth in satisfaction. It was as plain as the muzzle on his face: he was telling the truth. If he were lying, the inflammation of the muzzle's skin would give him away. Everyone in the room had to see that, had to know that despite Yenalb's ranting Afsan was telling the truth!

"He is *aug-ta-rot,* then," said Yenalb. "A demon. Only a demon could lie in the light of day."

Afsan spluttered. "A demon—?"

"Just as shown in the Tapestries of the Prophet," declared Yenalb. "Just as described in the scriptures. A demon!"

Fingers sprouted claws on half the assembled group. "A demon . . . "

"For God's sake," said Afsan, "I am not a demon."

"And what," said Yenalb, his voice dangerously edged, "do you know of God?"

"I mean—"

"You said God was a fraud, a natural phenomenon, simply a planet."

"Yes, but—"

"And now you invoke the Almighty to disprove your demonhood?"

Afsan looked left and right. Some of the assembled group had started bobbing up and down. The word "demon" passed from individual to individual.

"I am an astrologer!" cried Afsan. "A scholar!"

"Demon," said the crowd, harsh and low. "Demon."

"I'm telling the truth!"

"Demon." A chant. "Demon."

"A demon among us!" said Yenalb, spinning, his robes flowing about him. "A demon in our midst!"

"Demon," repeated the crowd. "*Demon.*"

"A demon who denounces our religion!" Yenalb's tail slapped the floor.

"*Demon. Demon.*"

Afsan's claws were out, his nostrils flared. Wild pheromones were free in the room.

"A demon who profanes our God!" Yenalb's wide mouth hung open, a rictus of ragged teeth.

"*Demon. Demon. Demon.*"

"A demon who has no right to live!"

Afsan felt the crowd surge forward, felt his own instincts coming to the fore, felt the room spinning about him—

"*No!*"

Dybo's voice shook the foundations of the room. Through clouded vision, Afsan saw that the Emperor was now on his feet.

Yenalb, crouched for a leap, turned his head to look at Dybo. "But Your Luminance—he is *poison.*"

"No. Everyone is to hold their positions. The first to move will answer to me."

Afsan felt his body relaxing. "Dybo . . . "

But the Emperor did not deign to look at him. He turned his back, tail falling off the edge of the pedestal. "Shut him away."

Chapter 30

Afsan thought he knew the basement of the palace office building well. After all, Saleed had worked there, as had many other court officials. But this was a part of it he had never seen. Two guards led him down a steep ramp into a dimly lit warren of rooms. Some of them had no doors at all, and seemed to be used for equipment storage. Others did have doors, of rough-hewn and pale *galamaja* wood, bearing the cartouches of service departments including janitorial and food preparation.

At the end of one corridor was a door whose cartouche depicted a triangle, three different-sized squares and two circles, all surrounded by a large square border. Afsan tried to fathom religious or royal symbolism in this, but finally realized it simply meant "miscellaneous storage." The door swung open, its hinges creaking as it did so, and Afsan was ushered in. It was a dank room measuring about ten paces by six. In it were some wooden crates, a broken wooden gear almost as tall as Afsan—it looked to be a damaged part from a water wheel—a single lamp hanging from the wall, and a shed snake's skin lying in one corner.

The guards turned to go.

"Wait," said Afsan. "What I've been saying is the truth."

No response.

"Please. You've got to listen to me."

One guard had exited. The other turned as if to speak to Afsan, thought better of it, and walked out as well, closing the splintery door behind him.

Afsan knew the door would be unlocked—the only reason to put a lock on a door would be to keep dangerous things away from children, and he couldn't imagine youngsters being allowed to play in this grungy part of the palace basement. But no doubt the taciturn and burly guards stood just outside, in case Afsan tried to leave.

What will become of me? Afsan thought. *They can't leave me here forever.* He wandered about the room, his tail swishing in the dust on the floor. He had assumed Dybo would be his ally, thought that once the Emperor had heard what Afsan had to say, all resources would be committed to the problem.

Time is running out, Afsan thought, and then, with a shudder, he realized that it wasn't just running out for the world. It was also running out for him personally.

Do they really think I'm a demon? Yes, the scrolls told of such beasts from ancient times, and again of the *aug-ta-rot* nay-sayers, who had ultimately been slain because they refused to listen to Larsk. But surely those tales were mere fantasy. *How can they be so blind, so terribly blind?*

Afsan wasn't the only one who knew the truth. Keenir knew it. Dybo knew it. The passengers and crew of the *Dasheter*—at least those with enough mathematics and brains to understand what they had seen—knew it, too. And Novato, sweet Novato, she also knew it.

Would they all remain silent? What punishments could be inflicted upon them if they did not?

Crime.

It was an odd word, an ancient word. Afsan had read about crimes in books from the past. During the great famine 380 kilodays ago, when half the plants died of plague, and, afterward, half the animals, there had been crimes, Quintaglios stealing food from other Quintaglios. He remembered the old punishment. Hands were cut off. In the 400 days it took to generate a new hand, the malefactor would usually learn his or her lesson.

Would they cut off my hands? It would be painful and awkward, but they would grow back. Who among those who knew would talk, would spread the word? Afsan felt sick at the thought of Novato, who created such magnificent instruments, losing her hands for even a short time. And Keenir had just finished regenerating a tail. At his age, that was a strain. One could suffer only so many such losses before the parts regenerated in malformed ways.

Maybe they were being wise in remaining silent.

But I cannot.

Afsan thought back to his moments of doubt aboard the *Dasheter,* high atop the foremast in the lookout's bucket, the pilgrims holding services below, the Face of God roiling above, wind whipping at him.

He'd thought to jump then, to plummet into the deck, rather than disturb the order of the world. But that was before he'd met Novato, seen her sketches, understood the magnitude of it all.

The world is coming to an end.

There was no alternative. Silence now would mean the end of the Quintaglio people.

I must find the strength to go on.

The storeroom had a musty smell. Afsan didn't like it, and he tried not to breathe deeply. He circumnavigated the room, touching objects, getting used to his new home. The cool stone walls, the rough wood of the crates: it was a harsh room, an uncaring room. His quarters near the palace had hardly been plush, but this was almost unlivable.

He leaned on his tail and let out a heavy sigh.

Rites of passage.

He'd been through them all now: leaving his home Pack and journeying to Capital City, beginning his profession of astrology, climbing the Hunter's Shrine, taking part in his first hunt, undergoing his first pilgrimage.

And Novato.

Sweet Novato.

His hand went up to the side of his head, feeling the small bumps made by his tattoos: the mark of a hunter, and, added by Det-Bleen aboard the *Dasheter,* the symbol of a pilgrim.

But maybe it wasn't just individuals who went through rites of passage on their way to adulthood. Maybe his whole species had to do that. He thought of the dark times, the cannibalistic reign of the earliest Lubalites, the frightening stories told in whispers. He thought, too, of current civilization, with its religion and superstition. And what is to come? What awaited the Quintaglio race, after its childhood's end?

In the lamplight, Afsan watched drifting motes of dust for a length of time that he did not measure.

"Permission to enter your territory?"

He looked up, startled by the voice coming muffled through the rough wooden door, a door no one had ever thought of equipping with a copper signaling plate. Still, the request was polite. He'd not expected any courtesy now that he was branded a demon. Eyes wide, Afsan replied, "*Hahat dan.*"

The door squeaked open. The two guards were still there, one on either side, but standing between them, wearing a red smock, was lanky Pal-Cadool, his friend the palace butcher. With his long arms, he was carrying a silver tray laden with hunks of meat. Steam rose from the pieces. A fresh kill.

"Hello, Afsan," said Cadool, bowing as much as the tray would allow.

"Cadool! It's great to see you."

Cadool moved into the room and set the tray on one of the packing crates. He returned to the doorway, but, much to Afsan's surprise, instead of exiting, he closed the door, shutting out the guards.

"I believe there is enough meat here for two," said Cadool. Afsan eyed the plate. *Yes, enough for two,* he thought, *as long as you're not as hungry as I am.* "May I join you?" Cadool continued in his protracted speech.

"You'd eat with a demon?"

Cadool clicked his teeth. "I don't think you're a demon." He reached down to the plate and grabbed a gobbet of meat. "Do you know the 111th Scroll? 'For there is grace in all Quintaglios, but none more so than the skilled hunter.' I'm one of those who went to feast on that thunderbeast you brought down, Afsan. A kill worthy of Lubal herself."

Afsan picked up a piece of meat, tossed it to the back of his throat, and swallowed. "Beginner's luck."

"You are modest. That, too, is commendable. I've heard also of the way you killed Kal-ta-goot."

"Then stories of the *Dasheter*'s voyage *are* circulating! You must have heard that we sailed around the world."

"That has been said, yes."

"And do you believe it?"

Cadool helped himself to another hunk, this one with an unpleasant vein of fat running through it. He worried it out with a fingerclaw before popping the meat into his mouth. "I don't know." Then he did something that didn't quite make sense to Afsan. He raised his left hand, unsheathed the claws on the second and third fingers, and spread his fourth and fifth fingers. Next he pressed his thumb into his palm.

"I'm sorry," said Afsan. "I keep seeing that sign, but I don't have a clue what it means."

Cadool nodded. "Where have you seen it?"

"The demons shown in the Tapestries of the Prophet. They're making that sign, aren't they?"

"You should know by now that those labeled 'demon' are not always deserving of that title."

Afsan's voice was small. "Indeed."

"Where else?"

"My cabin aboard the *Dasheter* had carvings on the outside of its door, carvings of the Five Original Hunters. Two of them were making that sign. And Captain Var-Keenir did it at one point."

"Anywhere else?"

"Pahs-Drawo made it after I killed a fangjaw. He's a hunter from my home Pack, Carno."

"Yes, I know Drawo."

Afsan's nictitating membranes fluttered. "You do?"

"He's here in Capital City, isn't he? Part of the delegation from Carno to honor the new Emperor?"

"Yes, that's right."

"I met him yesterday at a service."

"Yesterday was an odd-day. There are no services on odd-days."

"Umm, no. No, there aren't. This was a special service, held at the Hunter's Shrine."

"What kind of service would be held there?"

Cadool ignored the question, but made the complex hand sign again. "Watch for this sign, Afsan. There are more of us than you know."

"More of who?"

"*Us.*"

Afsan opened his mouth in question, but Cadool said nothing. Finally Afsan himself said, wistfully, "I thought that at least Dybo would be on my side."

Cadool clicked his teeth so rapidly in laughter that he almost *chewed* his food. The sight turned Afsan's stomach.

"I'm sorry," said Cadool, holding up a hand. "You're young, I know. But surely, Afsan, you can't be that naïve."

Afsan felt a tingling in his fingertips. He didn't like being laughed at. "What do you mean?"

"Dybo is the son of the daughter of the daughter of the son of the daughter of the son of Larsk, the prophet."

Afsan hadn't known the exact lineage of his friend, but the number of generations sounded about right. "Yes. So?"

"And Larsk is the prophet because he discovered the Face of God."

"Uh-huh."

"And Dybo rules now, and his mother, Lends, ruled before him, because their ancestor was divinely inspired to take the First Pilgrimage, to seek out the Face of God."

"So the story goes."

"And now you show up saying, wait, no, it's not the Face of God at all. It's just a natural object."

"I know all this."

"You know it, but you're not seeing what it means. Dybo and The Family rule through divine right, by the grace of God. You ask him to support you in saying there is no God—or at least, that the thing his ancestor discovered is not God. If it's not God, then Larsk was a false prophet. If he was a false prophet, then The Family has no divine right. If The Family has no divine right, then Dybo cannot rule the eight provinces and the Fifty Packs. For him to support you—or to allow others to support you—would mean abdicating his position."

Afsan leaned back on his tail, furious with himself. He'd vowed to better understand the way the real world worked, but, once again, he had failed. "I—I hadn't thought of it that way."

"You'd better. It's the only thing that will get you out of this mess."

"But the truth—"

"The truth is not the issue," said the butcher. "At least, not for Dybo. Not anymore."

Cadool popped one more hunk into his mouth, then pulled his weight off his tail and began to make for the door.

"Wait," said Afsan.

"I've got to get back to my duties."

"There's more."

"What do you mean?"

"There's more than just the fate of the monarchy at stake. There's more to it than just the Face of God being a planet."

"Yes?"

"The world is doomed, Cadool."

Cadool's inner eyelids batted across his dark orbs. "What?"

"The fact that we are on a moon, the fact that this moon is very close to its planet: it causes stresses. Stresses that quake the land. Stresses that have driven up the volcanoes. Stresses that will tear the world apart."

"Are you sure?"

"I have no doubt. I have seen what happens to moons that move too close to the world they revolve around. They break up into particulate rings of rubble."

"You have seen this? In a vision?"

"No, with a device, an instrument. It's called a far-seer. It magnifies things."

"I've never heard of such a thing."

"They exist. An artisan from Pack Gelbo in Jam'toolar makes them. Anyone can see what I've described by looking through one."

"Does Dybo know about these devices?"

"Oh, yes. He's used one himself, under my guidance."

"I doubt their manufacture will be allowed to continue." Cadool's tail swished. "You're sure of this? That the world will come to an end?"

"Yes."

"How soon?"

"Who can say? I've been trying to get a sense of how much worse the volcanism and landquakes are today compared to various points in the past. My guess, and it's only a guess, is perhaps three hundred kilodays."

Cadool's teeth clattered rapidly and he looked away. "Three hundred kilodays? Eggling, that's generations from now! Why worry about it?"

"Because—because we must do something about it!"

"Do what? Afsan, the future will take care of itself. Don't ruin your life for it."

"Ruin my life? Cadool, I *pledge* my life to this cause."

"That may literally become true."

Afsan reared to his full height. "That's a chance I'm willing to take."

"You're willing to go against The Family? That's treason."

"I'm against no one. I am *for* the truth."

Cadool shook his head, but then raised his left hand and gave the same hand gesture. "Remember this sign, Afsan. Trust only those who know it."

"But—"

"I must go." Cadool bowed quickly and departed.

Afsan had lost his appetite, but something told him it would be wise to keep up his strength. Over the rest of the afternoon, he ate the five remaining pieces of flesh, his mind wandering far between each one.

That night, Afsan again found himself suddenly awake, a thought having pushed itself to the surface.

Although Dybo had acquitted himself well enough during the thunderbeast hunt, the Emperor was neither tough nor strong nor fast. He was simply fat, and, although gifted musically, not particularly shrewd.

Was Dybo really the best of his mother's eight offspring? Really the one who ran fastest from the imperial bloodpriest? That bloodpriest would have chosen the eggling to become the next Emperor. If Afsan was right about the lineage of those who controlled the outlying provinces, the imperial bloodpriest ate none of Len-Lends's hatchlings. Rather, he or she sent the seven rejects off to be future provincial governors.

Perhaps a switch had been performed . . .

Perhaps, just perhaps, Dybo was the *slowest* of the offspring, the one *most* likely to be manipulated by the imperial advisors. Lends had been formidable indeed—perhaps too formidable for the priests and palace staff.

It would have been so easy a switch to make. The one that should have been in Dybo's place would still be alive, but had probably been sent to a distant province, perhaps isolated Edz'toolar.

Afsan could never prove it, could never even suggest it in public. But it was a disturbing thought.

Once again, he spent the rest of the night awake.

Chapter 31

Pal-Cadool knew the trick. He walked to the far side of the giant stone cairn that supported the Hunter's Shrine. Back there, its base hidden by carefully planted bushes, a stairway had been built. Quintaglios disliked stairs—the steps caused their tails to drag or bounce—but they did have their uses. Cadool parted the shrubbery and made his way up. It was still a long climb, but he reached the top only slightly out of breath, and the steady east-west wind cooled him quickly.

As a butcher, Cadool knew bones well. He always admired the structure of the Shrine, the special juxtapositions of femurs and clavicles, of tail vertebrae and chest riblets.

Inside, he could see hunt leader Jal-Tetex. She stood on the far side of the floating sphere of Quintaglio skulls. The wind was whipping too loudly for Tetex to hear Cadool's approach. The butcher tipped his body in homage to the skull of Hoog, patron of his craft, one of the five brown and ancient skulls at the center of the sphere. Then he spoke aloud. "Permission to enter your territory, Tetex?"

Tetex had been leaning back on her tail. She turned now, and Cadool saw in her hand a leather-bound volume. Embossed on its cover was the cartouche of Lubal: this was one of the forbidden books of Lubalite rites, a new edition, apparently, made possible by the recent introduction of printing presses. Still, no government-authorized press had produced *that* book.

"*Hahat dan,* Cadool," said Tetex, making no effort to hide the book. "You're late."

"My duties at the palace interfered, I'm afraid." He clicked his teeth. "When Emperor Dybo calls for something to eat, all other business must be put aside."

Tetex nodded. "Before stuffing Dybo, did you get a chance to see The One?"

"Yes. I took him food."

"He is well?"

"He's frightened and confused, but holding up."

"Fear is the counselor," said Tetex. "He is wise." She looked across Land, spreading out far below. "Now that you've spoken with him, have you any doubts?"

"None. Keenir was right. And so were you. He *must* be The One. He told me something today, something only The One would know."

"What?"

"He said the world is coming to an end."

Tetex's head snapped around to look Cadool dead on. "Are you sure?"

"He was quite plain. In three hundred kilodays or so, the world will end."

"Still that far away? But it is as the Book of Lubal said: 'One will come among you to herald the end; heed him, for those who do not are doomed.' "

Cadool made the ceremonial sign of acquiescence at the mention of Lubal's name. "It was all I could do to keep from touching him when he said it. I had my doubts until then, but no more."

"Does he know that you know who he is?"

"Tetex, I don't think *he* knows who he is. But I didn't give anything away. Of his own volition, he pledged his life to the cause."

Silence, save for the shrieking wind. Then Tetex spoke: "When I saw him on that first hunt, I *knew* he was special. I'd never seen a novice hunter with such skill, such determination."

"That thunderbeast he brought down was a giant indeed."

"A giant? Cadool, for the first time, I thought I was going

to die. There was no way we could defeat that monster—none! But Afsan succeeded. He saved us all. When Keenir returned with his stories about Afsan killing a serpent that attacked the *Dasheter,* and that fellow Drawo from Carno told us about Afsan bringing down a fangjaw on his own, I was sure. 'And The One will defeat demons of the land and of the water; blood from his kills will soak the soil and stain the River.' "

"But now they call Afsan himself a demon," said Cadool. "He was almost killed in the ruling room yesterday. Dybo's feelings are the only thing keeping Afsan alive, and who knows how long it will be before the imperial advisors convince Dybo to put him to death."

"But to kill a Quintaglio . . . "

"It's been done before, Tetex. In Larsk's time, the hunters who didn't accept his claims were executed."

Tetex nodded solemnly. "You're right. We must act quickly."

"Has word gone out with our newsriders?"

"They leave tonight."

"And Keenir?"

"He's loading provisions aboard the *Dasheter* now. At dawn, he'll set sail for the west coast to fetch Lubalites from there. When he landed there with Afsan, he told many hunters the story of Afsan killing the great serpent. He's sure that most will agree to come back here with him."

"That's still fifty days or so, round trip, even for the *Dasheter,*" said Cadool.

"That it is. But it'll take at least that long for any of those who the newsriders contact to assemble here. Everyone who knows the hand sign will receive the special call."

"Where will we gather?"

"At the ruins of the temple of Lubal, on the far side of the Ch'mar peaks."

Cadool's tail swept in a wide arc. "I hate that place—buildings half buried under lava flows."

"But no one goes there anymore; it's an ideal spot to wait for the others."

Cadool nodded. "I suppose." He looked back at the floating sphere of skulls. "Afsan himself did not know the hand sign."

Tetex blinked. "He didn't?"

"Not really."

"Did you show it to him?"

"Of course."

"Well, he knows it now," said Tetex.

"And that's enough?"

"We must pray that it is. There's little we can do for him without greater numbers. He has to hold on for sixty-one days."

Cadool looked puzzled. "Sixty-one?"

Tetex patted the cover of the book she held. "That will bring us to the traditional date of the feast of Lubal. At the fifth daytenth, we'll march into the Capital."

Chapter 32

Except for Cadool, who came once more with food, Afsan had no visitors for the next fourteen days. It was clear what was being done. Those who held sway with Dybo hoped the isolation would make him more willing to accede to their wishes. But a Quintaglio could take a lot of isolation before being disturbed by it. In fact, after the confines of the *Dasheter,* and the continual company of the delegation from Carno on his trip here, Afsan found being left alone with his thoughts a welcome change.

When he did at last have a visitor, it wasn't who he had hoped for. The door to the storage room burst open. Afsan leapt to his feet. Standing in the entryway, robes swirling, was Det-Yenalb, Master of the Faith.

Afsan did not bow. "I didn't expect to see you," he said.

"And I prayed my whole life never to see the likes of you," hissed Yenalb. "But now you are here, and you must be dealt with." He handed a piece of writing leather to Afsan. "I want you to draw your cartouche on this. I'll witness it with my own."

Afsan read the page. *I, Afsan, formerly apprentice to the Chief Court Astrologer, before that a member of Pack Carno of Arj'toolar province, hereby affirm without reservation the existence of the Divine, that She is the one true God, that She created all life, and that the Face of God is her true countenance and Larsk is a true prophet. I disavow any claims to the contrary, and renounce and rescind any statements I may have made in the past that disagree with the content of this declaration. I have placed my mark below voluntarily, without coercion, and of my own free will. May God have mercy upon me.*

Afsan handed it back to Yenalb. "I can't agree to that."

"You must."

"Or?"

"Or suffer the consequences."

"I've already lost my job and my freedom. What else can you do to me?"

"Believe me, child, you do not wish to know."

"You can't have me killed. That's against the teachings."

"A demon may be disposed of."

"If Dybo agreed with you that I was a demon, I would be dead already. Therefore, he doesn't."

Yenalb made an unpleasant sound. "It'll take more than sophistry to save you. The sacred scrolls confer extraordinary powers upon my office. I can select any fate I wish for you."

"You threaten me with death? You would commit *murder*?"

"You yourself dispatched a crewmember aboard the *Dasheter,* so I'm told. A fellow named Nor-Gampar, wasn't it?"

"That was different. He had gone into *dagamant;* he was crazed."

"And perhaps you are becoming crazed even as we speak. Perhaps I will have no choice but to rip your throat out."

"I am as calm as one could be, under the circumstances."

"Are you, now?" Yenalb stepped closer to Afsan. "I am a priest. It's my job to whip individuals or groups into a frenzy. I could set you off with a few choice words, or incite those guards standing out in the hall."

"Dybo would never permit that."

"Are you sure?"

"You'd be found out. The first time he, or someone else, asked you what had happened to me, you'd be discovered."

"Would I?"

"Of course! Your face would flush blue."

"Would it?" Yenalb's teeth clicked. "Not every person can be a priest, you know. It takes a special disposition, special talents, special ways. Have you ever seen a priest's muzzle show the liar's tint?"

Afsan stepped backwards quickly, widening the space between them. "No . . . you're saying that you can lie openly? No. It can't be. You're just trying to make me nervous, trying to frighten me into agreeing to recant."

"Am I? Do you wish to put the issue to a test?" Yenalb stepped closer again. "Agree to the words on that piece of leather, Afsan. Save yourself."

"I am trying to save myself. And all of us. Even you."

Yenalb's tail swished. "You are so young. And, except for your current delusion, so bright. Recant, Afsan."

"Even if I did draw my cartouche on that document, what would that prove? Anybody who asked me if I was sincere in my change of mind would know in an instant that I wasn't; I at least cannot lie openly . . . and for that I'm grateful."

"Grateful to whom, Afsan? I thought you didn't believe in a God."

"I mean simply . . . "

"Yes, I know what you mean. Of course, you'd have to leave Capital City; indeed, we'd have to eject you altogether from the Fifty Packs. No one could see you again."

Afsan's jaw dropped open.

"Why so shocked?" said Yenalb. "Surely it's better than death. You're an extraordinary hunter; we've all heard the tales. You'd have no trouble fending for yourself. Why, you could even continue to pursue your astrological interests. I'd arrange for you to have your—what are those corrupt things called?—your far-seer to aid in your studies."

Yenalb waited a few moments, letting that sink in. "And," said the priest, in a studied, offhand way, "we could even arrange to find a volunteer companion for you. I understand you have a friend in Pack Gelbo who shares some of your interests, and some of your heresy." Afsan's head snapped up. Yenalb made a great show of trying to remember. "Now, what was her name? Something exotic, I seem to recall. Novato? Why, yes, I believe that was it. Wab-Novato."

Afsan felt his pulse quickening. "How do you know about her?"

"There are delegations here from every Pack paying tribute to the new Emperor. I learned from Det-Zamar, the priest you traveled here with, that you had visited Pack Gelbo before going to Carno. The delegates from Gelbo were more than pleased to answer a few questions for the Master of the Faith." Yenalb turned his muzzle to face Afsan directly. "Think of it, boy! Put your mark on that declaration, and then you and your friend can go safely, under my authority. There's plenty of land on the southern shore of Edz'toolar where the two of you could hunt and live and study in absolute peace."

"But we'd never see anyone else?"

"That's a small price to pay, isn't it? I'm offering you a way out, Afsan." The priest looked at him as if wondering whether to go on. "I was fond of you, boy. I had taken an interest in you; went to Saleed on your behalf to help arrange your pilgrimage. You seemed so bright, and, well, if perhaps a bit absentminded, at least always polite and eager. I never wished you any ill." Gently he proffered the writing leather again. "Take it, Afsan. Put your mark on it."

Afsan did take the sheet and read it once more, slowly, making sure he understood the weight of each glyph, the significance of each turn of phrase. It was a tempting offer . . .

He unsheathed the claw on the longest finger of his left hand, the one he used to draw his cartouche. Yenalb produced a small pot of ink from a pouch in his robe and began to pry off the cap.

But then Afsan unsheathed his remaining claws and with a swat of his hand sliced the leather document into strips. They dropped to the floor, forming an overlapping array in the dirt.

Yenalb thumped his tail in fury. "You'll regret that decision, Afsan."

Afsan crossed his arms over his chest and leaned back on his tail. Sadly he said, "Part of me always will."

Chapter 33

The central square of Capital City was filled with a latticework of Quintaglios. Each stood as close to the next as protocol would permit, meaning that, viewed from an elevation, such as the wooden platform Afsan found himself on, their heads formed points at regular intervals throughout the square, two paces between each one.

Dybo was noticeably absent. It was his orders, or at least orders that he had approved, that had brought Afsan here, but the Emperor apparently did not have what it took to watch.

It was small comfort to Afsan that Dybo had apparently had difficulty coming to a decision: it was now twenty-six days since Yenalb had visited Afsan in his tiny prison, and yet Afsan was sure Yenalb had called for this immediately after that meeting.

Six guards had accompanied Afsan, each twice his own bulk. That was far greater an escort than Afsan needed, but it seemed that the public was to be shown that Afsan was much more dangerous than his thin form would indicate. The guards had goaded him with violent shoves, pushing him up the ramp and onto the platform. And now that he was here, the hastily erected wooden structure creaking beneath him, two of them were tying him to a post, his arms lashed together behind the rough wood, his tail strapped to the planks.

The ties, made of armorback hide, were drawn so tight that Afsan felt a tingling in his hands, a numbness in his fingers. His claws were extended, but he could no longer feel their presence.

At the end of the platform, a Quintaglio even younger than Afsan beat slowly on a drum.

Afsan looked up. Overhead, against the purple sky, several large wingfingers circled.

Looking out over the lattice of heads, Afsan saw them parting, saw a pathway open up. Coming toward him, clad in swirling robes, bearing the Staff of Larsk, was Det-Yenalb, Master of the Faith. The crowd closed behind him.

Afsan's heart pounded.

Yenalb came up the ramp that led onto the wooden platform. The crowd cheered him with whoops and thumping tails. He had yet to look at Afsan.

In an instant, Afsan saw Yenalb's whole posture change; saw him rear up, standing as erect as possible; saw his features rearrange themselves into those of an orator; saw him adopt the posture he used in the Hall of Worship, that special bearing that helped him control others. The priest faced the crowd, raising his hands in benediction. He shouted a few words in outdated speech, speech from the time of Larsk's voyage, speech that harked back to the truth Larsk had discovered. Then, pointing at Afsan, he announced, "We have a demon among us!" The crowd swayed back and forth, literally moved by the words. "He comes to us from the darkest volcanic pits, from the place of smoke and liquid rock and deadly gases. He is a danger to us all!"

"Protect us!" shouted someone in the crowd.

"Save us from the demon," said another voice.

Yenalb lifted his hands, again made the sign of benediction. "Fear not!" said the priest. "I will indeed save us all from this demon." At last he turned toward Afsan. "You are Afsan?"

Afsan's voice was tremulous. "I am Sal-Afsan, yes."

"Silence! Tak-Saleed was a godly soul. You will not profane his memory by taking his name!"

Afsan looked at his feet, at his triple toeclaws digging into the splintery wood.

"Afsan, I give you one last chance," said Yenalb. "Release the poison within you. Recant!"

Afsan turned his head toward the sky. "The sun is out. You can see my sincerity. But even if it were darkest night, I would not take back what I've said. The world is doomed—"

Yenalb's hand slapped across Afsan's face, and, tied up as he was, he wasn't able to roll with the impact. He tasted blood in his mouth, his serrated teeth having smashed into the inside of his muzzle. "Silence!"

Afsan swallowed, looked away. And yet, in that instant, he realized just how controlled Yenalb's anger was, how orchestrated the performance. A backhanded slap? From a carnivore? Yenalb was deliberately avoiding using claws or teeth, pointedly refraining from drawing visible blood. He played the crowd the way Dybo would a musical instrument.

Yenalb turned to the audience. "The *dat-kar-mas*!" he shouted. Again the assembled group parted as a second priest, a female, came through, carrying a small jeweled box in both hands. She proffered the box to Yenalb. He opened it, the lacquered lid tilting back on tiny hinges. Inside was an obsidian dagger, lying on fine black silk. It glinted with lavender highlights in the sunlight. He reached in to pick it up and Afsan noticed Yenalb's claws extending as he touched it.

The priest held it over his head and turned it so the crowd could see. Gasps and hisses filled the air. Yenalb would not attack Afsan with his bare hands, for such a spectacle might indeed incite the crowd to instinctive violence. No, already the sight of a weapon—distasteful, cowardly, a tool of the weak—had quelled the crowd. And yet, Afsan knew that Yenalb could bring them to near-boil again with a few words or an appropriate gesture. The priest turned toward him. "What you say, demon, is a lie. Since you continue to claim to see things that are blasphemous, you give us no choice." He nodded at the guards.

One of them grabbed Afsan by the throat, claws sharp against his skin, his dewlap bunched painfully against his neck. Afsan tried to bite the guard, but another moved in, crushing Afsan's muzzle shut in the crook of her massive arm. His head was twisted sideways, and Afsan closed his eyes. He felt the planks beneath him wobble as Yenalb moved closer.

Suddenly, roughly, his right eyelid was forced open by strong fingers. Diffuse light came at him through his nictitating membrane, and then a shadow fell across him. Afsan opened the membrane to see more clearly. Coming at him, cold and sharp, was the black obsidian knife.

The dagger was filling his field of view, and he realized at last that he was not to die here, although perhaps that would have been better.

The pain as the mineral point lanced into his eye was incredible, stronger and sharper than any agony Afsan had known before. He frantically tried to escape, to free himself, but the guards were much stronger than he. His left eyelid was forced open, too. He quickly rolled that eye, trying to move the pupil as far up into his skull as possible. The last thing he saw was one of the moons, a pale and dim crescent in the afternoon sun.

Then a second stab, a second agony on top of the first.

And blackness.

Through the pain, Afsan felt something like jelly on his muzzle.

His head pounded. His heart raced. He felt nauseous.

Yenalb's voice rose above the sound that Afsan suddenly realized was his own screaming. "The demon can never again claim to see something that blasphemes our God!"

The crowd cheered. The strong hand at Afsan's throat pulled away. Pain throbbed through him. He tried to blink, but his eyelids had trouble sliding over his rent orbs. His body racked.

And at last, mercifully, he fell unconscious, sagging against the wooden post.

Chapter 34

Dybo apparently thought that what he'd allowed to be done to Afsan was a kindness, a gentler fate than having him executed. Indeed, the Emperor, in a gesture of his infinite mercy, let Afsan go, free to wander the Capital. Stripped of his rank, stripped of his home, stripped of his sight.

But free.

His eyes would never grow back. Bone and flesh, those could regenerate, but the eyes, the organs—damage to them was permanent, irreversible.

Afsan was determined not to dwell on his loss, and not to be a burden on those few who were willing to help him. He was learning to identify the sounds of the city: the clicking of toeclaws on stone paving; the thundering footfalls of domesticated hornfaces making their way down the streets; the chatter of voices, some near and distinct, some distant and muffled; the calls of traders trying to interest those wandering by in the trinkets and tools brought from other Packs; the tourists responding with interest, the locals hissing them down; the entreaties of tattooless beggars; the drums from the place of worship, sounded at the beginning of each daytenth; the identifying calls of ships down in the harbor. And behind it all the background noises, the things he had ignored most of his life: the whistle of the wind, the rustling of leaves, the *pipping* calls of wingfingers gliding overhead, the chirpings of insects.

And there were smells to help guide him, too: pheromones from other Quintaglios, the reek of oil from lamps, the delicious aroma of freshly killed meat as carts rattled by carrying it from the central butchery to dining halls around the city, the acrid smell from metalworking shops, pollens in the air, perfume of flowers, ozone before a storm.

He found he could even tell when the sun was out and when it was hidden behind a cloud, his skin reacting to the change in heat.

Pal-Cadool and Jal-Tetex became his constant companions. One of them was almost always with him. Afsan didn't understand why they gave so much time to looking after him, but he was grateful. Cadool had carved a stick for Afsan from a *telaja* branch. Afsan carried it in his left hand, feeling the ground in front of him. He learned to judge what each little bump meant about the path ahead, with Cadool or Tetex providing a running commentary: "There's a curb here; that's just a loose stone; watch out—hornface dung!"

Cadool and Tetex were practically the only ones willing to speak to him. Afsan had not been tattooed with a shunning symbol—his crime was heinous, indeed, but he had not been moved to mate with a rutting animal nor had he hunted without eating what he had killed. But, then again, there were only a couple of other blind Quintaglios in Capital City, and both of them were very old. Everyone could recognize Afsan immediately, the scrawny young adult feeling his way along with a stick. And, after what had happened to Afsan, it was little wonder that no one risked talking to him.

Afsan was no longer a prisoner, but nor was he an astrologer. A priest from Det-Yenalb's staff had taken Saleed's place, and no apprentice was needed, apparently. Cadool had made space for Afsan in his own small apartment, two rooms on the far side of Capital City.

Today, the twenty-first day since he had been blinded, Afsan detected a difference in Cadool as the butcher walked beside him. His voice was charged, and there was excitement in his pheromones.

"What's with you?" Afsan asked at last.

Cadool's long stride faltered a bit; Afsan could hear the

change in the way his friend's claws ticked against the stones. "What do you mean?"

"I mean, good Cadool, that you're all worked up about something. What is it?"

"It's nothing, really." Without being able to see the muzzle of the person speaking, Afsan couldn't tell if he was being told the truth. Still, since lying was futile in most circumstances, it tended not to occur to Quintaglios to try. Nonetheless, Cadool's words seemed insincere.

"Come on, it must be something. You're more stimulated than someone about to go on a hunt."

Clicking noises. Cadool's laughter. "It's nothing, really." A beat. "Do you know what time it is?"

Afsan had gotten good at counting and remembering the number of drums sounded from the Hall of Worship. "It's four daytenths past sunrise. Or it was, a few moments ago."

"That late?"

"Yes. Why? Are you expecting something?"

"We have to get to the central square."

Afsan had also become good at counting intersections. "That's eleven blocks from here, and you know how slowly I walk. Besides, I—I'm not comfortable there."

Cadool stopped for a moment. "No, I suppose you aren't. But this will be worth it, I promise." Afsan felt a hand cup his elbow. "Come along!"

Physical contact with others was something that Afsan was getting used to. His claws extended when surprised by a touch, but he managed to get them retracted within a few beats.

Afsan's gait was slow—he had to be able to feel the stones ahead of him with his stick—but with Cadool propelling him they made good time. Afsan ticked off the landmarks in his mind. The putrid smell meant they were approaching the town axis, down which the main drainage ditch ran. Soon they were close enough to hear the gurgling of the water. Next, the hubbub of the main market. The silence of the holy quarter. The smell of woodsmoke coming from the heating fires in the creche, a sure sign that they were indeed near the town's center.

And, at last, the sounds of the central square itself. A constant background of wingfinger pips: Afsan could picture the creatures perched all over the statues of Larsk and his descendants, preening their white hairy coverings, stretching leathery wings, occasionally swooping into flight to pluck an insect from the air, or to fetch a gobbet of meat tossed by a Quintaglio seated on one of the public stools that ringed the square. Normal vehicles were prohibited here, so that carriage clacking over the stones must have been passing through on palace business. Indeed, it must belong to a highly placed official, for Afsan could hear the distinctive squeak of a pivoting front axle—a newfangled luxury, found only on the most elaborate carriages. The carriage was pulled by at least two shovelmouths, judging by the methane stench and the click of broad, flat toeclaws.

Suddenly Afsan lifted his head—an instinctive gesture, an attempt to look up. The thundering call of a shovelmouth had split the air, but not from nearby, not the small ones that had just passed. No, it came from out in the direction of the Ch'mar volcanoes, away from the harbor—a bellow, a reverberating wail.

Soon the ground shook slightly. Giant footfalls. A herd of *something* was moving down the streets of the city. No, no, not a herd—the slamming feet were all of different weights, different strides. A collection of animals? And Quintaglios, hundreds of Quintaglios, running alongside, their voices growing as whatever procession this was approached the square.

There were more calls from shovelmouths, as well as the low roars made by hornfaces and the *greeble-greeble* of armorbacks.

Afsan felt his claws unsheathe, his tail swish nervously. "What's happening?"

Cadool's hand squeezed Afsan's elbow as he continued to steer him through the square. "Something that should have happened some time ago, my friend. You are about to be vindicated."

Afsan stopped and turned his unseeing face on Cadool. "What?"

"They're coming, Afsan. From across Land, your people are coming."

"My people?"

"The Lubalites. The hunters. You are The One."

"The one what?"

"*The One.* The One spoken of by Lubal as she was dying, gored by a hornface. 'A hunter will come greater than myself, and this hunter will be a male—yes, a male—and he shall lead you on the greatest hunt of all.' "

"I know Lubal said that, but—"

"But nothing. You fit the description."

"You can't be serious."

"Of course I am."

"Cadool, I'm just an astrologer."

"No. You are much more."

The procession was growing nearer. Afsan could feel the ground shake beneath him. The shovelmouth cries were deafening.

"Here they come," said Cadool.

"What's happening?"

"It's a stirring sight, Afsan. You should be proud. At the far end of the square, through the Arch of Dasan, perhaps five hundred Lubalites are entering. Young and old, male and female. Some are walking, others are riding on the backs of runners and hornfaces and shovelmouths and armorbacks."

"My God . . . "

"And they're heading this way, every one of them. Some of them I know: hunt leader Jal-Tetex, of course, and Dar-Regbo, and the songwriter Ho-Baban. And I believe that is Pahs-Drawo, from your home Pack of Carno—"

"Drawo is here?"

"Yes, him, and hundreds of others."

Afsan felt stones near his feet bounce as the vast procession crossed the square. Their pheromones hit him like a wall. Afsan's claws extended in reflex. *The hunt was on . . .*

"Afsan, it's glorious," said Cadool, his voice full of wonder. "Banners are snapping in the breeze, red for Lubal, blue for Belbar, green for Katoon, yellow for Hoog, and purple for Mekt. It's like a rainbow. And those who own copies have the *Book of Rites* held high in their right hands, in plain view. No more secret worship! The time has come."

"For what?" For the first time in days, Afsan felt panic because he could not see. "Cadool, the time has come for what?"

"For the religion of the hunt to rise again!" Cadool's words were almost drowned out by the approaching din. "Afsan, they're here, they're hailing you. Five hundred left hands are raised in the salute of Lubal—"

"The what?"

"The hand gesture! They're greeting you! Afsan, return the sign! Return it!"

"But I don't remember it—"

"Quickly!" said Cadool. He felt the butcher's hand on his, manipulating his fingers. "Retract this claw, and this one. Good. Now, raise your hand. Yes! Press your thumb against your palm—!"

The crowd went wild. Afsan heard his name shouted over and over again.

"They all want to see you," said Cadool. He barked something at someone in the crowd. Afsan heard heavy claws move across the stones. Hot breath was on his face. "Here's a shovelmouth. Climb onto its back."

Afsan knew these beasts well. They were commonly hunted by Pack Carno and occasionally domesticated. Adults were perhaps three times his own body length, brown, with pebbly hides, strange crests atop their heads (the shape varying from species to species), and mouths that ended in wide, flat prows. They could walk on two legs, but usually ambled about on all four.

"Here," said Cadool. "Let me help you." Afsan felt one hand upon him, then another, and, a moment later, a third and a fourth. His heart pounded at the strange touches.

"Don't worry," said a female voice he knew well. "It's me, Tetex."

They boosted him onto the creature's back, and Afsan wrapped his arms around its short neck. The thing's body expanded and contracted beneath him, and he could hear a faint whistling as the air moved through the long chambers of its head crest.

Unable to see, Afsan felt dizzy.

Suddenly the beast's flank shook, and Afsan realized that Cadool or Tetex had slapped its side, prodding it. The shovelmouth rose up on its hind legs, lifting Afsan into the air. It had a small saddle strapped to its back, and Afsan anchored his feet into that, so that he stood straight, in line with the animal's neck. Once the lifting had stopped, and his vertigo had begun to pass, he dared unwrap his left arm from the neck and repeated the Lubalite hand sign. The crowd cheered him on.

"The One has arrived!"

"Long live Afsan!"

"Long live the hunters!"

Afsan wished he could see them. It was all a mistake, of course, but it felt good—like basking in the sun after a satisfying meal—to be wanted by someone, anyone, after all he'd been through. He managed to find his voice and said, so softly that only the first row of onlookers could hear, "Thank you."

"Talk to us!" shouted a female's voice.

"Tell us how you unmasked the false prophet!" demanded a male.

Unmasked the false prophet? thought Afsan. "I merely saw things Larsk did not," he said.

"Louder!" said Cadool. "They all want to hear."

Afsan spoke up. "My training allowed me to see things that eluded Larsk."

"They called you a demon!" came a voice from far away.

"But it was Larsk who was the demon," shouted another. "It was he who lied in the daylight!"

Afsan felt his stomach churning. *Such words . . .* "No," he said, now raising his hand in a call for silence. The crowd fell mute, and suddenly Afsan realized that it was he who was really in control here. "No, Larsk was simply confused." *Like all of you . . .*

"The One is gracious," shouted a voice.

"The One is wise," cried another.

It came to Afsan that he would never again have the ear of so many. This, perhaps, was his one great chance to spread the word, to show the people the truth. For the first and maybe only time in his life, *he* was in command. It was a moment to be seized.

"You've heard my explanation of how the world works," he said, his throat aching from unaccustomed shouting. "We are a moon that revolves around a planet which we call the Face of God, and that planet, like all the others, travels in a circular path around our sun."

"Behold!" screamed a voice. "The lies of Larsk revealed!" The speaker sounded close to madness. The crowd was nearing a fever pitch.

"But hear, now, the most important message of all!" Afsan

dared raise both hands, briefly letting go of the shovelmouth's neck. "Our world is doomed!"

"Just as it was foretold!" shouted a drawn-out voice that sounded like Cadool's.

Afsan heard a buzz move through the crowd. "We have some time yet," he shouted. "Although the world's fate is sealed, we have many kilodays before its end will come."

"Kilodays to pray!" said another voice.

"No!" Afsan again balanced on the shovelmouth's back, holding both hands aloft. "No! Kilodays to prepare! We must get off this world."

The sounds from the crowd were of puzzlement now.

"Get off the world?"

"What does he mean?"

Afsan wished he could see them, wished he could read their faces. Was he getting through to any of them?

"I mean," he said, "that although the world is ending, our race does not have to. We can leave this place, fly to somewhere else."

"Fly?" The word echoed throughout the square in intonations ranging from puzzled to sarcastic.

"Yes, fly! In vessels—ships—like those in which we now ply the waters of this world."

"We don't know how to do that," called a voice.

"And I don't know, either," said Afsan. "But we must find a method—*we must!* It will mean changing the way in which we conduct our lives. We must give ourselves over to science, we must learn all that we can. Wingfingers fly; insects fly. If they can do it, we can do it. It's only a question of discovering their methods and adapting them to our needs. Science holds our answer; knowledge—real knowledge, verifiable knowledge, not superstition, not religious nonsense—will be our salvation."

The crowd, at last, was silent, save for the grunts of the beasts.

"We must learn to work together, to cooperate." He smelled their pheromones, knew they were confused. "Nature—or God—has given us a great challenge. We have trouble working side by side; our territorial instincts drive us apart. But we must overcome these instincts, be creatures of reason and sanity instead of prisoners of our biology."

Afsan turned his head in small increments from left to right, as if looking at each individual face. He could hear the hiss of conversation growing, a comment here, a question there, a remark from the back, an interjection up front.

"But, Afsan," came a voice, louder than the others, "we need our territories . . ."

Afsan held the shovelmouth's neck firmly so as not to lose his balance as he tipped forward in a concessional bow. "Of course we do," he said. "But once we leave this world, there will be room for us all. Our Land is but a tiny part of the vast universe. We're going to the stars!"

Suddenly another voice cut across all the others, a voice amplified and reverberating through a speaking horn.

"This is Det-Yenalb, Master of the Faith. Disperse at once. I have assembled those loyal to the Emperor and they are prepared to move upon the square unless you leave now. I say again: This is Det-Yenalb—"

The fool! Afsan felt pheromones from the crowd wash over him like a wave. His own claws extended. The shovelmouth gave a little yelp as their points dug into its neck. He could hear bodies jostling as Quintaglios, already packed too tightly, turned to face the priest. The situation was explosive.

"What are you afraid of, Yenalb?" shouted Afsan.

"Disperse!"

"What are you afraid of?" echoed the crowd of hunters.

Yenalb's voice reverberated back. "I fear for your souls."

"And I fear for the survival of our people," Afsan shouted. "Call off your supporters, Yenalb. Do you really want to send priests, academics, and ceremonial guards against the finest hunters in all of Land? Retreat, before it's too late!"

"I say again," said Yenalb. "Disperse. No punishment will be levied if you leave now."

Cadool's voice rose up, almost deafening Afsan. "Upon whose authority do you act, priest?"

Echoing, reverberating: "The authority of His Luminance Dy-Dybo, Emperor of the eight provinces and the Fifty Packs."

"And how," demanded Cadool, "did fat Dybo come upon his authority?"

"He is—" Yenalb halted, the final syllable repeating as it

faded away. But the crowd knew what he had intended to say. *He is the descendant of Larsk.*

"Larsk is a false prophet," yelled a female voice, "and Dybo's authority is unearned."

Shouts of agreement went up throughout the square.

"You will disperse!" said Yenalb.

"No," said Afsan, his voice cutting through the uproar. "We will not. Order your people to withdraw."

They waited for Yenalb's response, but there was none.

"Once first blood is spilled, Yenalb, there will be no stopping an escalation." Afsan's voice was going, his throat raw. "You know that. Order the retreat."

Yenalb's voice echoed back, but it had a different tone. He must have turned around to address those who were loyal to the palace. "Advance!" shouted the priest. "Clear the square!"

For once, Afsan was glad he could not see.

Chapter 35

Pal-Cadool looked up at Afsan, balanced atop the tube-crested shoveler. The One, still small and always scrawny, had eyelids closed over rent orbs. His voice, unaccustomed to addressing multitudes, had become strained.

Cadool then looked out across the square. The Lubalites filled most of the eastern side. Some were atop hornfaces, half hidden behind the great bony neck frills. Others were riding running beasts, both the green and the beige variety. Still others were on shovelmouths—hardly a fighting creature, but still a good mount. And a few hunters stood on the wide knobby carapaces of armorbacks, ornery plant-eaters mostly encased in bone.

But Cadool saw that the bulk of the five hundred hunters were on foot. They had been rapt with attention, drinking in the words of Sal-Afsan, The One.

But now those loyal to the Emperor, led by Det-Yenalb high on the back of a spikefrill, were moving into the square through the Arch of the First Emperor.

The hunters turned, those on foot swinging quickly around, those riding atop great reptiles prodding their beasts to rotate through a half circle. With grunts and hisses the animals obeyed.

Cadool guessed there were seventy paces between the two forces. On this side, 500 hunters. On Yenalb's, perhaps 120 priests, scholars, and palace staff members, each atop an imperial mount.

The palace loyal were a sorry lot: many of them had lived soft lives, relying on butchers such as Cadool himself to do their hunting and killing. No, they were no match for the Lubalites, either in number or skill. But their mounts were fresh, not exhausted from the long march to Capital City. Cadool took a moment to size up the animals they rode. Armorbacks had daggers of bone coming off the sides of their thick carapaces and had solid clubs at the ends of their muscular tails. A hunter would never use such a club in battle, but scholars and priests might indeed sink so low. One swing from an armorback's tail could stave in a Quintaglio skull.

And then there were the hornfaces, with three pointed shafts of bone protruding from the fronts of their skulls: a long one from above each eye and another, shorter horn rising from the tip of the muzzle. In his time, Cadool had seen many hunters, either too daring or too careless, gored by such beasts. Even Dem-Pironto, who, excepting Afsan, was the finest hunter Cadool had ever known, had been felled that way. Further, the great neck shields, rising like walls of bone from the back of the animals' skulls, would help protect the scholars and priests.

And then there were the spikefrills, such as the one Yenalb was riding. These were a rare breed of hornface with long spikes of bone sticking out of the short bony frill around the neck. They had only one real horn, a huge one sticking up from the snout, although there were small pointed knobs above each eye.

But even as he tried to make a critical assessment, Cadool realized that his own control was slipping away, his blood coming to a boil.

"Advance!" Yenalb had shouted through his brass speaking cone. "Clear the square!" The palace loyal began moving slowly. The square was crowded; their mounts jostled each other. Beasts that size could crush the foot or tail of a Quintaglio without noticing a thing.

It's madness, thought Cadool. *Absolute madness.* And then he growled, low and long—

• • •

Afsan felt the ground shaking slightly, knew that imperial mounts were starting to move toward him and the hunters. The air was thick with pheromones. He didn't want this, had never wanted it. All he'd wanted was to tell the truth, to let them see—see what he no longer could see.

The blind leading the blind.

Afsan felt his claws unsheathe.

Cadool charged, pushing through the crowd of hunters. Other Lubalites were lunging forward, closing the gap between themselves and the imperial contingent. Being on foot, Cadool had greater maneuverability than those upon mounts. He and a hundred others surged ahead, three-toed feet kicking pebbles and dirt into the air, a cloud rising around them.

Cadool's heart thumped in time with his footfalls. The hunt was on!

Forty paces. Thirty.

The air filled with wingfingers, rising in droves from statues at the periphery of the square. Their squawks, like claws scraping slate, counterpointed the dull thunder of feet pounding the paving stones.

Twenty paces. Ten. Cadool could smell them, smell their stimulation, smell their fear.

Five paces—

He leapt, kicking off the cobbles, flying into the air, cutting across the distance between himself and the closest of the opposing forces, one of the ceremonial imperial guards, straddling the back of a hornface.

The tri-horned brute bucked at seeing the screaming Quintaglio flying toward its flank. It tried to move to the left—

—and crashed against an adjacent hornface, this one of the rare variety with a boss of bone where the nasal horn would normally be—

Cadool hit the tri-horner's huge side, rippling waves moving through its tawny flesh, radiating from the impact point.

The butcher's claws dug in, pulling him up onto the beast's back.

The imperial guard, a female slightly bigger than Cadool, fumbled to get out of her saddle—

—and Cadool's jaws snapped down upon her throat.

He released the leather restraints holding her dead form to

the beast's back and let it slide to the stones below, splattering them with blood—

—and then leapt from the back of this hornface to the adjacent beast, his feet forward, toeclaws out, smashing into the chest of its horrified rider, a scholar Cadool knew slightly, knocking him to the ground.

He swung to look at the skirmish line. Every imperial loyalist was engaged by a Lubalite. Jaws snapped. Claws tore. Blood washed stones, dappled the hides of mounts, smeared muzzles of individuals on both sides. With a bone-crunching crack, Cadool saw Pahs-Drawo from Carno dispatch a loyalist atop a running beast, but then watched in horror as Drawo himself fell victim to a choreographed lunge by Yenalb's spikefrill, the beast's huge nose horn impaling Drawo, running through his gut like a fingerclaw through rotted wood.

Yenalb stood on his hind legs atop the spikefrill, dewlap puffed into a giant ruby ball—

Cadool was sickened. To be stimulated in *that* way by this . . . Chest heaving, vision blurring, Cadool had one last clear thought before he gave himself over to the madness: Yenalb was his.

Afsan knew there was nothing he could do, but he tried anyway. The cries of wingfingers, the thunderous calls of shovelmouths, the pounding of feet all drowned his words.

"Stop!" he shouted in the loudest volume his raw throat could manage. "Stop!"

But it would not—*could* not—stop.

Suddenly Afsan felt the shovelmouth he was standing on buck wildly in panic. Afsan shared the beast's emotion as he found himself catapulted through the air. In his perpetual darkness, he had no idea where he was going to land. Air whipping about him, he quickly rolled into a ball, tucking his muzzle into his chest, wrapping his arms over his head, retracting his legs as much as possible, and folding his tail up and around.

Screams . . .

His own . . .

And then he hit—

• • •

Cadool slid down the rump of the boss-nosed beast, lashed out with his claws to stop a toppled loyalist who tried to intercept him, and made a dead run for the high priest.

Det-Yenalb had been shouting orders through his speaking cone, but each successive proclamation became less recognizable speech and more animalistic hiss and growl. His spikefrill had tipped its head low and was using a stubby forefoot to pull what was left of Pahs-Drawo off its nasal horn.

Suddenly Yenalb became aware of the charging Cadool. He yanked on the two largest of the giant spikes that protruded from his mount's neck frill, as if to get the beast's attention. It looked up, Drawo now discarded, just in time to try to intercept the butcher. The spikefrill's beak snapped viciously at Cadool, but Cadool danced and weaved to stay out of its way.

The square was too crowded. The spikefrill couldn't turn enough to get at him. Cadool leapt again, this time grabbing two of the spikes coming out of the crest of bone around the beast's neck. He used these as handholds, pulling himself up onto the creature's back. Yenalb tried to push him off, but the priest was no match for the butcher, none at all . . .

Cadool opened his jaws wide, let out a primal roar, and—

This is for Pahs-Drawo!—

Snapped his mouth shut on Yenalb's dewlap, ripping it open, air hissing out—

And this *is for Afsan!—*

Taking a second, deeper bite into the priest's meaty throat, serrated teeth ripping through muscle and cartilage and tendons, a semi-ten of Cadool's fangs popping free as his jaws banged closed against Yenalb's cervical vertebrae—

And this is for the truth!—

But suddenly the animal beneath him was shaking—

—the whole square was shaking—

Through the haze of instinct, Cadool thought some great monster—a thunderbeast giant, like the one Afsan had felled on his first hunt—had made it into the city, the guards having left their stations to be here.

But, no, the rumbling continued, the shaking growing more pronounced, the horizon jumping wildly—

• • •

Afsan was sure he had lost consciousness upon hitting the ground, but for an instant or for many daytenths, he couldn't tell.

He heard the crowd rioting around him, screams of Quintaglios pushed into fighting rapture.

Afsan's left side hurt badly. He knew he'd cracked some of the ribs that were attached to his backbone, as well as some of the free-floating ones that normally lay across the belly. He'd also knocked out a few teeth . . .

And then, suddenly the ground began to shake. *I'm to die here,* he thought, *crushed under some giant beast, in the same square I thought I was going to die in all those days ago.*

But the shaking wasn't because of footfalls, wasn't because of stampeding reptiles.

The ground shook—

—and shook—

Animals screamed.

Landquake.

Cadool listened to terrified roars of the animals, then stole a glance at the cobblestones below. Pebbles and dirt jumped.

Fear washed through him. In an instant, his fury was forgotten. He looked at the corpse of Yenalb, flopped on the back of the spikefrill, twin geysers of blood shooting from where the nearly severed head still joined the chest. Cadool pushed the body from the spikefrill's back, letting it fall to the heaving ground. The head twisted around as it landed, facing backwards. The beast next to the spikefrill—an armorback whose old rider was cowering in fear—panicked as the land continued to quake. It moved backwards, trampling what was left of the high priest.

Throughout the square, Cadool could see statues tottering on their pedestals. As he watched, Pador's great marble rendition of the Prophet Larsk wobbled back and forth a few times, then toppled to the stones, crushing a hapless hunter beneath it.

Many of the riding beasts were bucking, and it was only a matter of time before a stampede would begin. Some of the Quintaglios were already hurrying to get out of the square, even though it was probably better to be here in an open space rather than near any buildings.

For an instant, Cadool thought the spikefrill was bucking, trying to throw him from its back, but he realized in horror that the whole square was lifting, heaving, like a slumbering monster shuddering into wakefulness.

The One! thought Cadool. *What about The One?*

Several of the hornfaces near him turned and charged out of the square, their round feet crushing whatever happened to be beneath them. But Cadool was a butcher; he knew the ancient art of guiding animals.

Standing erect on the beast's back, he grabbed firmly onto an upward-angled spike on either side of the frill.

Spikefrills, like all hornfaces, had ball joints connecting their massive heads to their bodies. Using the long spikes like the prongs on a captain's wheel aboard a ship, Cadool steered the mighty beast.

The spikefrill moved, Cadool and his mount acting as one, sailing through the sea of Quintaglios, riding high and fast and firm through the rippling waves of the landquake—

"Out of my way!" shouted Cadool above the screams of the crowd, but most Quintaglios and animals were too deep in panic to heed his words. The spikefrill cruised forward, toward the east side of the square.

Cadool glanced back. In the distance, fools were trying to exit through the Arch of the First Emperor. He watched as the arch's keystone rattled its way up and out, and then came crashing down. The rest of the arch stood as if suspended for half a beat, and then the huge cut stones fell. Splats replaced screams in mid-note. Dust rose in a great gray cloud.

His mount sailed on, Cadool's hands firm on the animal's spikes. Standing upright atop the beast's massive shoulders, he could see clear across the square. But where was the face he sought? Where?

Three Quintaglios were in the way, apparently dazed. Cadool dug the single claws on the back of each of his feet into the spikefrill's hide, driving it on. Two of the Quintaglios managed to stagger out of the way; the spikefrill, in a surprisingly gentle gesture, nudged the third out of its path with a sideways motion of its pointed beak.

Afsan's shovelmouth was nowhere to be seen. Had The One gotten away safely?

But no. At last Cadool spotted Afsan, on his side, lying in

the dirt. He was surrounded by a ring of hunters, muzzles out, teeth bared, forming a living shield around The One, even in the panic of the landquake not willing to leave him. His tail was a bloody pulp, apparently having been trampled by some beast in a panic to escape before the hunters had been able to protect him.

The ground heaved again, and Afsan looked briefly like he was convulsing. If only that were true, thought Cadool, at least it would mean he was still alive. There was blood on his face and a huge bruise on the side of his chest.

Cadool pushed against the spikes, commanding his mount to tip its head. Grabbing a spike halfway down the frill, he swung himself to the ground and hurried over to Afsan.

The hunter closest to Cadool bowed concession and got out of his way, opening up the protective ring. Cadool rushed in, stones still rippling beneath him. He placed his palm above the end of Afsan's muzzle to see if he was still breathing. He was. Cadool mumbled four syllables of Lubalite prayer, then spoke Afsan's name aloud.

No response. Cadool tried again.

Finally, faintly, confused: "Who?"

"It's me. Pal-Cadool."

"Cadool . . . ?"

"Yes. Can you stand?"

"I don't know." Afsan's voice was hissy, faint. "It's a landquake, isn't it?"

"Yes," said Cadool. "The fight is over, at least for now. The loyalists are running for safety." Most of the hunters had run off, too, but Cadool was glad that Afsan hadn't been able to see that shameful sight. "You must try to stand."

Afsan raised his muzzle from the ground. A small groan escaped his throat. "My chest hurts."

"I'm going to touch you; let me help."

Cadool's hand went under Afsan's left arm. He saw that Afsan was too dazed or too weak to have his claws respond to the intrusion. He rolled the ex-astrologer slightly, then gently brought his other hand under Afsan's other arm. The ground rattled again, and Cadool simply held Afsan until it subsided. The screams of the Quintaglios were fading; many were dead or dying, many more had retreated far from the edges of the square. Cadool dared look up. The new statue of

Dybo's mother, the late Empress Len-Lends, was directly behind them, rocking back and forth on its pedestal.

"Get up. You must get up." Cadool helped Afsan to his feet.

Suddenly the air was split by a crack greater than any thunder. The ground shook even more violently. Even the hunters who had been shielding Afsan ran off in panic. Cadool pulled Afsan to his feet and propelled him to the left. The marble Lends crashed down, hitting exactly where Afsan had been lying. Chips of stone bit into Cadool's leg.

He looked for the source of the massive explosion. There, in the distance, the rightmost of the Ch'mar volcanoes was erupting, black smoke spewing into the air.

"We must move quickly," said Cadool. "Trust me; let me guide you." He put one arm around Afsan's shoulders and cupped Afsan's nearest elbow with his other. They began to trot in unison, small moans escaping Afsan's throat with every footfall.

A second explosion cut the air. Cadool glanced backwards. The top of another of the Ch'mar mountains was gone. The sky was filled with a hail of pebbles, some even falling this far away, here in the square.

Head over heels, cobblestones scraping skin, landing in a heap with Afsan . . .

"I'm sorry, Afsan!" Cadool shouted above the roar from the volcano, "I wasn't watching as carefully as I should. Come; the Ch'mar peaks are erupting." He grabbed Afsan's arm, hoisted him to his feet. But Afsan's pace was more cautious now, holding them both back. Cadool tried as best he could to keep them moving.

Through his pain and despite the exploding mountains, Afsan heard something. He lifted his muzzle. A sound was coming at them from the direction of the harbor.

Five bells . . .

Two drums . . .

Five bells . . .

Two drums . . .

Alternating loud and soft, bells and drums, bells and drums, the sound he'd grown sick of during his pilgrimage—

—the identification call of the *Dasheter*.

"Cadool," said Afsan, some strength returning to his voice, "we must hurry to the harbor."

The roar behind them continued. "What? Why?"

"I hear the *Dasheter*. We can escape by water."

Cadool changed course immediately. "It'll take us a while to get there."

"I know we don't have much time," said Afsan. "I'll try not to slow us down."

Cadool's firm hand propelled them on. "I was wondering what had become of Var-Keenir. He had pledged to be here for the march of the Lubalites. Trouble upon the waves must have delayed him."

"He's here now," said Afsan. "Hurry!"

They ran through the streets of Capital City. Some Quintaglios seemed to be going the same way they were; others ran in different directions. Afsan heard the wails of children as they passed the creche.

At last he felt a cold wind on his face; the same steady wind that, thankfully, was blowing the smoke from the volcanoes away from the city. It meant they were out of the lee of the buildings, and must now be overlooking the harbor.

"It's there, Afsan," said Cadool. "I see the *Dasheter*." They started down the long ramp to the docks. "The waves are higher than I've ever seen; *Dasheter* is rocking back and forth like—"

"Like a student bowing concession to everyone he passes," said Afsan, finding the strength to click his teeth once. "I know that feeling well. Hurry!"

As they got closer to the docks, Afsan could hear the crashing of the waves, louder now than the roar of the volcanic explosions to the west.

"Careful," shouted Cadool. "We're about to step on the gangway." There were several others on the *adabaja* planks, jostling to get aboard. This was no time for worrying about the niceties of territoriality.

Afsan felt spray on his face, and almost lost his balance as he stepped onto the little bridge of planks leading up to the ship, swaying, swaying—

Up ahead, Cadool saw a short, pudgy figure scurrying up the gangway.

Dybo.

The Emperor escaping. Cadool thought briefly about rushing forward and pushing him into the choppy water before he could make it to the ship's foredeck.

And there, up on deck, old Var-Keenir helping the Emperor board!

Of course. Keenir had been cut off aboard the *Dasheter* for some sixty days. At the time he had left Capital City, The One hadn't yet been blinded. All Keenir knew was that Dybo's intervention had saved Afsan from being executed in the throne room by Yenalb—

Suddenly the ropes holding the gangway to the dock snapped. The planks swung across the open space, and Afsan and Cadool were dunked into the water.

"Climb!" Cadool shouted. Afsan's mangled tail was still bleeding, and the waters around him were stained red from it. Guided by Cadool, Afsan grabbed hold of the first plank, his claws digging into the slippery wood, gaps having appeared between each board as they began to slip down the ropes. He hauled himself up, hand over hand. Cadool did the same. Up above on the deck, looking over the railing, Cadool could see Keenir and Dybo. Much to his surprise, both were leaning over the side, helping those still on the dangling gangway get over the railing and onto the ship. Afsan and he pulled higher and higher, the planks like thick rungs in a ladder. The *Dasheter* rocked. Cadool felt his knuckles smash as the gangway slapped against the ship's hull.

Higher. Farther.

"I don't . . . know . . . if I can . . . make it," Afsan wheezed.

"It's not far!" shouted Cadool. "Hang on!"

The ship swung back, the gangway dipping into a crashing wave. Cadool felt chill waters on his legs and tail.

Soon hands were all over Afsan, hauling him aboard. A moment later, the Emperor himself reached out to Cadool, helping to pull him onto the deck of the *Dasheter*.

Cadool turned and looked back. On the sandy black beach, many Quintaglios stood helpless. A few were trying to swim. Other boats were turning, heading out of the harbor into open waters.

Two other Quintaglios were hauled aboard with lifelines, but then Keenir ordered the ship to set sail. "We've got forty people on board now," he said to Dybo in his gravelly voice. "Any more and we risk a territorial frenzy of our own."

The *Dasheter* bucked under giant waves. The four sails, each depicting an image associated with the false prophet Larsk, snapped loudly in the wind.

In the background, silhouetted, Cadool could see the tumbled and broken adobe and marble buildings of Capital City, and behind them, a false red dawn as lava spewed forth from the Ch'mar volcanoes.

Chapter 36

Pal-Cadool took stock of the situation. Afsan was sprawled on the *Dasheter*'s heaving deck, exhausted. Two members of the ship's crew were bent over The One, wrapping his twitching tail in soft hide, cleaning his face and arms with precious pieces of cloth. Emperor Dybo had disappeared below deck. Captain Var-Keenir stood nearby. When Cadool had last seen Keenir, the sailor's tail had been pale from recent regeneration. It was now the same dark green as the rest of the captain's skin, his injury completely healed.

Keenir, wearing a red leather cap, nodded at Cadool. "You saved The One."

Cadool shook his head. "No, Captain. He saved me."

Keenir looked down at the prone form. "There's somebody here who'll want to see him." He headed off down a ramp that led below deck, the timbers beneath him creaking under his bulk. Cadool gripped the railings and watched the continuing spectacle of the eruption, black clouds puffing into the sky. Like Afsan, he'd been summoned to Capital City as a young adult. But that had been so long ago, the Capital was the only place Cadool called home. His tail swished back and forth as he watched the city die.

He was startled by the sound of small *peeps* behind him. Turning, Cadool saw Captain Keenir, followed by a female who was slightly older than Afsan, and coming up the ramp behind her, one, two, three . . . *eight* egglings, half walking, half stumbling. Measuring from the tip of their snouts to the ends of their tails, none was longer than Cadool's forearm. They made small sounds of wonder, completely oblivious to the spectacle unfolding on Land—in fact, Cadool realized, they couldn't see it over the raised sides of the ship.

Afsan was still prone on the deck. A sailor had brought him a bowl of water. Cadool, exhausted, nodded gratitude to the fellows attending Afsan but Keenir motioned for them to move aside. The female's face showed alarm at the sight of the fallen Afsan, and she rushed to him. The babies stumbled along behind her. Cadool moved as close as propriety would allow and cocked his head to listen.

"Afsan?" said the female's voice, full of concern.

The One lifted his head from the deck. His voice was raw, ragged. "Who's that?"

"It's me, Afsan. It's Novato."

Afsan tried to lift his head further, but apparently was too tired. It slipped back onto the planks. One of the babies waddled over to him and began crawling up onto his back. "What's that?" said Afsan, startled.

"It's a baby."

"It is?" His whole body seemed to relax. "I can't see, Novato."

She crouched low to look at him. Her eyes narrowed as she examined his face. "By God, you can't. Afsan, I didn't know. I'm sorry."

Afsan looked as though he wanted to say something—anything—but the words would not come. There was a protracted moment between them—

—broken, at last, by a second baby, perhaps emboldened by the first, climbing up onto Afsan's thigh.

"Is that *another* one?" asked Afsan, his voice full of wonder.

Novato was a moment in replying, as if she had been reflecting on Afsan's loss. Finally: "It is. Her name is Galpook."

Afsan reached an arm over to stroke the tiny form. Galpook made a contented sound as Afsan's hand ran down her back. "Is she yours?"

"Yes. And yours."

"*What?*"

"She's your—" her voice faltered for an instant, and then the word came out, an unfamiliar word, a word rarely spoken—"*daughter.*"

"I have a daughter?"

"At least."

"Pardon?"

"Afsan, you have *three* daughters. And five sons."

"Eight children?"

"Yes, my Afsan. Eight. And they're all here."

"From that night?"

"Of course."

Afsan's hand stopped in mid-stroke. "But—but—the bloodpriests . . . ? Do you know about them?"

"Yes," said Novato. "I'd understood some vague details before, and Keenir explained the rest to me."

"But, then, with the bloodpriests, how can there still be eight children?"

"Well, the eggs hatched aboard the *Dasheter,* and there are no bloodpriests here. But even if there were, your children would be safe. You are The One, Afsan. Bloodpriests come from the hunter's religion, and no hunter would eat your children."

"You mean all eight get to live?"

Novato's voice was joyous. "Yes."

Another baby had crawled onto Afsan's back, and the one who had first journeyed there had made it all the way to the dome of Afsan's head, her thin tail lying beside Afsan's right earhole.

"I wish I could see them."

"I wish you could, too," said Novato softly. "They're beautiful. Haldan—that's the one on your head—has a glorious golden coloring, although I'm sure that will darken to green as she grows older. And Kelboon, who is a bit shy and is clinging now to my leg, has your eyes."

"Ah," said Afsan, in a light tone. "I knew they'd gone somewhere."

"The others are Toroca, Helbark, Drawtood, Yabool, and Dynax."

Cadool knew Afsan would recognize the names: astrologers of the past who had made great discoveries. "Those are good names," Afsan said.

"I'm pleased with them," said Novato. "I never dreamed that I'd get to name my own children." She moved Haldan aside and spoke softly to Afsan. "I've missed you," she said.

"And I you," said Afsan, who appeared to be reveling in the sensation of the three babies crawling over his body. "But I don't understand why you're here."

"Keenir knew you were The One. So did someone named Tetex here in Capital City."

"She's the imperial hunt leader," said Afsan. "But I am not The One."

Novato reached out, stroked his forehead. "The One is supposed to lead us on the greatest hunt of all, and Keenir tells me you want to take us to the stars. That sounds like a great hunt to me."

Afsan had no reply to that.

"In any event," said Novato, "Keenir, Tetex, and other influential Lubalites are convinced that you are The One. When you got in trouble with Yenalb, the *Dasheter* set sail for the west coast to fetch hunters from there to support you. When Keenir returned to Jam'toolar, he anchored again at the Bay of Three Forests, where he'd let you off after your pilgrimage. My Pack was still near there. He heard from Lub-Kaden that I'd laid eggs fertilized by you. Keenir convinced the *halpataars* of Gelbo that you really are The One." She glanced up at the gruff old sailor, standing a few paces away. "His word can lift dragging tails everywhere, it seems. He got them to release all my eggs from the creche."

Afsan said, "You arrived just in time."

Keenir spoke at last, his voice gravelly and low. "We meant to be here earlier, but bad weather delayed us as we rounded the Cape of Belbar."

"Captain? You're here, too? It's good to hear your voice again."

"It's good to . . . hear your voice again, too, egg—Afsan."

Afsan clicked his teeth. "You may call me eggling, if you like, sir." He brought his hand up to find Novato's, still stroking his forehead. "I'm so glad you came," he said to her, "but . . . "

"But now you must sleep," she said. "You look exhausted."

Keenir stepped forward. "Let me take you below deck, Afsan. You can have my quarters."

"Thank you," Afsan said. "But I'd prefer my old cabin—the one with the carving of the Original Five on the door—if that's still available. At least I know its layout."

"As you wish," said Keenir. "Do you need a hand getting up?"

"Yes. Novato, can you gather the children?"

"Of course." She lifted Galpook off Afsan's head, the baby letting out a *peep* when picked up. With careful taps she scooted the others off Afsan. Keenir reached his hand out to Afsan but realized after a moment that Afsan couldn't see it.

"I'm going to touch you," Keenir said, "to help you up." He gripped Afsan's forearm.

"I'm sorry, Novato," Afsan said as he rose, his voice a wheeze, "but I really must get some sleep."

"Not to worry." She touched his arm lightly. "We have all the time in the world."

Chapter 37

Afsan stretched out on the floor, trying to relax. Keenir and Cadool insisted on having him examined top to bottom by Mar-Biltog, who, although no healer, was at least trained in emergency procedures. It was clear, Biltog said, that the lower portion of Afsan's tail would have to be removed so that the crushed bones could grow back whole. They'd wait until his strength was up, and until they got to a proper hospital, before they did that. He was given water and bowls of blood, and he heard someone drawing the leather curtain across the cabin's porthole, but that, of course, was an unnecessary gesture.

At last, they left him alone.

Afsan slept.

Later, he did not know when, he was awakened by a sound at the door to his cabin.

Muffled by the wood, a familiar voice said, "Permission to enter your territory?"

"Dybo?" said Afsan, groggy and still weak. "*Hahat dan.*"

The door swung open on squeaky hinges and Afsan could hear the footfalls of the Emperor crossing to the part of the floor on which Afsan lay.

Afsan tried to lift his head, but his strength had not returned. His chest still hurt.

"How are you, Afsan?" said Dybo.

"Tired. In pain. How would you expect me to be?" Afsan was surprised at the anger in his own tone.

"No different than that, I suppose," said Dybo. "I'm sorry."

"Are you?"

Afsan heard the boards creak as Dybo's weight shifted. He assumed the Emperor had crouched down to better see him. "Yes."

"What about Capital City?"

"Heavy damage, of course. But some buildings are still standing."

"The palace?"

Dybo was quiet for a moment. "It was leveled."

"Then what becomes of your government?"

Afsan thought he heard Dybo's teeth click together. "Governments endure. My power was not vested in a building."

"No. It was vested in a lie."

Dybo's tone was surprisingly gentle. "Was it? My ancestor, Larsk, was the first to sail halfway around the world. He was indeed the first to stare upon the Face of God. If it hadn't been for him, you wouldn't have made your voyage, wouldn't have discovered the things you discovered. You say the world is doomed—"

"It is."

"Well, if that is so, it is knowledge we owe at least in part to Larsk." Dybo's teeth clicked again. "Governments endure," he repeated simply.

"No," said Afsan. "No, they don't. Or at least yours won't."

"Won't it?"

"It can't. *Nothing* will endure. The world is doomed."

"You persist in that?"

"You saw what happened today."

"The land shook. Volcanoes erupted. That has happened before."

"It's going to happen again and again and again and it will get progressively worse until this world cracks like an egg."

"Do you really believe that?"

"Yes, Dybo. I really do." Afsan paused. "Saleed knew the truth. Before he died, he knew."

"Well, what would you have me do?"

"Do whatever must be done. You've got the power."

"Perhaps. The Lubalites came close to taking Capital City today."

"You would have taken it back eventually. You were unprepared, but the other provinces would send aid to restore you."

"Yes," Dybo said slowly. "I imagine they would."

"After all, aren't the provincial governors your mother's brothers and sisters?"

"What?"

"Aren't they?" said Afsan.

"No, they're not."

"Perhaps. Being blind is a two-way street. I can't see whether you're lying. But, then again, I don't have to take everything I hear at face value, so to speak."

"You've become a lot more sophisticated, Afsan."

"I have. It's part of growing up."

Dybo's voice was soft. "Yes, it is."

"In any event," said Afsan, "all that matters is that the governors of the other provinces are loyal to you. Only five hundred Lubalites could be mustered from all of Land. That few couldn't have held power long."

"In that, you're right," said Dybo.

"I'm right in all of it," said Afsan.

"Are you?"

"You know I am."

Dybo's voice came back differently; he must have turned away from Afsan. "I know you *believe* you are right. But I have to be sure. What you're asking for requires enormous resources, enormous changes in every facet of our lives. I have to know that it's really, absolutely true."

Afsan rolled onto his side, trying to find a posture in which his chest didn't hurt so much. "You'll find my notes in my quarters back in the Capital. Even if the building was destroyed, sift through the rubble for them. Have Novato, or any learned person, take you through the equations, show you the inevitability of it all. It's more than just what I believe, Dybo. It's true. It's *demonstrably* true."

"It's all so hard to grasp," said the Emperor.

Afsan wondered again if he was right, if Dybo really was the slowest and dullest of the eight children of Lends. If that were so, would he be up to the task? Could Dybo lead his people in the direction they needed to go? Now, more than ever, the Quintaglios required a true guiding force, someone who could take them into the future.

"I have faith in you, friend Dybo," Afsan said at last. "You'll see, you'll understand, and you'll do what is necessary."

The timbers creaked again: Dybo shifting his weight.

"I want to do what's right," the Emperor said.

"I hope you will," Afsan replied.

"When you're well, I'm going to appoint you as my court astrologer."

Afsan sighed. "A blind astrologer? What good would I be?"

Dybo's teeth clicked lightly. "For generations, Saleed and his predecessors worked in the basement of the palace office building, out of sight of the stars. Can a blind astrologer be that much worse?"

"I—I still harbor much anger against you, Dybo. I can't help it. You allowed my eyes to be taken."

"But I prevented Yenalb from taking your life."

"For the time being."

"Didn't Cadool tell you? Yenalb is dead. There's much confusion about who was responsible, of course, but the high priest was killed in the battle in the central square. It doesn't matter who did it, I suppose; everyone was in *dagamant*. No charges will be laid."

Afsan felt his injured tail twitch. "Yenalb is dead?"

"Yes."

"And who appoints his successor?"

"The priesthood has its own rites of succession. They will name the new Master of the Faith."

Afsan let air out noisily. "Well, I doubt it will be a moderate. Still, this may indeed be a new beginning."

He felt a hand on his shoulder, briefly. "It is. Whenever you're ready, we can go back into the city."

"How do you mean? Where are we now?"

"Back at the docks. The *Dasheter* is moored. The eruptions have stopped, and what lava did make it into the city has been cooled by rainfall and has hardened into rock."

"What about Novato?"

Afsan could hear Dybo make a sound with his mouth. "Ah,

Novato, yes." The old tone of teasing was back in the Emperor's voice for a moment. "You rutting hornface. Mating out of season. You should be ashamed."

"What will become of Novato?" Afsan asked again.

"She's committed no crime, in my view. She's free to do as she pleases."

"Free to go back to her Pack of Gelbo? Back to the far side of Land?"

"She could have chosen that, yes. But she did not."

"What?"

"Well, my chief astrologer is going to need an assistant. There is much you can do still, of course, but, well, your condition—" Dybo paused briefly. "I asked her if she'd like to stay here in the Capital, helping you. She said yes."

For a moment, Afsan felt his heart lift, felt a joy he had thought he would never feel again. But then, at last, he shook his head. "No."

The boards groaned again as Dybo changed positions. "I thought you'd be pleased. She told me about how you met."

Afsan rallied some strength. He pushed up off the floor, and got to his feet. His tail was too badly hurt to lean back on, so he reached out with an arm to steady himself against the wall. "I am pleased that she wants to stay. But being my assistant is not a fitting job for her. She's brilliant, Dybo. Her mind is"—he searched for the appropriate term—"far-seeing."

"Keenir says the same thing about her. But if not your assistant, what?"

Afsan turned his head to face in the direction the voice had come from. "You're committed to my vision of the future? Committed to getting us off this world before it's too late?"

Dybo was silent for several heartbeats. Then, at last, decisively, the syllable ripe with firmness: "Yes."

"Then make her director of that operation. Put her in charge of—what to call it?—of the Quintaglio exodus."

"That project will take generations."

"Perhaps."

"You believe she is the best person for the job?"

"Without question."

Silence, except for the creaking of the ship's lumber, the lapping of waves. "I'll do it," said Dybo at last. "I'll assign her that task, and all the resources she needs." Then: "Are you ready to go up on deck?"

"I think so."

"Let me help you." Dybo reached an arm around Afsan's shoulders, and let Afsan reciprocate. The young astrologer's weight sagged against Dybo. Together, they made it up the ramp and out onto the deck, the steady breeze playing over them. Afsan felt hot sun on his muzzle.

He heard a squeaking of wheels coming across the deck, then, a moment later, Novato's voice. "Afsan, are you all right?"

He nodded in her direction. "I'm still in pain, but it's getting better." His teeth clicked. "I finally understand what Keenir went through. It's awfully hard to walk properly without a working tail." He wished he could see her. "How are the egglings?"

"They're fine; they're right here."

"Here?"

"Keenir found a wheelbarrow down in one of the cargo holds. It's not an ideal stroller, but then the creche operators told me they don't make strollers to hold eight children." She paused for a moment. "It looks like all of them except Galpook are napping."

"Let's go," said Dybo. He and Afsan started walking toward the connecting piece that led up to the *Dasheter*'s foredeck. After a moment, Afsan could hear the squeaking of Novato's wheelbarrow and a couple of little *peeps,* presumably coming from Galpook.

"Where are we going?" asked Novato, coming up beside them again.

Wingfingers were singing overhead. Afsan could tell by the way the Emperor's voice sounded that he had tipped his muzzle up at the sky.

"To the stars," Dybo said.

ABOUT THE AUTHOR

Robert J. Sawyer has been selling science fiction since 1979, but took a long detour into the world of magazine and corporate writing before beginning to write SF novels. Orson Scott Card called Rob's first book, *Golden Fleece,* the best science fiction novel of 1990, and it won the CompuServe SF Forum's HOMer Award for best first novel of that year. Rob's next two novels, this book and the forthcoming *End of an Era,* deal in quite different ways with his beloved dinosaurs—his original career goal was to be a paleontologist. His short SF has appeared in *Amazing Stories, The Village Voice, Leisure Ways,* and the anthology *100 Great Fantasy Short Short Stories,* edited by Isaac Asimov, Terry Carr, and Martin Harry Greenberg. Rob also writes and narrates documentaries on SF topics for CBC Radio's *Ideas* series, reviews SF for the Toronto *Globe and Mail,* and is *The Canadian Encyclopedia*'s authority on science fiction. He lives in Toronto, Canada, with his wife, Carolyn.